ACKNOWLEDGEMENTS

Long is the list of friends and family who helped bring these stories to life, but I have to mention a few. Many thanks go to Mike Pontarelli, authors Steve Karas, Michael DeAngelo, and Lou Anders, and Dean B.—my number-one story consultant. Finally, my wife and motivator in chief, Marilyn, deserves a shout out. You have my love, appreciation, and deepest gratitude.

This one is for Steve M, who's been with me on this journey from the very start.

HAIR OF THE DOG

DEAN KASTLE

Edits by Michael DeAngelo

First edition 2024

CONTENTS

CHAPTER ONE

Geth awoke in darkness. Memories of angry fists, of road dust, and an iron door tumbled through his head. It was a while before he remembered where he was, and when he did he wished he could forget.

The Tower of the Moon.

Landed yourself right up calamity's asshole this time. It took something special to book a reservation in Pellon's most infamous prison, and yet Geth had managed it. Windowless confines excluded all sunlight, but a trap door in the ceiling opened each night to expose the moon's baleful eye. The weight of it, it was said, could drive a man mad.

But Geth reckoned it was hunger that would kill him before anything else. His belly ached so bad even his teeth hurt. By the ragged breathing to either side, he knew he wasn't the only starving bastard in there either.

"Hey, you," he addressed the darkness, "when do they feed us around here?"

The darkness made no reply. If anything, it got quieter.

Geth scooted across the knotted wood floor, reigniting pain in each limb. He bit down a curse, reached a hand through the blackness until he touched an oily shoulder. "I said—"

"Ahh!"

"Easy now—"

"Ahh!"

Geth let the poor bastard slip further along the curved stone wall. *Mad as a castrated piglet, that one.* He settled back against the cold stone of his prison, stomach no better off for the exchange. *Maybe I can eat one of them.*

Or maybe an end in the tower was exactly what a gutter-born sellsword deserved. Geth croaked a mirthless laugh. He had to applaud the gods their timing, presenting the bill for a lifetime of misdeeds only *after* he'd fallen in with a righteous cause. He thought of King Hadean back in Towerrock, surrounded by the Ilar siege, trapped among questionable allies. Then there was Phelan, jailed for his own transgressions, and Neary, Kerrel, and the rest of the dead-man dozen.

"Gods all be damned!"

But anger only made Geth hungrier. He took a deep breath. *They have to feed us*, he reckoned. *To stretch out the torture if nothing else*. Eyes were useless in the utter dark, so he cocked an ear. Prison mates wheezed to either side. The sound of heavy breathing seemed to echo from somewhere beneath him as well.

A cellar? Could there be food down there? Geth frowned. He ran a hand along the timber under his rump. Feeling around the curve of the walls—over stinking, yammering madmen—his fingers found an opening in the planks where a curling stone stairway plunged along the edge of the walls into the tower's depths.

But instinct paused the big warrior where he was. For all the reeking bodies and limited space, not a prisoner lingered within yards of that stairway. Geth tapped the top step. *What are you hiding?*

There was an easy way to find out.

Feeling his way back from the edge, Geth crept through the darkness toward the wheezing of his nearest cellmate. Grabbing the shrieking bastard with both hands, he dragged him across the floor and dropped him straight through the hole.

"Ahh!" Thuds and curses sounded on the way down, followed by scrambling noises as the man hurried back up. "How dare you lay hands on Lord Wels!"

"Sorry, er, my lord." Geth thought it best to play along. "Forgive the accident."

"There will be a reckoning! Once my men have freed me, there will be a reckoning for this indignity!"

"I just—"

The one called Wels lowered his voice to a hiss. "Do you know what lies below? An *unspeakable* evil."

Now we're getting somewhere. "You wouldn't stow *me* down there, would you?"

"I just might!"

"And there's no food down there either, I reckon."

"Certainly not! When my men arrive, you'll find out for yourself."

"C'mon now, friend," Geth lowered his voice, tone conspiratorial. "Are you telling me you're planning a bust out? How will your men get past the guards? Must've been dozens of them."

A pause. "For now."

"For now?"

"Since your arrival. When no one comes for you, the number will lessen."

Geth opened his mouth, but Wels wasn't done.

"And when my followers come, they will come in swarms! They will breach the walls, storm the parapets…"

Geth's ear had turned toward the spiral stair. The lord's rants seemed to have roused whoever—*whatever*—lay below. From the opening in the floor, the scuff of leather on stone announced a footfall at the top step.

No matter how Geth strained his eyes, it was impossible to see through the darkness. But there was no mistaking the tension in the air. He sat up on the balls of his feet and listened. What sounded like two separate patterns of breath echoed through the dank prison. The prisoners stirred. Jostling for position, if Geth wasn't mistaken. Then they went still. If they had been quiet before, they went utterly silent now.

Like hunted prey.

"Where's our new friend?" a voice said.

Geth held his breath. One of the pair passed him by no more than a yard. The noise of a struggle broke out a few feet away, followed by a gasp, a shriek, and the familiar ranting of Lord Wels.

"Hands off! You'll pay!"

"This one will do," a second voice said.

Wels's indignation turned to a piteous wail. "*No!*"

By the echo off the tower's lofty rafters, Geth reckoned the fight had turned desperate. Heavy breathing became panting, followed by grunts and more terrified cries. Something tore. It wasn't until Geth recognized the slapping of flesh that he understood what Wels had meant by 'unspeakable.'

"Sick bastards."

Geth edged forward through the dark at a crouch, hand outstretched until he touched a gyrating body. Anticipating the swing of an elbow, he skipped to one side, threw a fist into where the man's exposed ribs would be. Wels squealed and scampered away as his tormentor staggered off him.

By then the second rapist had made a grab for Geth with both hands. Expecting a blow of some sort toward his midriff, Geth swatted downward with his left hand, reached out with his right to grip a ragged shirt. Something sharp sliced his left palm—the strike he'd expected—but he caught hold of a wrist and held on tight. With his right hand, he yanked his enemy in close, grabbed the back of the bastard's neck, pressed his own forehead against the man's temple in a wrestler's hold.

Even in that squalid pit—maybe especially so—there was comfort in the familiar feel of combat, the push and pull as Geth grappled. He felt half-alive again. What wasn't so familiar was the weakness in the knees that sent him backpedaling under his enemy's press.

"Damn you, Awer!"

Using the bastard's own momentum, Geth released his grip on the neck, swung his right arm under and turned to bend and throw the rapist overhead. The thud of flesh on timber, followed by a hollow grunt, told Geth his enemy had landed flat on his back, lost his wind. Geth pummeled with one fist where he thought the sonofabitch's head would be, but in the darkness missed, running splinters into his knuckles as he punched the floor. The blackness came to his aid a heartbeat later as a kick from the second man scraped past his right side, granting a warning and ample time for Geth to sweep the man's standing leg, crumpling him beside his fellow.

But that was everything Geth had. Panting, legs shaking, he edged backward until his heels touched the wall. He strained to hear over the blood pumping in his ears for the rapists' next advance. Gods be praised, the only thing he heard was the scuff of feet descending stone stairs.

The frenzied howls and unintelligible babbling of the other mad bastards continued well after the two rapists returned to their lair. *Bloody animals.* Geth licked the cut on his hand and sank down to his rear, back against the wall. The taste of blood only made his hollow middle ache more.

"Least you could do is thank me!" he called into the darkness.

The chatter of the crazies subsided. The voice of Lord Wels answered, his tone sincere. "I *am* a great lord you know."

"Whatever you say."

"It won't be long before my servants break me out. Serve me well in here, and I just might bestow upon you a mantle of power."

"I'll keep that in mind."

Some other moonstruck fool babbled to Wels about a similar promise. "You said you'd make me a prince!"

"Shut up!" By the sound of it, Wels had slapped him. "We're still in here, you twit! What shall you be prince of? The latrine?"

Geth laughed too soon.

"Radmus is already prince of the latrine."

Thram's balls.

Geth blew out a sigh. Mad as the dear lord was, Wels was clearly a good deal better off than some of the others. Geth didn't doubt he had been a lord once—a traitor no doubt, but a lord, nonetheless. And he was someone to talk to.

"So, when do we get food, er, *my lord*?"

"Soon. Our day begins."

With the groan of pulleys, the roof above opened wide to admit the pale light of a waning moon. After the complete blackness that preceded, it was like a brilliant gem. The other prisoners stirred, began talking to themselves.

It was only a half-moon above them, but its light offered Geth his first look around. The belly of the tower was a bare stone enclosure, twenty feet across, perhaps. Bats hung from timber rafters another forty feet up. Besides himself, he counted a dozen prisoners huddled against the walls. At least one of them was already dead. The living weren't much more than sacks of bone and hair themselves. If Geth was a big man compared to healthy folk, among this lot he was a giant.

To one side, a heavy iron-plated door with a slot near the base marked the entrance to the prison. Opposite that, across the planks of the floor, the cellar stair twisted down into darkness. The stone bench of a latrine sat to the right. As Geth watched, a wispy-bearded fellow shuffled over to squat atop the narrow hole.

"Oh, for Thram's sake!"

The nutty bastard pissed all over the seat then wiped his arse with his own ragged shirtsleeve.

"Lord of the latrine," Wispy-beard muttered, well-pleased. Geth supposed this must be Radmus. Another prisoner—this one short with bony bumps all over his scalp—dipped his head as Radmus passed then squatted with a sigh directly in that puddle of urine.

Geth studied the tower's other denizens as well. The nose-picking, the howls, the misplaced chuckles, the one-sided conversations. They were mad alright, but there was a certain order, a set of laws that governed. They didn't fight, they didn't take from one another, as far as he'd seen. The same laws prevailed in the streets where orphans and unwanted children like himself had come up.

But even in the gutters of Old Sorn, just miles from where he sat now, he'd never been so hungry. "Hey Wels, when do we get food?"

Wels licked his lips. By his sideways glance, Geth had some indication of what to expect when the slot in the door creaked open.

"Come and get it, you miserable sonsabitches!"

Through the slot, several apples rolled along the wood floor, followed by what looked like half-eaten trenchers of bread, scraps of bone, and other refuse Geth didn't immediately recognize. But the crazies poised on the balls of their feet, held their place rather than lunging after it. Geth paused, following their lead. Footfalls sounded on the stone stairway and the first of the two rapists peeked his head up over the rim of the hole.

Now was the time to strike, with the foul bastard exposed, Geth reckoned. A boot to the nose would drop him square on his friend below, allowing the big warrior to jump down among them, maybe break a rib or two with his heels then smash them both to a pulp. Problem solved. Except that he was almost too weak to stand. And to fail was to die. He took his cue from Wels and the rest, watched and waited.

These two, now here were living men. They moved like predators, eyes daring a challenge as they climbed up to the center of the chamber. The one was heavy-boned, pig-like in the face, the other lanky, with a nose that must have been broken a dozen times. That one carried some sort of shank, the weapon that had cut Geth's hand, he reckoned. Together the pair probably outweighed the lot of the other prisoners combined. But Geth was still a bigger man than either. The lanky one passed the weapon over, crouched down to begin gathering up food as other prisoners quivered in place, watching and whining.

Pig-face turned a menacing stare on Geth. "Watch yourself," he said, voice like a pig's grunt indeed.

Geth rose to his full height, crossed his arms as if that hadn't taken every ounce of his strength. He met Pig-face's eye with an unflinching stare. Broke-nose let his friend watch his back, kneeling to shout into the door-slot.

"C'mon, I hear the lot of ya out there! Don't be so stingy with the leftovers! Your justicar wants us tortured, not dead! Otherwise, we'd a' been hanged."

Laughter echoed from outside. Something clinked, followed by a groaning sound, and the slot opened. More scraps fell through. Broke-nose gathered these, escorted by his friend toward the stair. When Geth saw how few morsels they'd left for the rest though, he took a step forward to cut them off midway. A low growl rose from his throat.

A look passed between Broke-nose and Pig-face. How would they get back down with their hands full and fight him off at the same time? Geth dropped his hands to his sides, flexed his fingers, heaved his broad chest.

Only anger gave him the strength to even fake it. But it worked. Broke-nose let go a couple trenchers and a single apple which rolled across the floor toward Radmus, who pounced on it almost face-first.

Geth stood firm. The rapists exchanged another look. They weren't used to a challenge, didn't want to risk it, even two against one and armed.

Pig face dropped a few more crusts and apples to one side and growled. "That's all you get."

With the other mad bastards already clawing and biting each other over the scraps, Geth had no choice but to let the pair go before all the food was gone. Grabbing a prisoner in each hand by the scruff of the neck, he smashed two of them together until a couple trenchers and a wilted wedge of cabbage fell loose. There was a bit of gravy still on the crusts, the tang of salt like heaven on his tongue.

The two he'd robbed sat watching sullenly as he scarfed it down and licked his fingers. "What? You bastards owe me. Which one of you ate my share while I was out cold, huh? I should murder the lot of you."

There was nothing in that threat though. The weight of food in Geth's stomach had lightened his mood already, turned him giddy almost. The others seemed to feel it too, chatting to themselves, humming, scratching meaningfully at the walls.

"Let's kill the guards," one of them said. That started off a chain of helpless giggles from the others.

"Let's starve them," offered another. "We'll pull one through the slot then give *him* leftovers!"

More laughter. When the voice of Lord Wels spoke, it was softer but full of purpose. "It's the others we should kill." He flicked that sideways glance of his at Geth. "Crush them. The one who did that would sit at my right hand once we are out."

Geth smiled, partly at Wels and partly at the backbone these poor creatures mustered after just a few scraps of food. Any other time, he would have killed both the guards *and* the two downstairs without hesitation. But now? He wasn't even sure how long he could stand.

He hadn't missed the way their captives had answered the call of Broke-nose either. *Jailor and jailed like ass and undercloth?* Only shit could come from an arrangement like that.

"So, there's no way to get outta here, huh?" he said out loud.

He'd directed the question toward Wels, but it was Radmus who answered. "Doomed we are. Never to see the Eye of Creation again."

Wels snorted. "Speak for yourself, princeling. I shall be out quite soon. Don't worry, you shall still be lord of all things shit and piss."

Geth chortled, but Poor Radmus gave a somber nod. Geth turned back to Wels. "How you gonna manage the escape, your majesty?"

"A lord has servants to do his biddings. They will find a way."

"And how 'bout a lowborn criminal such as me? What if I wanted to break free of this hellhole as well?"

Wels's sighed as if the answer was obvious. "You must remain in good graces, count on my benevolence."

"So, there's no other way?"

"The Old One, perhaps," said Radmus. "The Old One may know a way."

"The Old One?"

Wels glared at Radmus, but Geth was already studying the other prisoners, preening their dirty beards, searching for crumbs. "Which one is the Old One?"

Wels shooed Radmus off. "He's not a vassal of mine. He lives down below."

"And those two—I mean, the *unspeakable evil* doesn't bother him?"

Wels leaned in, voice low. "Not him. He's *mad*."

Geth's eyes narrowed but he could see Wels was serious. "Tell me."

"He can talk inside your head, without making a sound. He doesn't eat, he doesn't feel the cold, or the heat, or the weight of..." Wels licked his lips.

Geth finished for him. "The moon."

"When it's full." Wels nodded.

Geth thought that through. It seemed a far-off chance that anyone, least of all another prisoner, would have any inkling of how to escape. Why, then, would he still be inside? But mention of the Old One teased Geth's curiosity, not least how it happened Pig-face and Broke-nose left the man untouched. Perhaps there was something to it. Geth had met more than one sorcerer in his day, capable of the sorts of things Wels described.

But in his current state, Geth knew there would be no venturing into the lair below, in search of the Old One or anything else. He needed more food, rest. Until then, he'd just have to hope the two below didn't make a move of their own.

CHAPTER TWO

There was a rhythm to life in the tower—if such an existence could be called living—and Geth fell into it. The closing of the hatch above signaled the start of the blackness, nighttime, hours of stillness, sleep. The opening of the same, whether to a bright moon or fainter, overcast evening, began the day. Food came then, their one tiny joy.

Geth felt some measure of his strength return. He thanked the gods. Those two bastards below weren't going anywhere unless it was to Vorda's cold hall where he sent them himself. And eventually, he reckoned, that's exactly what he'd have to do.

For now, though, a stalemate ensued. Geth didn't venture down into their lair, and they didn't climb up except when their meager scraps came tumbling through the slot in the door. Geth had taken to gathering up a reasonable amount before they arrived, though he still left them far more than two men's share. He wasn't ready for another fight just yet. Neither were they, gods be praised.

This pattern wasn't much disturbed until the full moon a week later.

"Nothing more than a thief and a liar!"

"Ahh!"

"Liar! You lie!"

A disagreement between Radmus and the bony-headed one had escalated 'til the pair went after each another with fists, nails and teeth. Geth watched, amused by the howls of the bystanders as much as the tussle itself. Within those close stone walls, however, the commotion soon became more than his eardrums could bear.

"Enough!" Tossing Bones in one direction, Radmus in another, Geth stood between the pair. They licked their wounds, still breathing heavy. The cries of the others died down.

"Lord Crusher," Bones said, "He lies! It was all lies. They just threw me in here. I stole from no one! Make him say it!"

"*You* are the one who lies! A thief *and* a liar! He is, Lord Crusher. You know it well." Radmus stood, knuckled sternum puffed out. "Those are words you can rely upon, good sir. I too was a lord before being hauled to this abysmal place."

Geth snorted. "Everyone's a lord all of a sudden. Even me."

"Now, I myself," Radmus went on, "I did nothing, Lord Crusher. Nothing but question the choice of a captaincy and away they took me. I—"

"Oh, for Thram's sake, shut up! Tell it to Wels if you have to, before it's you that gets crushed."

A chuckle from Wels floated over Geth's shoulder. "You're a lord now. That title carries responsibilities with it."

Geth cursed him. This was what his fight with the 'unspeakable evil' had earned him. Their improved nourishment too, the protection they enjoyed.

"I can't solve your problems! You hear me, you sons-abitches!"

But he had no choice really. There was no way to escape it. The incessant chattering, the pawing, the begging. It was a relief when the hole above closed that night.

The moonlight, he'd come to understand, really did have a powerful effect in the tower. Perhaps it was because of the close confines, or their starvation from light. Perhaps that bright orb issued a sort of magick—a magick the tower amplified. Whatever the case, it was like liquor in the veins. At first it calmed, offered a high. But with time it dragged a man down like a weight, making desperate, wounded creatures of an already desperate lot.

But the darkness could drive you just as mad as the moonlight. Geth supposed that was why the prisoners mostly slept in those hours. At times someone would burst into off-key singing or senseless mutterings. These, he'd come to realize, were efforts to avoid a festering sickness in the head. As the days went by, Geth started doing it himself.

"Anyone can steal in the dark, Phelan says." Geth knew he was talking to himself but didn't care. "The darkness brings out the dark side of a man's nature. If you want to be a professional, well, you've got to learn how to do it in broad daylight."

Geth laughed at the irony of such a thought, here where the sun really never did shine. Huddled against the walls, some of the others laughed too, an echo of their shared madness. *Poor, crazy bastards. Poor me.* But the clink of keys and the scrape of iron shook the mood off him as the tower door sprang open to reveal a sliver of a night landscape outside.

Geth sucked in a breath. In an instant it was gone, consumed by black iron as the outer door to the anteroom shut. Three guards entered the enclosure. A fourth remained to stand watch beside the outer door.

"Out of the way! Move, filthy whoresons!"

They came for the dead man. Clubs and boots cleared a path through cowering prisoners. The nearest two were ordered to drag the corpse into the anteroom. Once there, they received a kick in thanks before the door slammed shut. The outside door clanked and as quick as they'd come, their captors were gone.

Pathetic whining and fervent curses trailed the guards.

"What are you complaining about?" Geth said. "Good riddance." That corpse had been there several weeks, he reckoned, mouth agape, stinking against a patch of wall even the crazies avoided. And for Geth, the opening of that door fueled a surge of hope. The sight of those moonlit hills, the purple, star-speckled sky... It was like a light at the end of this hopelessly dark tunnel.

What's more, it gave him an idea.

Bless you, Thram! Thank you, Mighty Awer! Finally, he had something he could use. *Three men with clubs plus one at the door.* That one, he'd wager, held the keys. All he had to do was get them to open the door again.

But how?

The answer was obvious.

Kill a man, that's how.

The days passed. Geth's mind worked. The leftovers had, indeed, decreased. So, too, the noises outside, both of which indicated Wels had been right about the lessening of the guards over time. Four distinct voices were familiar by then. Geth surmised these were all he had to worry about. *Four guards.*

He thought of Umbel, of Phelan, of Hadean. Of his dozen, and the fight ahead of them. He had to get back. But killing a man wasn't so straightforward, even for him.

Just kill one of these bastards and have done. He snorted a grim laugh. "These men are dead already, truth be told."

The animals stirred. They were mad, not deaf. And like an animal, there was an innocence to them. Oh, they'd done something to land themselves in this place, Geth reckoned, just as he had. But if he was going to kill anyone, he'd rather it be Broke-nose or Pig-face.

Going after the rapist below just wasn't an option though. Not yet.

How long do I wait? They need me back in Umbel.

You really want to kill Radmus? Or Bumpy or Wels?

Awer be praised, the door groaned open the following day before he had to make a decision.

"Go on harper, make yourself at home!" came a rough voice. Two of the same four guards dragged a teary-eyed fool across the threshold, dumping him flat on his face in their midst. Geth rose to the balls of his feet, tried to peer past them. He cursed. It was too soon; he wasn't ready. As quickly as the door had opened it had clanked back shut.

"Thram and bloody Awer!"

The noise elicited fresh whimpers from the newcomer. "Don't hurt me! I'm the minstrel of King Elius himself. It won't be long before he calls for me. He'll rue the mistake. I might be able to curry some favor for those who treat me well."

"Sure you will." Geth settled back against the wall. "Best mind your manners for now though."

Before he could prepare the scratch any more for his new life, the clink of the slot in their door cut him off. Several bruised fruit, stale crusts and wilted vegetables tumbled in. Geth gathered up a share before Broke-nose and Pig-face arrived, but there was a tension he could feel beyond the normal frenzy of feeding time. As always, Geth stood to his full height, menacing best he could manage as the pair stooped to gather the generous share he'd left them. Rather than watch him, however, they flicked glances from the harper and back to one another. The moon was still bright, high in the night and lighting the place well enough to read the hunger in their eyes.

The poor bastard hardly noticed, head buried in hands, but Geth knew what they wanted. The others left the harper alone, relieved—the despicable bastards—to know the attention wasn't on themselves. Geth gnawed at a stale crust, unsure how he'd react himself if "the unspeakable evil" came for the man.

The hole in the door soon closed and night began. The harper whimpered in his sleep. But there were real life things in the tower worse than any nightmare.

Despite the tension at feeding time, when the dark hours came, Geth fell asleep. He dreamed.

Palladine laughed in his ear. Geth struggled against the bonds at his wrists. The twin trackers took turns pelting him with jagged stones from their slings.

"You've been charged with murder," Palladine said. "Did you think Hadean would forget you killed his closest kin?"

"I did what had to be done," Geth said. "I'll go back to him and beg his—"

Another stone landed, cutting him short. The twins laughed.

"How are you going to do that? You're mine now. I've got you right where you belong."

A throat cleared and Geth looked up to meet the gaze of Hadean's dead uncle, blood crusted at the corners of his mouth. But it was Palladine the dead traitor addressed, not him.

"He's killed so many already. What's my death? What's one more? Sometimes it's the only way."

Eldric had gone before Geth could reply, replaced by Phelan, shackled at wrist and ankle. "Am I a murderer or not?" Geth asked him.

Phelan nodded, eyes somber. "As much as I'm a thief."

"But every murder isn't the same. You know that. I had to kill. I have to."

Palladine snorted. "A kingdom is governed by law—"

A hand reached over from somewhere behind Geth to swing him around with surprising strength.

"Wake!"

Geth found himself looking into the urgent, deep-set eyes of a silver-haired stranger. "Who—"

"Now!"

The scuff of something on stone sounded in Geth's ear and like a rider emerging through a patch of fog, he came awake. Not a moment too soon. Another noise sounded. Even in the dark, Geth recognized the echo of feet on stairs. Just at the same time, his ears detected the heavy breathing of someone even closer.

Pig-face.

Geth rolled to one side. A nasty thud sounded from the spot where he'd been lying, followed by a curse. Geth scampered away on all fours until he'd landed square on top of another sleeping form. The wails of the emaciated creature beneath him betrayed him and he skipped away again though the dark.

Blood pumped in Geth's temples, surged through his arms, his thighs. He cocked an ear, hands outstretched, feeling through the inky blackness for an oncoming attack. Wheezy, nasal breathing put Broke-nose somewhere just ahead of him now. Not waiting, Geth crouched to sweep a leg forward. The move caught an ankle, tripped the sick bastard's just as Geth'd hoped. Rather than lunge after the man now and maybe impale himself on that shank, he threw another kick, met something meaty, then retreated further into the darkness.

"Just give us the harper and we're done!"

By the sound of it, Pig-face was somewhere to Geth's right. The shuffling of disturbed prisoners made it hard to say exactly where. Broke-nose was still cursing only a few yards away.

"We're done when I say we're done!" Geth sidestepped as soon as he'd spoke, before they could close on him. "And I'm just getting started!"

"Whoreson bastard! Can't you mind your own business?"

"We'll gut ya!" That from Broke-nose, just a few yards away. He'd been following the sound of Geth's voice all the while. "We'll skin your hide, ya big dumb bastard!"

Geth circled further to his left. By the sound of it, Pig-face and Broke-nose had come shoulder to shoulder near the center of the enclosure. Smacking or kicking each sleeping body he passed, Geth riled the animals of the tower. A din of feral shrieks filled the room, making it impossible for anyone to hear much of anything.

"It's you who'll be crushed in the end, you fool!"

Footfalls on stairs sounded their retreat. Geth sank down to the seat of his pants, spent, even if hatred had fueled him much longer this bout than the last. He'd started a war that first night defending Wels, a war in which there could be no peace until one side was destroyed.

But nowhere was Geth at home more than in war. He laughed into the darkness. *And at least now I know who to kill.*

CHAPTER THREE

Geth remained alert until the hatch above opened and their day began. He thought of the silver-haired vision that had saved him, of the feud with Pig-face and Broke-nose. Down in their lair, they whispered back and forth, plotting their next move, Geth reckoned, just as he plotted his.

When feeding time came, Geth took the best scraps for himself and ate them immediately. He doled out the rest for the crazies, leaving none for his enemies. They rose cautiously from below, Pig-face in front with that shank of his. He eyed Geth from across room, noted the missing leftovers, and snorted a laugh. Coming up behind him, Broke-nose crouched on the floor near the slot in the door.

"I need a favor! Ya hear me?"

Geth cursed. He hadn't seen that coming. He should have attacked as they came up the stairs, he thought, not for the first time. Pig-face held his weapon at the ready, waiting. It was too late now.

"You know what it costs," came the reply of one of the guards, a wet-voiced fellow Geth called Spittle. "I need something from you if you want to be my favorite."

A glance between Pig-face and Broke-nose indicated some exchange.

"I did it last time!" Pig-face grunted.

The door groaned open, and their argument was decided. Broke nose cursed. To Geth's disbelief, a club-bearing guard let him out before slamming the iron closed once more.

Son...of...a...bitch!

Geth looked to Pig-face. He had the vile bastard alone now. And yet there was no point attacking when the guards stood just beyond the door, ready to come to his aid.

But what could have bought such an alliance? A slurping sound echoed from the anteroom through the slot and Geth knew. "Selling yourselves now?"

Pig-face watched him warily. Geth considered rushing the bastard right then, but it came to him suddenly that he only needed to wait a few seconds more. His chance to escape was when that door opened again. Phelan and Hadean needed him, the others too. The only thing that stood in the way was two filthy rapists and a few club-bearing guardsmen.

Red-handed Awer, pitiless god of war, lend me strength!

Geth closed his eyes, recalled the night scene—freedom—that he'd seen the day before. The sounds from the anteroom ceased and the door groaned open, to admit Broke-nose, Spittle, and a second guardsman. Geth charged.

"*Argh!*" In those close quarters, he crossed the distance in a heartbeat. Pig-face barely got his hands up before the force bowled him backward into not one, but all three of the bastards behind him. His weapon went flying. Broke-nose cursed as he tumbled sideways into the stone doorframe. Geth landed directly on top of the flailing arms of Pig-face and the two guards, jabbing with thumbs for eyes, swinging at the soft spot under the arm, chopping at throats.

He stomped with both feet as he struggled to rise. Hands clutched at his feet, his calves. "Sneaky bastard!"

Spittle cursed. "Help! Belo, get *in here!*"

That was exactly what Geth had hoped for. Broke-nose came from behind with a punch at the back of his head, but Geth absorbed the blow, on all fours still, flailing with both feet, scrambling to his knees and off the pile. He reached the anteroom, made it up on one foot. The second door swung open, just in time. Geth cocked a fist to meet the entrance of the next guard, but a blinding orange light seared his eyes, sent that blow off target.

Something heavy cracked against a forearm raised against the blinding glow. "Ahh!"

Still reeling from the torchlight, Geth shut his eyes, used his other senses to grapple with the guard in his path. His left hand caught the man's club-arm. His right sent a body-blow to the bastard's gut. Knuckles scraped across the iron of a metal-studded bodkin. A gust of cold, clean air washed over Geth and he aimed a head-butt from mere inches away into this last foe, sending him staggering back.

"Out!" He slammed the bastard to one side, tried to squeeze past. One foot landed on packed dirt outside.

But the bastard slid down to his rear, clutched at his trailing leg with both arms. Vise-like grips at his elbows and waist caught him as he was gang-tackled from behind.

"*Nooooo!*"

Geth teetered, feet slipping out from under him. He landed flat on his stomach, halfway over the threshold. With his left hand he clawed at the earth. His right elbow shot backward to find a jaw, but they caught that arm, pulled him onto his side. An impossibly-wide night sky reeled overhead, and Belo arrived from outside to kick at

the crown of his head. Inch by inch, they dragged him back
inside.

Geth sat half-propped against the shit-stinking lip of the
latrine, unable to move. Every part of his body hurt, but
thank the gods, he was alive.

"Thank Palladine."

He spoke out loud, to himself. Just like the crazies.

"And why's that?"

"Because he's the only reason you aren't dead. He didn't
put you here to find a swift end. He put you here to suffer."

"You mean *us*."

Geth closed his eyes, forced himself silent. *Palladine
wins if I go mad. Palladine wins. Phelan, Hadean and the
rest all lose.*

He felt the pain in his limbs, used it to ground himself.
"Hey, Wels. Where are you? Can't have gone far."

The shuffle of knees and hands on floorboards announced a tentative approach. "What...what is it?"

"Don't be such a scared rabbit. I'm too tired to hurt you
even if I wanted. Now gimme some water. I know you keep
a damp rag around."

Wels produced the rag for Geth to wring out a few drops. "You almost made it, Lord Crusher. I've never seen anyone get so close. Maybe The Old One has, but I haven't."

Geth swallowed a bitter laugh. "I had it good out there, you know, for a fatherless sword-for-hire. I'd made a new life, under a good king. Sure, we were losing the war. We probably still are. But I had a *home*."

"We need good kings. Not the kind who lock us in such places as these."

But Geth wasn't listening. His mind wandered from Phelan and their first days in Umbel, to young Hadean at the head of the army, to Neary and the lad Kerrel and rest of the file—shield-brothers that had fought by his side. If he died, what became of them? He closed his eyes to gather whatever strength he had left. No doubt he'd be fighting again soon, until this little private war of his ended.

"The Old One would have liked to see that," Wels was saying.

Geth opened his eyes, turned to face him. "See what?"

"The outside."

Geth frowned. *The Old One.*

Was he a fool for thinking he could still win?

But a witch for an ally?

Might change the game.

Getting down below wasn't going to be easy though. Geth was battered and exhausted, lucky not to have lost an eye or a few teeth. It would be a struggle just to rise and make the descent into 'the unspeakable evil's' lair. He'd have to draw the two rapists out beforehand as well. And that would require a sacrifice.

The hole in the roof closed before he could muddle through the details. Pig-face and Broke-nose would come up that ladder to finish him off in those dark hours, Geth reckoned. That's what he would've done in their place.

It left him no choice. He called down into their cellar before they could make their move. "Hey Pig-face! Broke-nose! You can have the harper. You hear me? I'm calling a truce."

A faint rustle of movement sounded below.

"You hear me? You can have him. The harper is yours!"

A panicked voice cut through the dark. "What do you mean? What does he mean? They can have me?"

The scuff of feet on stones sounded, punctuated by Broke-nose's wheezing breaths. "Watch yourself, Crusher. You don't want to get it even worse."

Geth forced a laugh. "Those limp-wristed bastards don't know how to give a beating."

Whether a little bravado made them think twice about trying to finish him off, Geth didn't know, but it made him feel better. He moved through the dark so they couldn't pinpoint his position just in case. Offering up the harper seemed to have their attention anyway.

"Where are you minstrel?" Pig-face had joined Broke-nose somewhere near the top of the stairs. "Come here, boy."

Geth listened, his mind's eye picturing the game of cat and mouse as Harper scrambled through the dark to elude his pursuers. The others went silent, leaving the sorry scratch to his fate lest they attract any attention themselves. The shuffle and scrape of the chase lasted only seconds before they nabbed him.

"Wait! Please! Almighty Shaper, save me! Oh, Sweet Selel!"

The sound of punches and groans echoed off the stones as Pig-face and Broke-nose subdued their prey. Geth waited, listening. Something tore—trousers no doubt—then soft crying. Geth lingered until the slapping of flesh began, masking his own careful footfalls. He descended the curved stair into the tower depths.

The first thing Geth noticed was how much warmer it was. *No wonder the bastards claimed the place*. It was broad and empty as far as his groping hands and careful footfalls could tell, with a latrine of its own to one side, judging by the stench. Geth followed his nose in that direction, feeling around the edges of the bench but finding the opening no more passable than the latrine up above.

"Never wanted to crawl out through the shitter anyway," he muttered. The floors were paved with stone as well. Best he could tell there was no hidden opportunity for escape down there, unless it was hidden within the mind of the Old One.

"Where are you, friend?" he whispered, mindful not to be heard up above. "I mean no harm."

A sigh answered off to Geth's right. The sound of Harper's violation halted briefly. Geth wondered if he'd squandered his time. When the noise resumed, followed by nasty laughter, he surmised the sick bastards had only paused to switch places. The minstrel grunted, a piteous noise, but the crying had stopped. Geth forced that out of his mind and made his way toward the Old One.

"Wels says you may know a way out of this hellhole," Geth breathed. "Any truth in that?"

"A way out? There are many ways out."

The Old One's speech came thick, as if he hadn't used his voice in some time. There was an accent to it Geth couldn't place, and yet it was somehow familiar as well. It was a moment before he remembered the silver-haired stranger from his dream and the voice that had roused him. "You *want* to help me, don't you?"

"The easiest way out is death. Don't need my help with that. The guards will have you out within the month."

"I'm working on it already."

"Or you could wait for wind and sun to tear down the walls. That's another way."

Geth snorted. "Afraid I don't have that kind of time."

The Old One answered with a string of gibberish in a tongue Geth had never heard. *Nutty as the rest of them.* Geth reached forward as gentle as he could to rest a hand on a thin, bony shoulder.

"Listen, I almost made it out yesterday. Is there nothing you can tell me? When do the guards sleep? How might I lure them in? Anything. Or maybe you can use your...powers."

That sigh again. "So many years," the Old One said. "So many mistakes."

Geth waited but there was nothing more. He turned for the stairs, directed a crude gesture heavenward. "A pox on your sense of humor, Thram."

Wait!

Geth froze, rooted in place by the command in his head. His palm tickled as the sensation of something hard and curved sprang into his mind. He squeezed his grip, but nothing was there.

"Find it," the Old One said, aloud this time.

Geth dropped down to all fours. The slapping of flesh overhead quickened, neared its crescendo. He searched the ground. Nestled in a crack between the base of the pavers and the wall, his fingers touched a sharpened length, half-buried in ages of dust and grit.

A stick? A bone of some sort?

A human rib.

Above him, Broke-nose and Pig-face were laughing. Aching, frustrated, quivering mad, Geth's hand closed on the weapon. His injuries shot fire through him, but that only stoked his anger, channeled it into his hands and arms, right to the bony point in his grasp.

He sucked in several quick breaths. In a few painful springs he was back up onto the timber floorboards. Harper seemed to be putting up a bit of a struggle, earning curses from his assailants, who weren't done with him. Moving toward the noise, Geth reached forward through the dark until his hand touched a back. A powerful thrust put that sharpened rib in among a few others.

"Die!"

By the wheezy gasp, Geth knew it was Broke-nose he'd sent thrashing to the floorboards, the fall wrenching his weapon from his grip. He'd have to fight Pig-face hand-to-hand. The big bastard was already fumbling toward him through the dark.

"Double-crossing whoreson!"

A sharp intake of frightened breath told Geth the harper still stood between them. Hurling the poor fool forward, he let Pig-face waste a blow on the minstrel, then skipped right to attack from the side. An outstretched hand found Pig-face's shoulder. Fearing the bastard had recovered his own shank from the day before, Geth hurried to wrap him in a bear hug, trying to lock both arms at his side. But Pig-face had one hand up before Geth could trap it. A trail of pain burned across the big warrior's triceps as a stab from his enemy glanced wide.

"Shit!"

Geth jumped back, out of reach. A whoosh signaled another near miss with that weapon. Geth backpedaled, wary of the stairway opening, left with no other choice but to retreat. Howls had erupted from the crazies by then, ample noise to cover his footfalls as he searched out the latrines by nose to reorient himself.

"Ahh!"

Geth stepped on someone, stumbled, landed on his rump and let out a grunt. Radmus, posted by the latrines as always, had accidentally tripped him. Pig-face closed the space.

"Gah!"

The sickening noise of flesh being mauled sounded. Radmus's cry came too late for Pig-face to realize he'd gored the wrong man. Geth rolled to one side, sprang to a crouch and lurched forward toward the place where Pig-face's knees should have been. In the darkness he missed his mark, ramming a solid thigh with his head instead, sending them both stumbling in opposite directions.

Another slash whooshed past before Geth could find his feet. Luckily, Pig-face had misjudged his position. The big warrior countered with a rush forward, grappling with Pig-face somewhere near the center of the chamber. Geth flailed with his left hand for the weapon in Pig-face's right, but missed. An overhand stab bit into Geth's shoulder blade before he found that arm, clutching it tight.

They grappled, pushed, and pulled. Stars burst through the darkness as Pig-face slammed a headbutt into Geth's face. Still, Geth didn't let go of that shank hand. Blood ran down the big warrior's back and he felt his strength ebb, vying for leverage against Pig-face in the dark.

Betting it all, he released the hand, slid lower to grip around the bastard's waist. Before the weapon could go up and stab back down, Geth arched his back. He used the last remaining strength in his legs to hurl both Pig-face and himself overhead and backward in wrestler's fashion.

The ground came up to meet him right where Pig-face had gored his shoulder. Pain shot through the wound all the way to his skull, and he knew no more.

CHAPTER FOUR

H e didn't hear it, but he felt it. The tugging of the moon. The hole in the roof had been opened. And he was still alive.

The fight with the pair from below flashed through Geth's mind and he scanned the room for danger. Broke-nose sat propped against the opposite wall, bone shank still protruding from his side. Radmus lay dead-eyed and limp beside his latrine. Pig-face had disappeared.

"What in the name of Thram...?"

Geth's eyes skimmed over the crazies a second time, past the iron plated door, toward the opening in the floor leading down to the cellar. He crawled to the edge and peered down. A single thick foot stretched out from the deep darkness below onto the moonlit steps. The awkward lay told Geth all he needed to know. With the luck of Awer

Red-Hand, Geth had thrown Pig-face straight down the stairs.

But a wheeze across the chamber could only have come from Broke-nose. Geth struggled to his feet, tested his legs with a tentative step forward. The crazies looked on warily, silent, afraid. Broke-nose eyed his approach with a hateful stare.

"You'll die when they—"

Geth knelt beside him, jammed the protruding end of that shank as deep as it would go, slapping away a weak protest. Broke-nose's eyes bulged, a hand clawed for Geth's face, but he caught the fingers in his mouth and bit down until he tasted blood. Geth's vision blurred. He collapsed on the floor. Broke-nose slouched over in the other direction. The big warrior only regained consciousness when someone propped him back up.

"Eat this."

It was Wels, an apple core in hand. Geth nibbled the meager remains, drank from a damp rag wrung out over his tongue. "You've killed them. Both of them. I dub you Prince of Apples, Lord Crusher. Lord and Prince."

Geth heaved a sigh. "Both dead?"

Wels nodded.

The part of Geth that had gone mad wanted to giggle. Or cry. Could it be the gods had shown a merciful side?

No, they had more tortures lined up. Of that, he was sure. Their appetite for suffering would be whetted once more when the slot opened at feeding time and the guards found their two favorites missing.

An eternity passed. Geth fought off mad imaginings, painful memories, and aches all throughout his body. The tower had gone silent, all eyes watching him. Across the enclosure, the harper seemed to have recovered from his own ordeal, eyes open but faraway. Perhaps the lot of them had surmised the same thing as Geth: he'd soon be as dead as his enemies.

The noises outside started about the time the slot should have opened. At first it was just voices, then what sounded like angry shouts. *How can they already know?* The bone shank in Broke-nose's side made a sucking sound as Geth pulled it free, the only weapon to be had with Pig-face's lost below. He closed his eyes, breathing slow, waiting. Several loud cracks sounded. The door groaned open.

Geth clawed up to his feet, determined to die standing at least.

"Shit on you, Awer. Yet I'll spill this blood for you one last time."

It wasn't Spittle or Belo that came for him, however, but a lanky, grey-headed bastard with an axe in one hand, a ring of keys in the other.

"You in here Geth? Sergeant?"

Geth's mouth hung open. "I've lost it. Or I'm already dead."

"There you are." The vision of Neary crossed the chamber to wrap an arm around him, usher him toward the door. "Hurry! We captured three of the guards but one of 'em got away. He'll be back with more troops before long."

"Neary?"

"Uro and Thram, you smell terrible!"

It was real. And he was alive! "Ha!"

Geth laughed like a crazy. He couldn't stop himself. Empathetic giggles echoed from the other prisoners around the edges of the chamber. From outside, a bright voice cut through the chatter.

"What should we do with these three?"

Neary hauled Geth through the antechamber to breathe the cool fresh air. Geth's head reeled with the vast openness of the star-speckled sky overhead. Only Neary's arm around him kept him from teetering over.

"Sergeant Geth, did you hear me? What should we do with the guards?"

Geth blinked. "Kerrel? Thram's balls, is that you?"

The lad grinned. "By the grace of the gods. But what about the guards?" He motioned to a trio in dirty white tabards, bound and gagged, starring malevolently at them from their seat on the grass.

"Give me that axe."

Neary raised a hand. "Hold on. I promised King Hadean we wouldn't kill anyone, Umbel and Pellon being sworn allies and all."

"He's right," said Kerrel. "But they'll know who broke in now, won't they?"

Geth ignored that, turned back toward the doorway to holler inside. "Come out you mad bastards! Wels! Harper! All of you, come out!"

The harper came first, eyes on Neary. For the first time, Geth noticed that Umbelman wore the white as well. But one look at the bound guards convinced the harper. He dashed off into the night.

Wels, however, only came to the edge of the threshold. He stood there shaking.

"Come on Wels—*Lord* Wels." Geth pulled him out by the elbow. "Your followers have arrived, just like you said they would."

"My followers?"

Neary's hand was on Geth's arm again. "The guards Geth, we gotta go. I messed up, shouldn't have spoken Hadean's name. Do we take them with us?"

"Take the guards?" Geth shook his head. "We take Wels. The guards stay here, to answer for their crimes."

With the help of Kerrel and Neary, Geth dragged the three cursing jailors toward the tower door. Spittle seemed to be pleading mercy through the rag in his mouth but Geth's fist across the back of the skull shut him up. He pushed them one by one in among the prisoners, hands still bound. Taking Neary's axe from beside the mangled doorframe, he began the climb up a set of stairs leading to the roof of the tower.

"Where you going, Sergeant?" Kerrel called.

Geth hadn't enough breath to answer. Panting and sore, it took all he had to put one foot in front of the other until he reached the tower summit. He raised his axe, smashed the light-covering hatch clean off its hinges. From below, the screams of the guardsman echoed up amid a cacophony of crazed laughter.

They took Wels with them, two men per horse, down from the Tower of the Moon and into the surrounding countryside. Each jostle sent pain stabbing through Geth's body, and Wels squealed with fright from his seat behind Neary. But such haste was called for. The guard that had escaped would be back before long with watchmen from the town of Sorn, just a few miles below. At least that one hadn't heard mention of King Hadean.

"Wait!" Geth tugged at Kerrel's arm to rein in as they came to the bank of a shallow brook. He slid from the saddle with a groan. "If we follow this upstream, it'll take us straight into the town of Sorn."

"That's right under the tower's nose," Kerrel said. "It's away from Sorn we're headed."

"We'll never outrun them, not in this condition. But I know somewhere we can hide."

"Hopefully that harper will lead them astray," said Neary. "That might buy us time."

He spoke sense. Geth thought of Spittle and the other guardsmen, their fate at the hands of the crazies. With any luck they were already dead and their prisoners free. The more prisoners to escape, the harder the job of tracking them all down.

At Neary's insistence, they walked the horses right down the middle of the stream to throw off any pursuit using hounds. Geth's legs about froze, but the pain kept him from slipping into unconsciousness again. After a good mile splashing through the mud and over slick stones, Geth came to a place he recognized. He motioned them up the side of a shallow bank.

"Nobody knows these grounds better than Phelan," he said, "but if I'm right, Tumbledown Wall should be just around the next bend."

Rounding a curve in the stream, the orange twinkle of lanterns appeared ahead. They led their mounts through a gap in the crumbling fortification that had once encircled the town to arrive among the night-quiet lanes of Sorn, moon-washed cobblestones bright against the deep shadow cast by tenement after leaning tenement. Geth struck course into the darkness, out of sight. Cutpurses slunk back into doorways as the four of them passed, the clop of horse hooves the only sound until faint laughter and off-key singing floated to Geth's ears. He pulled up in front of a well-lit tavern on an otherwise silent row.

"We're looking for the Lady Largess," he told the doorman. The man looked them over, shook his head and went inside.

"Is this what I think it is?" Neary asked.

The big woman that came through the doors answered his question. Her dress was a garish purple and much shorter than the season demanded. She greeted them with

a hungry smile, one hip thrown out, neckline split to display her immense cleavage.

"What can I do for you lads this evening?" Her fingers
tousled the end of a yellow curl hanging down between
those huge breasts. "Looks like you could use a hot bath.
And gentle hands to do the scrubbing."

Neary looked to Geth. Kerrel's jaw dropped open. Wels
cleared his throat but by then she'd recognized her son.

"Gods above and below, is that you boy?" Her mouth
screwed up, face gone all shrewish. "Well, I've never been
more ashamed."

Geth was too spent to care. "We need a place to sleep.
And yes, we can pay."

CHAPTER FIVE

G eth awoke to a bright morning. *Too* bright. He backed away from the window into a shaded corner, dizzied and confused. Empty bottles of liquor and perfume cluttered a sideboard across the low-ceilinged chamber. The smell of face-powder choked the air. Only when Wels snorted in his sleep from the floor beside Geth's bed did it all come back to him.

The poor bastard was filthy beyond description. Looking down at the blood and grime on his own tattered rags, Geth reckoned he looked just as bad. The world was a different place under the Shaper's bright eye. He'd almost forgotten how different.

Easing himself into the sunlight, Geth let those rays melt away memory of the tower. He lay there for some time with just Wels's snores for company. Neary had left on some errand, but Kerrel came knocking at the door with a pair of tankards, two steaming bowls and several plates resting on a wooden tray.

"Breakfast!" He cleared a space on the sideboard and set the food down.

Wels bounced up like a spring. "Praise the Gods!"

Geth wasted no time either, shoveling meat and barley bread into his maw. The taste of sweet, bitter ale moved him almost to tears.

"Gods all bless you, Kerrel."

"Take some soup. They say it's good to build strength."

Geth reached for more pork instead. "I'll eat something solid while I still have teeth."

Wels was happy to slurp down both bowls of broth himself. Geth pushed the tray away only after he'd filled himself to bursting.

"How'd you pull it off?" he asked Kerrel. "Pretended to be Paellians?"

Kerrel beamed. "We couldn't figure any other way. Neary wore the white and played guardsman. I was the captured thief, bound at the wrists. But the way he stole those white tabards, I tell you it's him should have played the criminal. He walked us up to the place, got to arguing with the jailors. That got their attention. There wasn't supposed to be any new prisoners, you see?"

"Course not. They don't stow just anybody in that hell-hole."

"Things got a little loud. With all eyes on Neary, I was able to club a couple of 'em from behind."

Geth whistled.

Kerrel didn't look abashed at all. "We took down a third guard too, but the fellow with the key to the first door got away. They keep the two keys separate it turns out. For security I reckon. In the end, we just smashed the lock off with that axe. Another fellow had the key to the inner door. And then we were in."

"You've got the makings of a fine soldier, Kerrel. I mean that. And I won't forget what you've done for me."

"And I—" Wels belched loudly from his seat on the floor, "won't forget this meal, young sir. I ate like this every day once, you know. Succulent meats, fine wine. Ladies as fine as our dear hostess."

Geth muttered a curse. The food and ale were something but mention of his mother brought him back down to the well-worn mattress beneath him. As if by magick, the woman herself appeared in the doorway.

"We won't be here long," Geth said before she could start. "Just need a place to rest up for a day or two."

"Sure you do."

"Listen woman, the last time I was here I burned half this town to settle your debts. It's you that owes *me*."

"Well, that was useful. But there are four of ya. That'll cost."

"They're just here for some food and some rest. They're not here for a tumble, *Miss Largess*."

"They'll be wanting a tumble before long. And in the meantime, I'll need something for the work I missed last night. And the room."

Geth opened his mouth, but Kerrel reached under his tunic to count out silvers. Mother watched closely. She seemed a bit fresher than the last time Geth had seen her. Perhaps the night off had helped. Gone were the circles beneath her eyes. He smelled no beer on her breath either.

But her tongue was as thorny as ever. "That all you got?" She eyed Kerrel's coin.

Geth passed the silvers himself. "That's plenty."

"You're forgetting the food. And baths. I won't let you leave without a bath." She shook her head. "Worst you've looked in years. I'm not gonna ask what you've fallen into."

"Neary will have more coin when he gets back. No need to panic."

She hefted Kerrel's silver in one hand before tucking it away. "I suppose this will do for now." She threw out that hip once more, batted her lashes at his friends. "But if anyone sees anything they like, just remember it's only a coin toss away."

Neary returned within the hour, a bundle under each arm. He emptied a sack full of woolens, boots and a pair of travel cloaks onto the bed. Geth fingered the plain, country-style tunic. Neary had shed the white tabard he'd been wearing for similar dress but when Geth started to change, the lanky Umbleman wagged a finger.

"Not yet," he said. "You've had food and drink. Now it's time for soap and water."

Every muscle and joint still hurt but Geth managed to limp downstairs. The rags he wore had stuck to the dried blood of the wound on his shoulder blade and fresh blood ran down his back as his he yanked it free. Neary inspected the wound, washed it clean, and stitched it himself.

"Damn that hurts," Geth swore. "I'd kill you if I didn't love you so much."

"Keep it clean and you should be fine. It's not pretty though."

"You should see the other guy."

Steaming water awaited. Geth eased into one of the sealed troughs the brothel used as baths. Kerrel brought

Wels downstairs and forced him into a tub of his own. He resisted at first, but judging by the giggles, his lordship didn't regret it.

"Now there's a pretty flower," he said, pawing at the bony girl who arrived with their towels. Her painted lips parted in a smile, and she bent nearly double in a curtsy to expose her modest cleavage. Geth shooed her away and sent Wels back upstairs with Kerrel soon after, before he could purchase a tryst on Neary's tab.

Geth let the water soak in. He felt like new man almost. He'd rested, eaten and drank. Splashing warm water on his cheeks, he accepted a razor from Neary and went to work on the matted tangle on his face.

"Phelan hates it, but I'm keeping the mustache."

Neary chuckled, but Mother arrived in the doorway before he could make any quip. Geth would have shooed her off except for the tray of food she carried. At least the suds covered his nakedness.

"I'm sure you're hungry," she said. "Gods know you could use some fattening up."

"I guess this means you've already met Neary here. And his coin purse."

"Speaking of which, I'll need a deposit for the night." She set down the tray and held out a hand. "How much longer you plan on staying anyway?"

"Shouldn't you be out in the common room working the guests? Or you figure there's easier coin to be made shaking us down?"

"Nothing in life's free, boy. I don't have to tell *you* that."

Not even the love of a mother. Neary handed over several more silvers and she left the way she'd come. Geth watched her exit with a scowl.

"Won't be long before she bleeds us dry."

"It's alright Geth," Neary said, apologetic, like it was somehow his fault.

"It's not—"

"Doesn't mean anything. We've all got secrets, not that it's anybody's business."

Geth didn't bother arguing. He knew. Of course he did. Perhaps it was a family resemblance, or the sort of banter that only exists between family. He heaved a sigh. "Growing up with her, I don't know, maybe I should be thankful. Could be that made me stronger. She didn't have much love left over for me each day, not after sharing it out all night."

"Geth—"

"But I did have someone, a man of faith called Mather. He treated me well. Fed me, clothed me when he could. Even taught me to read."

Neary cracked a wry grin. "To read the Omnibus you mean."

"Well what kind of cleric would he be if he didn't?"

They shared a smile.

"It's alright, Geth," Neary said. "We're alright. Don't worry about her. If I told you how much coin the king gave us, you'd shit right there in your bathwater."

Geth blinked. Shame turned to pride at mention of Hadean. But the shame soon returned, thinking of his friends, the men he'd left behind. Even if it was against his will.

"I owe King Hadean. For letting the two of you come after me. And for a lot of other things."

"Melagus said he was better off without you." Neary snorted a laugh. "Called you a 'masterless dog.' After all you've done."

"Not the first time he's called me that."

"Maybe that's why Hadean sent us over the walls in secret. He didn't want to hear about it from the Asp."

"Over the walls? The Tooth was already under siege by the time you set out?"

Neary nodded.

"How'd you even know I'd been taken?"

"That bastard Palladine made it a point to send word back to Hadean."

"Of course he did. Highborn asshole."

"The Ilars swept down not a day after you disappeared," Neary went on. "But it wasn't hard getting down and out by rope. The river was frozen; we crossed easy enough. Sneaking past the Ilars would have been a tough one, but they hadn't really got set up on the west bank yet. There's no bridge there after all."

"Still, it was a risky thing you did."

Neary waved that off. Quietly competent, as always.

"Phelan told you where to find me, I reckon. But tell me, he still behind bars?"

"He is. And I worry for him, Geth. When the stores start running low, you can bet it's the prisoners who'll feel it first."

"Seemed to me like the cellars were bursting when I left." Geth frowned. "Not to mention all the timber and such. You reckon they didn't gather enough? We knew the siege was coming."

"Aye. But the king let too many villagers and townsfolk inside the walls. Couldn't leave 'em to the Ilars, could he? He'd ordered them south. You think they listened? Once the first homestead burned, they all ran for the Tooth."

Geth grimaced, mind working. He knew it was winter, but he couldn't say how long he'd been gone. There was a good chance Towerrock was running low on stores already.

"And the dozen?" he asked. "Inside the fortress as well?"

"Safe and sound." Neary smiled, like a fortress under siege was someplace anyone would want to be. "Now, the countryside?" the Umbelman continued, "the tribes were already busy pillaging when we left. Sword and fire to everything in their path."

"Bastards."

"An army at Waterset kept them from the south though. Lord Brant's men. And Towdric of Turey Hill. A few others."

"The same bastards that held out on Hadean in the first place," Geth said. "All except Brant."

"That's right." Neary's smile had gone. He looked like he wanted to spit, a nasty habit he'd probably picked up from Geth himself.

"We had the numbers to give 'em a go, didn't we, between Towerrock and Waterset?" Gethg shook his head. "If those cowards had answered the call."

"But they sat tight, away south. Brant included."

Geth cursed out loud. The water had begun to grow go cold. He rose dripping from the tub and reached for a towel. "They're waiting for Hadean to lose his grip on the realm."

Neary said nothing, but there were wits aplenty under those grey locks. He knew the truth of it as well as Geth.

"No need to send assassins after him now," the big warrior went on. "Hadean will be losing liegemen with every farmhouse that's burned. Every day he hides behind Towerrock's walls, his enemies grow stronger."

CHAPTER SIX

Despite his frustration, exhaustion got the better of Geth. He slept through most of the afternoon. Only the sound of hurried footfalls in the halls of Mother's brothel woke him, hand moving for his sword before he remembered Palladine had it now. On the floor at the foot of the bed, Wels snored, oblivious. Kerrel and Neary were nowhere to be seen.

Geth moved to the window, cracked a shutter to find several white-cloaked Paellian soldiers milling about in front of the inn.

"Thram's crooked cock..."

The door creaked behind him. Geth whirled but it was only Neary.

"Lilies."

Geth frowned. "Too many for my liking."

"They're asking around. But we should be alright. I spread enough silver to make sure everyone keeps quiet."

"They won't keep quiet for long. They'll be offering a reward soon, I reckon. And I wouldn't trust my own mother once she gets wind of that."

Wels sat up, rubbing his eyes. "Did someone say 'reward'? I do reward my liegemen richly."

Neary flicked a glance in the lord's direction and back. He grimaced. If he had more to say, he thought better of it.

Geth had plenty to think about already. They couldn't stay much longer, that was clear. For his part, Geth would have ridden for Umbel directly from the Tower of the Moon. But even after the day and half of rest, he wasn't sure how hard could he travel.

And then there was the matter of Wels. After so long a stretch in the tower, a whole month's rest might not be enough to prepare the man for the road. *Uro's puckered ass.* They couldn't leave him, and yet Geth knew they couldn't take him along either. Cracking the shutters again, the sight of a familiar shaved pate down on the street didn't improve his mood.

"Puckered, stinking, pockmarked ass!"

Palladine, the whore of justice himself, was there. Memories of a vomit-reeking hood, of countless beatings, and of the black pit of the tower sent a shudder through the big warrior. He summoned his indignation, stoked it to a rage until it melted away the icy ball in his stomach. A voice in his head told him he'd never be free until he'd had his vengeance. But another reminded Geth that he was in no condition to deal with Palladine, let alone the lilies he'd brought along.

The door creaked again as Mother backed into the room, closing the door behind her. She turned to face him, hands on hips. "You've really stepped in it this time, haven't you? Do you know how much they're offering for your hairy hide?"

"You won't turn me in."

"Ha! Someone else will beat me to it. That new bitch, Brena, or the horsegrooms—one of them will put it all together before long. They've got your description down pretty good."

"Looks like they're leaving," Neary said from the window. He sighed.

Mother just snorted. "Those lilies may be leaving now, but that high country captain of theirs doesn't seem like the sort to give up easy."

"High country?" Wels sucked in a breath. "*Palladine* is from the high country!"

"Sounds like I'm not the only one familiar with the bastard."

Mother sighed. "Listen, I'm not here to get your wine sack all tangled. I'm just here to give you some advice."

Geth raised an eyebrow. "And what's that?"

"It's time to go. This may be your one and only chance to get the hell out of here."

Their belongings were few. It wasn't a quarter of an hour before Geth and his friends had thrown on their cloaks, purchased provisions, and assembled in the hallway. The only loose end was Wels.

Neary must have seen Geth eying his lordship. "We can't take him with us," he told the big warrior. "You know that. He's about as mad as a three-legged tomcat. And it doesn't look like he'd last a half a day on the road anyway."

Geth didn't argue. An idea had begun forming in his head. With any luck, it would solve this problem along with a few others.

Mother met them in the stables. "The girls are already whispering."

"We're leaving now." Geth nodded toward Wels. "But this man needs to stay. Can you hide him? I'll pay in advance."

"The lilies—"

"Palladine's looking for me, not him. Just make sure someone hears how your good-for-nothing son has left for the Golden City."

Mother's eyes narrowed, but in the end she nodded. As long as they lined her pockets, she'd do it, of that Geth was certain. He turned toward Wels.

"I have to leave, Lord Wels. But Miss Largess will look after you for a time."

Wels looked Mother up and down. Geth didn't want to guess what was going through his mind. He bent over her hand to kiss it.

"I would be happy to remain in the company of our dear mistress, Lord Crusher."

"Gods watch over you." Geth turned to his mother. "Thank you. I mean that."

Her mouth opened. Probably about to utter something snide, Geth reckoned, but for once she held her tongue. They left her with enough silver to make her eyes go wide and headed down the alley behind the inn toward the city's nearest exit.

It was dusk, the streets and lanes busy as laborers and vendors made their way back home or to the tavern of their choice. If Palladine had posted any kind of watch, the lazy bastards did a poor job of it. Geth sat atop one of their two mounts, trailed by Kerrel on the other. The city shrank behind them. Neary reined them in from on foot in front of them. The north-south road crossed their path just a few furlongs ahead.

"Seems we've made it out of Old Sorn, but where to now?"

"Umbel of course," Geth said. "Home."

"Best we choose our route then."

Geth frowned. "You're asking whether we take a ship or look for another horse and journey over land?"

"That's right." Neary gave a nod. "But it all depends on what we've got planned once we get there. There's only two ways it can go. We can try to sneak into Towerrock and get back to the king. Or join up with Lord Brant or Towdric in the south."

"Thram's cock can join up with Towdric's ass."

Kerrel snickered but Neary's face screwed up, thinking. "So, we look to buy another horse and strike west across the Flats. That will take us into the northern vales."

"Last time, I made the journey by ship," Geth said.

"A ship would get us to Umbel in half the time, but we'd still have to make the journey upriver to get to the Tooth."

Geth thought that through. He looked from the lanky oldster to Kerrel and back. "There's no point sneaking back inside Towerrock, is there? If it's even possible. We'd just be another set of mouths to feed. We can't help the king from there."

"So, we take the west road out of Pellon you think?" Neary asked.

"No. From here, we head north. Palladine will figure out I had help from Umbel breaking out. He'll expect us to move west down the King's Passage or south toward the sea. But he won't expect us to go north."

Kerrel looked confused. "I thought your mother was already sending them east, toward the Golden City?"

"She is. And maybe that decoy will work."

Neary eyed Geth. "We still need to head west eventually."

"Eventually," said Geth. An idea had begun forming in his head—a crazy idea—but he kept it close for now. "In the meantime, we head north, through the high country and all the way to Turia."

"Turia?"

"Before I set out for Ilia with Phelan," Geth explained, "there was talk of gathering a few fighters from the Sworn

Realms, if only to harass the Ilar siege, put fear into those tribesmen that ventured out to burn and rape Hadean's lands."

Neary nodded that grey head. "Hit and fly."

"And kill wherever we can. With a few dozen Turian fighters, we'll be able to give it back to those leather-stinking bastards, one inch of steel at a time."

They traveled a few hours into the night, slept in a dilapidated cottage, and climbed back in the saddle again the next morning. Neary and Kerrel took turns riding the one horse while Geth rode the other. Much as it galled him, he didn't have his strength to take a turn on foot.

But he thanked the gods he hadn't been tempted to bring Wels. With any luck, the plan taking shape in his mind might draw Palladine out before he had the chance to dig deeper, uncover the poor bastard's hiding hole. Neary's voice shook him from those thoughts before he could dwell on it.

"So, you think we might scare up some swords in Turia?"

"Maybe." Geth kept his eyes on the road ahead. "I spent a few years among the clans, made a few friends. I might have stayed longer if my liege hadn't got himself run through."

Neary clicked his tongue.

"Then again, maybe not. In Turia, you see, you're an outsider ten miles from your own front door. They never really accepted me, even if I'd earned a full measure of their respect. Once Selden was gone, I had more enemies than friends. Feuds last for generations up in the mountains, and with Turian steel at every hip, you can imagine it was never the best place for the likes of me."

Neary grimaced, hearing that.

By Geth's own admission, there were holes in the plan you could drive a caravan through. The Umbelman could see them himself, but friend that he was, he let it lie.

Two days wending past winter-brown fields took them within sight of the snow-capped Priene Mountains, the border with Turia. Geth felt his strength returning even with the rigors of the journey. For that, he was thankful. On the third day, they arrived in the high country.

At midday, Geth stopped them at a village inn to get directions and gather supplies. He purchased a bottle of White Adus spirits and tucked it in among their saddle bags. Ignoring a raised eyebrow from Neary, he steered them west down a side road for several hours before halting them early for the night.

"This hollow should be enough to keep the wind off us," he said. "Let's get some rest. I want to be up early."

Neary harrumphed. "You ready to tell me what's going through that head of yours?"

"We need another horse."

"A horse? That's what this is about?"

"That, and Palladine."

Neary started a fire, shaking his head and muttering as he piled kindling on the little flame. Kerrel stepped away to tether the mounts. That lad would walk through a brick wall if Geth ordered it, but if he was going to do this, now was the time to tell them.

"Look, we can't be sure if Mother was able to send Palladine off to the Golden City. But I have an idea that will get his attention for sure." He knelt next to Neary to prod the fire, sending a wisp of red embers up into the evening sky.

"And this idea will get us another mount?" Neary asked.

"It will get us even, too." Geth grinned. He drew out the bottle of spirits, took a burning swallow, passed it to Kerrel. The lad managed a tiny sip before passing it on to Neary. The grey-headed fighter downed a hearty mouthful and muttered another curse.

"Something tells me this liquor's for burning more than our throats," he said.

"Palladine will be expecting us to turn either west or south, right?"

Neary and Kerrel exchanged a look, waiting.

"Well, my idea is to get his eye turned up here, north-wards. Once we know he's headed this way, we can head south, even circle back for Wels."

"But how's he going to know we're up here?" Kerrel asked.

A curse from Neary cut Geth short before he could answer. "Bloody High Country."

The big warrior couldn't help but smile. "Neary, why don't you tell him?"

CHAPTER SEVEN

A part of Geth wondered if the tower had permanently addled his wits, but even Neary agreed his plan laid out pretty neat. They needed a horse. They needed Palladine's eye off their actual path. And Geth needed to get a lick in while he had the chance.

"So, we burn down Palladine's house," Kerrel repeated, "but not before letting them see your face?"

"And steal a horse."

It was almost morning. They rode under a moonlit sky, through vineyards and past rows of manicured hedges until they reached a wall surrounding a large homestead situated on a hill out in the countryside. It was quiet, the roosters yet to crow. The wall, Geth reckoned, was more to keep out foxes and wolves than anything else. He climbed its modest height to get a better look inside.

A few out-buildings flanked the manor house—barns, a granary, a stable. Geth beckoned Kerrel to join him, showed him the layout. They jumped back down together.

"Alright," Geth told him. "You go in, set the granary on fire, and back over the wall with you. I'll head to the stables."

Kerrel frowned. "Why the granary and not the house?"

It was Neary who answered. "If we set fire to the house, there's no telling who gets burnt. Much as we hate the man, we didn't come here to kill Palladine's grandmother."

"They'll all head for the fire once it gets going," Geth said, "As soon as it's alight, I want you, Kerrel, back over the wall and waiting on your horse. I'll ride out once the place is good and panicked."

"You'll need the gates opened beforehand," Neary said. "You don't want to have to dismount to get it unbarred. I could slip over the wall with you and make sure the way out is clear."

Geth cocked an eyebrow. "Know a little bit about cattle rustling, do ya?"

"What can I say? I've been known to find a bit of mischief now and again. That's how I ended up doing penance at Point-fort."

"Thank the gods for that. I'd be dead without you. Now, if everyone's ready, let's move."

Kerrel went first, padding toward the granary. Geth jumped down next. His feet landed at the base of the wall with the soft crunch of boots on gravel. Neary came down slow but silent.

They split up. Geth listened for the low growl of dogs or the challenge of a watchman, but none came. Wealthy folks even kept their dogs indoors, he reckoned. Running at a crouch, he reached the stable. Horses snorted in their dark stalls as he paused to let his eyes adjust.

The smell of smoke hit Geth's nose, and the first dog started barking. *Good.* Kerrel would be back over the wall by now if everything was going to plan. The fire drew the dogs, followed by an angry voice, first shushing the animals then crying out in dismay. Other voices sounded as men and women rushed for buckets and water. Geth moved quietly down the aisle of the stable, passing draft animals and a few tired looking steeds until he arrived in front of a dappled grey with a proud neck and a defiant eye.

"There now, boy," Geth whispered. "I promise I'll be a better friend than that cunt, Palladine."

He had the beast saddled in moments, but a voice from behind cut him short. "You picked the wrong horses to wrangle, Turian." A sword hissed from its sheath to underscore the threat.

Geth turned, slow, brazen. "How's that?"

"Because these are the horses of Lord Palladine, captain of the first host, and hand of justice. You'll wish you'd been hanged when he's done with you."

"Palladine, you say?" Geth spat. "Never heard of the bastard."

The man edged forward, blade in hand. He wore no beard—Paellian style—but his close-cut silver hair signaled he was a soldier. Master-at-arms of the estate, Geth reckoned. The perfect man to kill.

"Fire the granary then make away with the horses, eh?" the old soldier was saying. "That's a worn out trick." He inched closer, sword-arm steady. But he didn't call for help.

Eager to handle things himself? Greedy sonofabitch. "I think I'll name my new horse Palladine," Geth goaded. "After your master. And what're you called? Might as well name that piebald gelding there after another nutless sonofabitch."

The attack came as Geth expected, a skip forward and a straight thrust, waist high. Twisting to his right with the speed that always caught his enemies by surprise, Geth let the tip whistle past. From inside the reach of that blade, he threw a jab forward, snapping the old soldier's head back. A left hook dropped the master-at-arms, and Geth hurried forward to kick him in the face before he could cry out. The blade clattered to the ground as the crusty bastard clutched at his bloody face.

Geth wasted no time, snatching it up. The master-at-arms had made it up to one knee as that blade came to rest against his neck.

"Turian whoreson."

"I hope you like this face, because it's the last one you'll see."

Instead of cutting his throat, however, Geth lowered the blade to stab under the man's ribcage, where the blood runs dark and thick. The old scratch groaned, collapsed to one side, hand at hsi side.

Geth knelt to wipe the blade on the hem of his cloak. "Don't want it to rust on my way to Turia."

"You'll pay." The master-at-arms winced around the words. "They'll skin you alive."

There was still some life in the man, just as Geth hoped. He climbed on the back of the grey. Two men appeared in the doorway behind the injured soldier, but Geth kicked his new mount to a gallop and scattered them with his exit, new sword in hand, never more alive.

CHAPTER EIGHT

G eth gathered up his friends, lead them through fields, across streams, and, eventually, down quiet lanes once it became clear they'd thrown any pursuers. He'd trodden these paths many times as a sword-for-hire on his way to and from Turia. Only Phelan knew the back roads of that region better.

On these paths, they avoided any chance of running into Palladine on his way northward. He'd know it was no coincidence what had happened, and he'd choose the quickest route. If things went according to plan, he'd continue north after that.

"The bastard that donated this sword," Geth slapped the naked blade thrust through his belt, "he's done a job for us. With his dying words he'll tell everyone exactly what I look like and that I was headed to Turia. I made sure of it. That will buy us the time we need to throw Wels across the back of a horse and be gone."

"But what if Palladine's man died before they found him?" Kerrel said.

"He didn't die. Not right away. I stuck him in the liver. A wound like that will fetch the harrows, but it could take a whole day."

Kerrel wasn't stupid. There were plenty of ways things could go wrong, in truth. But Geth reckoned the two men in the doorway had managed a look at him as well. At the very least, they'd tell the tale of a Turian horse wrangler, a man who'd likely be headed back to Turia. That was the tale Geth wanted them to tell.

"So, we're going back for him?" Neary asked. "To Sorn?"

Geth nodded and his friends didn't question him. The steed beneath him felt good. So too the sword at his waist. For the first time in a long time, he wore a smile.

The tiled rooftops of Sorn appeared on the horizon two days later. As a precaution, Kerrel waited with the horses on the outskirts of town while Neary and Geth returned to Mother's brothel, the Acorn and Branch. Sneaking in the back, Geth found Mother upstairs bidding farewell to a client.

"I'll be holding my breath 'til next time, my love." She blew a kiss to the paunchy, middle-aged man with saggy breeches and a dumb grin on his face. "Don't keep me waiting long."

"Never, Mistress. Never."

Saggy stepped past Geth and Neary with hardly a glance up. Mother's face went tense when she saw them.

"It wasn't my fault."

Geth and Neary exchanged looks.

"Someone must have told." Mother wrung out her hands. "I swear it wasn't me. I don't like it when people die."

Geth blinked. "Where's Wels?"

Mother's face twisted up. She started crying. Motioning them back to her room, she smoothed the rumpled blankets and collapsed into a seat on the bed, head in hands.

"It wasn't a day after you left." She spoke through her hands, sobbing. "They just stormed in and grabbed him. That bald one and a pair of twins with a country look about them."

Her big frame shook as she cried. Geth swore. He didn't doubt she was playing it up, for fear of his anger or that Neary might want some of his shine back, but there was real emotion in those tears. Mostly. For all her faults, the woman really didn't like violence. Never once that Geth could remember had she struck him as a child. He might have been better off if she had.

"Do you know where they took him?" He sat down beside her on the bed.

"Everybody knows. He's in the temple square, nailed up for all to see."

Poor Wels. Palladine had done a job on him. By the look of things, both his arms had been broken and at least a few fingers. When they'd wrung out all they could, Palladine and his boys drove spikes through his shoulders and pinned him against the side of Vorda's temple in the great square at the city center.

Geth eyed him from an alley mouth across the way. He had no curses this time, his anger was a cold one. A good thing too; Palladine would have watchers in the square. He'd noted the big warrior's temper, Geth reckoned, and fully expected him to barge up to the temple and pull his friend's body down.

"You think he talked?" Neary asked.

"Sure. But he didn't know anything other than the fact there were three of us."

"He may have heard us talking about King Hadean."

"Palladine already knows my connection to Umbel."

They moved under a cobbler's awning across the busy, stone-paved plaza, pretending to look at boots. Geth pulled at the end of his mustache through the scarf wrapped over his head and mouth, a makeshift disguise. He searched the eyes of passersby despite himself. His gut told him his business with Palladine wouldn't be over until one of them was dead. Maybe not even then.

"If our business in the high country worked," he told his friend, "Palladine will think we've headed to Turia. At least for the time being. If he comes looking for me in Umbel, I'll be ready this time."

Neary didn't press. Geth started them back the way they'd come, eager to have that scarf out of his mouth. He'd deal with Palladine by and by, but not until Hadean, Phelan, and all the rest were safe.

Neary took the lead as they walked, perusing the wares of stall after stall, buying provisions for the journey ahead. Food, waterskins, a bedroll for Geth. And a tent. They'd need that, especially on the Flats. It would be two weeks before they reached Umbel.

They headed straight for Kerrel and out of Sorn when they were done. This wasn't the time for goodbyes. If Palladine had eyes on Wels, he likely had eyes on the brothel as well. He'd left Mother with the coin they'd earmarked for Wels. That would have to suffice.

The same sort of back roads that had carried them south from the high country now took them west across Pellon. They slept in their tent each night and avoided villages as much as possible, reaching the western edge of the kingdom and the brown expanse of the Flats after three days.

"I reckon we've made it," Geth told Neary, stoking the fire on their first night beyond the borders of Pellon. Across from him, the grey-headed Umbleman wrapped himself in his blankets against the wind. Kerrel had already fallen into the deep, drooly sleep only a lad of his age could manage.

"In twelve days," Neary answered, "we'll reach Umbel."

"I wanted to thank you, Neary. Again. For making the journey and busting me out of that hole. Any longer in that place and my doors would have come all the way off the hinges."

"I wish we could've got you out sooner. But we had to bide our time, learn the comings and goings of the place. That took a good fortnight."

Geth eyed him from across the flames. "Not just anyone could have pulled that off. There's a lot more to you than a farmer-turned-soldier, isn't there?"

Neary waved that off.

Geth laughed. "Wish we had some White Adus. I bet there's a story there."

"Not one I'm proud of. But getting sent to the Boundaries was the best thing for me. Got me straight. Got me married and with a plot of land as well."

The Umbelman's eyes went distant, spoke to his loss. Geth changed the subject before the man could get to thinking on all the Affliction had taken.

"Well, you saved my life. And together we'll save more. Only problem is we're heading back to Umbel with nothing to show for it. No soldiers at our back to help the fight."

"What are you thinking?"

"I'm not saying we change course and join those traitors down in Waterset," said Geth, "but I can't see how we do anybody any good from inside Towerrock either."

Neary offered that sage old nod of his. "We need men."

"We need men. And I have no idea where to get them."

The fire crackled. A steady wind blew the flames in mad circles, but it stuck tight and kept burning. Some trick of Neary's, setting up the logs a certain way.

His voice broke the silence. "I think I know where we might find a few stout lads."

Geth looked up.

"There's a town called Stoney on the western edge of the Flats, just inside the borders of Umbel. Folk in those parts mind to their own business. They've got a decent wall around the village proper and I daresay they won't have left it. For Towerrock, Waterset, or anywhere else."

Stoney. It was something. But first they had to cross the wind-blasted scrublands of the Flats. According to the Omnibus, those lands were laid bare in the great battle of Angerfields, when a folk called the Elder Race attracted the fury of the gods. Deep rents in the earth still remained as evidence. Phelan would have been a better companion to ponder the topic, but Neary just nodded or shrugged in his usual stoic way. At least Geth had Kerrel to spar with each evening, training the lad and building his own strength back at the same time. The boy was like a younger version of Hadean, a natural fighter. It brought back good memories.

The great east-west trade route known as the King's Passage carried them toward Umbel until Neary veered them off its course ahead of a broad winter-grey wood. "This is where we turn north. We're right on the edge of Umbel, but a straight ride through the Aldwood will only take us to Turey Hill, Towdric's lands. We don't want a run-in with Crookbow and his highwaymen either."

"In the forest?" Geth asked.

Neary turned his eyes north. "It's that direction will take us to Stoney anyway."

Two days would see them to the town. They took shelter in a crofter's cottage, the first sign of civilization in those distant reaches of the realm. It was a damn sight warmer than their tent, and a good thing too. Several inches of snow came down overnight, a possibility Geth had almost forgotten about in southerly Pellon. Winter had arrived, and with it a bone-numbing chill. When the chimney smoke of Stoney finally tickled Geth's nostrils, he was ready for a night at a well-provisioned inn.

"You really think we'll be able to gather fighters here?" he asked, leading his grey up a rocky hillside toward a settlement on what looked like the remains of some ancient fort. They'd passed a few empty homesteads, but the one person they'd seen, a young shepherd, steered his flock away at their approach.

"Don't be fooled," said Neary. "They're here, watching our every step. Now if we manage to come away with anyone, that's another matter."

Geth eyed their surrounds as they climbed Stoney's hill. Forested mountains could be made out purple and hazy in the north. *Ilia*. A pair of bowmen wrapped tight in their cloaks called down from behind the town's man-high wall as they neared the crest.

"What's your business?"

"Well, we're not Ilars, are we? You gonna let us in or not?"

The gate to the town was wooden but stout. It swung open with the creak of heavy timbers. Geth stared, surprised by the dense cluster of snow-blanketed rooftops inside, the wide village green.

"Could be five hundred people in here," he said out of the side of his mouth.

Neary nodded. Kerrel just took in the sight. A woman with a fine shawl and a neat grey braid had already started toward them. An old soldier wearing Umbel green and a frown followed in her wake.

But not before the first of the two bowmen from the wall hurried over. "It's the king's Paellian! I saw him at Copper Ridge." He turned to Geth directly. "I saw your duel with the Ilar champion, er, my lord."

The lad hurried to salute, but Geth waved that off. "I'm no lord, just another brave warrior like you." He squinted as if trying to recall something. "Copper Ridge though. That's right. The men of Stoney made a name for themselves there. Fought like savages."

The bowman's face lit up, but the shawled woman met them there, in the middle of the green, before he could reply.

"King Hadean's men, are you?" she asked. Around the green, watercarriers and shopkeeps stopped to watch.

"That's right," said Geth.

"And what's your business in these parts?"

"Just here for food and rest."

"Then all will be well. I'm Landren, lady of Stoney. And as such, the keeping of these folk rests on my shoulders. To that end, I must tell you our rules before you get comfortable."

Geth frowned. "Rules? Are the king's men not welcome here?"

"These are times of war. And in war, people must look out for themselves. Our rule is this: any friend of the realm seeking shelter may find it here. But only for one night."

"One night, eh?" Geth looked to Neary and back to Landren.

"That's all. Tomorrow, you move on. Only those who have sworn their oaths to Stoney may stay."

"To Stoney?"

Landren nodded. "And me."

CHAPTER NINE

Stoney's inn, the Goose and Gander, was a hidden gem. The steaming soup, the deep brown ale—Phelan would have loved the place, except for the lack of working girls to work the patrons.

But Landren's words about leaving in the morning rang in Geth's ear. If he swore anything to that woman, it wouldn't be an oath.

"Sure is quiet in here," he told Neary, eyeing the empty tables.

"It's the lady." The Umbelman grimaced into his cup. It couldn't have been because of the taste.

"You think so? Think she's keeping the village folk away from us?"

"Has to be. Should be at least a drunk or two at the bar. Just look at the innkeeper."

Geth flicked a glance toward the red-cheeked propri-
etor. The poor scratch stood drumming his fingers for-
lornly on the polished surface. If Neary was right, the three
of them were costing the man a lot more than they were
spending. On a good day, there could have been dozens of
people shuffling in for a seat by the fire and a drink.

Geth hailed the man over. "Hello, friend. You know
how to run an establishment, if I'm allowed a say so. And
I've seen my fair share."

The innkeep managed a nod.

"You get any news in these parts?"

"Some."

His answer was a guarded one, but after a moment of
thought, he came all the way from around his bar to stand
behind the empty chair at their four-seater. Perhaps he
hoped a bit of news might see them to their room now that
they'd eaten and drank.

They asked him about the war, the king, and anything
else he might know. In a few words, he confirmed all that
Neary had told Geth back in Pellon. The Ilars had marched
south to lay siege. Brant and Towdric held the south.

"Not pushing north," Red-cheeks told them. "Not being pushed either. Upriver from the ferry at Waterset, the
tribesmen roam free. But not here in Stoney."

"What about the mountain-holds out west?" Neary asked.

"Haven't got a messenger pigeon from the Tooth in a while. Who can say?"

Geth nodded. "Have you heard anything about the Ilars, who came south—who's forces are set up where?"

"They all look pretty much the same to us. But one of the lads did say their woman chief hadn't been seen. Some speculation around that. I don't know enough to make sense of it."

Geth sent the innkeep back to his barrels for another round of ales. "You hear that? By his account, Vriana's missing. You think there's any truth to it?"

Neary and Kerrel exchanged looks. "Nobody saw her banners when the siege first rolled in," the older man said. "But everyone assumed she'd gone further south to hold Brant's army in check. Or cause some other sort of mischief."

Geth pulled at his mustache. The door to the inn creaked open before he could think on it more. That scowling old soldier held the door for Lady Landren's entrance, pushed in, almost, by a blast of cold air. Thankfully, they got the door closed again behind them. Landren didn't wait for an invitation, seating herself in the empty chair at their table.

"I trust you've enjoyed a good meal." Landren eyed the pile of empty bowls, mouth twitching in something like a smile. "I was hoping you might share any news you've heard in return. We don't get many travelers from Pellon."

Geth snorted. She'd already put together that they'd arrived from the east, not the south. No telling what else she knew. "What can I tell you, m'lady?"

"I wonder what business could have drawn you to the East? That's an awful long distance from the fighting, especially for the king's great champion."

"Seems you know a few things already. More about me than I know about you, at any rate."

Landren didn't so much as blink. "This town depends on me. I make it a point to know things."

Red-cheeks arrived with that second round of ales, plus a mug of tea for the Lady. She took a sip, looked up at Geth, waiting.

"Well, I was sent to Pellon to fetch swords," he told her. "Sworn allies and such, this being a war."

"Sworn allies," she repeated, watching him like she was looking for tells. "Well, it does seem we could use more swords, as you call it."

"The ships won't sail for another month though," he lied.

"So late in the season?" She wasn't stupid.

"Help is on the way, rest assured. King Hadean has plenty of friends, long may he reign." Geth lifted his tankard. Neary and Kerrel followed suit. Landren copied the gesture with less enthusiasm.

"It's good you've got men on the way," she said after another sip at her tea. "Because you won't find any here. The king's got most of our boys up in the Tooth already. We don't need his green-cloaks coming to scrape up the rest."

Geth nodded. "I reckon those men are heroes, standing beside their king in these times. The war is out there, after all. And it won't win itself, even once the lilies arrive."

"I take it you'll join the fight again yourself?"

Geth didn't know if she was angling for his oath, and the three extra swords that would bring her, but he squashed the idea. "As soon as I can."

"Will you join the lords Towdric and Brant then?"

"Do I look like a coward?"

Landren sniffed. "Someone needs to protect the south. If no one plants in the spring, how will we eat in the fall? And the whole of the north will lie fallow at this rate with the king hiding in his fortress."

Geth swallowed a sharp reply. Had the ladies and lordlings of the countryside already begun to turn on Hadean? Maybe it was just this one old hag.

"I hear you have pigeons. I'll want a message sent to Towerrock."

"We do. But I don't lose my birds for free. We haven't got many left."

"Name your price. Just address a message to the king and tell him, 'The masterless dog has slipped his leash. He's roaming the yard.'"

He paid the lady an exorbitant amount for her pigeon, haggled with the innkeeper for more supplies, and they retired to the stable. Hadean's silver was finally running low, but Red-cheeks let them sleep among the beasts for free. Anything to get them out of his common room.

"Thieving old wench," Geth grumbled as they bedded down in the hay.

Kerrel was asleep in seconds, but Neary loosed a sigh. "I guess we won't be staying long."

"True. But that doesn't mean we won't get what we came for."

Neary rolled on his side to meet Geth's eye.

"They knew me," Geth told him. "You heard that bowman when we arrived. They'll be talking about us, what we did at Copper Ridge."

"You think that might be enough?"

"There are always fools that answer when the drums of war start beating."

"I guess I'm one of them." Neary said. "We both are."

"We may have answered, but we're no fools. This war came to *us*. It's the folk of Stoney who are fools if they think it won't come to them too."

Stable or no, it was as good a night's sleep as Geth had had in weeks. The animals and the hay kept the place warm. In the morning, they packed up and left the Goose and Gander. A bright sun gleamed off the previous day's snow, the village green bustling with lads fetching water, girls minding toddlers, grown folks clustered in knots against the cold, beginning their day with some gossip.

Whatever the topic, the appearance of Geth and his friends trumped it. Stoney's townsfolk fell quiet. If there was any chance of plucking a few fighters from this lot, the big warrior reckoned this was it.

He nudged his grey toward the well near the center of the green. They filled their skins, but Geth made sure to push back his sleeves despite the frigid air, revealing the blue ink wrapped around each forearm. There was something alluring about those tattoos, in Umbel anyway, where they knew little of the Mog. He washed his hands, drank deeply, then climbed up into the saddle and kicked his mount in a slow, purposeful circle of the snow-crusted green.

"People of Stoney," he called out. "You may have heard there's a war going on. Well, I'm going out to fight it. If anyone else wants to kill Ilars before they come to kill you, you can join me."

Landren arrived with a face as stony as her town, but Geth turned his mount toward the gate before she could speak. Neary and Kerrel followed in his wake.

"Now what?" Kerrel asked, pulling up alongside as they started downhill.

"We leave."

"That's it?"

"Not too fast. They need to see which way we're headed in case it snows again and covers our tracks."

The same young bowman that had stopped them on their way into town stood waiting for them halfway down the hill. "Where to, Captain?"

Geth flicked his head downhill. "I reckon we'll make camp nearby somewhere. Once we get our bearings, we begin the hunt."

"For Ilars?"

Geth nodded. "We lost some good lads at Copper Ridge. You were there, you know as well as anyone. I'll not stand by while the same bastards that killed my friends rape their wives and burn their homes."

The bowman blinked, but Geth just saluted with fist to heart, waved Neary and Kerrel on.

They rode through patches of melting snow until they came upon an empty homestead with a stable and a well just a few miles from the town. The owner must have retreated behind Stoney's walls. Or been killed. By the next morning, the bowman and several others had found them.

"I'm Drayic," the bowman said. He tugged at the end of his green cloak. "I've fought before and I'm ready to fight again. We all are."

"Then you've come to the right place." Geth clasped hands with each of them. It was a paltry force, seven odd ball villagers—and two of them women besides. Far less than what he'd hoped for. But Geth didn't voice that even to Neary.

"Brings us up to ten," he told the Umbelman out of the side of his mouth as they settled in. "Almost a full file."

"Reminds me of our file back at the Tooth."

Geth met Neary's eye. They shared a smile.

What they didn't have in weapons or experience, Geth reckoned, they'd make up for in knowledge of the land. Drayic was the only one with a sword, a former green-cloak. Who could say why he'd left, but guilt or something else brought him back with purpose in every stride. And judging by the bows and full quivers, the lot he'd pulled together knew more than their share about hunting. Geth nodded, sizing them up. Had the gods actually thrown him a bone this once? A band of archers might be exactly what he needed to harass the tribes.

The hunt began the next day. Remote as Stoney seemed, it was only a hard day's ride from Iyengar and his siege of the Tooth. Geth marched his makeshift troop straight toward it.

They hadn't traveled ten miles before the scent of smoke hit their noses. Geth sent Drayic out ahead to scout the source. He came back huffing but wearing a grin.

"It's Ilars, Captain. Four of 'em!"

Four. Geth reckoned he'd never get a better chance to break this lot in. They followed Drayic back quietly the way he'd come. There was no need. From the edge of a snowy clearing Geth looked on as three drunken tribesmen hooted and spread fire from cottage to barn to shed of a small compound. A fourth Ilar seemed to be passed out against a tree bole, wrapped in his cloak, wineskin in his lap.

"String those bows," Geth said, voice held low. "It won't be easy to hit anything from here, but this is what we're gonna do. Kerrel and I will sneak around to the right. Ladies, you come with us. But first let down your hair. You won't need any weapons other than that."

"What's the plan, Captain?" the first of the girls asked, a redhead with a no-nonsense chin and men's trousers.

"Call me Geth."

"What's the plan, Captain Geth?"

The big warrior just shook his head. "Alright, this is what we're gonna do. I want you, er..."

"Red,"

"Red, right. I want you, Red, and you—"

"Loura,"

"—Loura, to let down your hair and come in from the right like you've just arrived home. And what a shock it is for two defenseless girls to run into Ilars? Those bastards will come after you faster than you can shout."

"They'll come after her," Red said, hooking a thumb at her friend.

Loura, blushed. Indeed, she had pretty lashes, and a nice wave to that dark hair. But the way she gripped her bow, Geth wouldn't want to cross her. One of Drayic's boys clapped her on the shoulder and they shared a laugh.

"Now, the distraction will allow Drayic and everyone else to sneak up a little closer from over here, where we are now. Once the Ilars start the chase, you girls scream and run back the way you've come. Kerrel and I will be waiting to spring out of hiding once you run past. If any of them avoids the arrows, we'll mop up."

"What if they get wise, turn and run the other way?" Neary asked.

"Good point. You better take a couple lads and move out to the left, just in case."

It was a simple plan and easy to understand. The kind that worked. They took up positions and Red and Loura moved in, hands at their mouths like they'd just hurried home to find the place on fire. The sight of a woman's hips snared the Ilars exactly as Geth knew it would.

With hoots and cries, the three standing tribesmen pointed and gave chase. The arrows came flying almost immediately and two of them went down. The one against the tree died before he could stand, but the third was still hard on the girls' heels, oblivious, when the pair rushed past Geth's hiding spot.

Before the big warrior could stand though, Kerrel had surged by him, sword flashing. The tribesman ran headlong into a hacking stroke that broke his arm and dropped him. A tidy thrust finished the job.

Kerrel stood over the dead Ilar, sword red, as the man bled out on the snow. Geth whistled. He looked up as the rest of the band trotted out into the clearing toward their dead enemies. No less than a half dozen shafts protruded from each of them.

"Bows down," Geth told them. "It's over."

CHAPTER TEN

They'd done it. Modest as it was, Geth couldn't call it anything less than a victory. They'd killed enemies, taken weapons, spoils, and supplies, without so much as a scratch. The only shame was that an arrow had pierced that skin of Ilar berry-wine, curtailing any hope of a celebratory drink.

But the smoke and heat from the burning buildings forced them to retreat anyway. Geth raised his blade and took the four Ilar heads before they left.

"Like at Point-fort?" Neary asked, recalling an expedition north before this war had even begun.

Geth nodded. "A tithe, for the folk of Stoney."

They stowed their plunder at their homestead beneath the town and made straight up the hill toward the green. Drayic, Red, and the others strutted all the way up, grim trophies gripped by the hair. Sentries on the wall watched wide-eyed.

Landren met them at the gate. "You really are a fool." Smoldering eyes flicked from the Ilar head in Kerrel's grip and back to Geth. "You'll bring the wrath of the tribes down on us. And at the same time steal the very fighters we need to defend ourselves."

"Stay calm, woman. We're not staying. This is just a token to remind your folk that they can be wolves if they want, not sheep."

"The only thing you'll remind anyone is that we're *here*. Stoney survives by staying out of sight."

"Hiding, you mean."

"Would you rather we had joined Hadean, weighing him down with yet more mouths to feed? Or should we have trudged south, to starve through the winter?"

"You've already made your choice."

"All for naught." The lady snorted, flicked that grey braid over her shoulder. "You've brought attention to Stoney already."

She turned. Geth followed her eyes toward the inn. Several men in Umbel's green crossed toward them. Catching sight of the big warrior they all started shouting at once.

"Sergeant Geth!"

"You're here!"

"We've found 'em!"

"Ha!" Geth hooted for joy. He'd never been so happy to see those seven ugly faces. It was easy to forget about Landren amid a storm of embraces, back-slapping, and hand-clasping.

"How did you find us?" Geth asked finally.

"King Hadean got your pigeon," said Hack. "I'm not sure Melagus was happy, but the king told us straightaway and asked if we wanted to go over the walls. The river's still froze solid so we just slunk down by rope and creeped and crept along the ice until we were south of the siege."

Geth squeezed a shoulder, and a smile parted the Umbelman's pimpled face. Hack, Bird-man, Blink, Sweaty, Dodger, Red-eye and Baby—the remainder of the Dead-man Dozen. Landren watched with a scowl, arms crossed, that old green-cloak at her back like always. Geth waved the boys toward the gates, speaking loud enough for the lady and everyone else to hear.

"C'mon, men." He turned to Drayic and the rest. "But we leave those heads here. There's more where they came from."

Introductions were made, news exchanged. Three more lads from Stoney caught up with them at the homestead as well, bringing their numbers to twenty. They had the makings of a proper warband. Finally. After a night's rest, Geth had them up and marching to resume the hunt.

"I have a message from Phelan," Hack told him on the road. He looked over both shoulders and whispered. "He said to hurry and win this war before he starves."

Geth frowned. "Stores running low already?"

"He wasn't starving, not yet. Not with us around to sneak him a bite. But the whole of the Tooth was already on half-rations when we left."

Geth didn't like the sound of that. Less than two months in and already tightening their belts? He looked at his little troop. With twenty fighters, and more than a few of them trained green-cloaks, at least he could finally do something about it.

But Landren's fears weren't misplaced either. Geth reckoned he wasn't doing anyone a favor if he kicked the hornet's nest then led a swarm of Ilars back to Stoney. He marched his little war band south and away.

If he'd learned anything from his time among the Mog, it was that you couldn't kill what you couldn't catch. They hadn't the steeds that defined the way of life of the horse-borne tribes of the east, but they had excellent archers and scouts. Between his dozen and Stoney's folk, they knew the land, the roads, and the towns. The Ilar habit of sneaking away in small groups to plunder presented an opportunity as well. The tribesmen traveled without fear but were few in number. They weren't hard to find, track, and slaughter.

Geth kept the band moving all that week, hitting targets on either side of the river, north as far as the Boundaries, south nearly to Waterset. Most dwellings they came across had already been burned and looted, but they found a few intact to provide shelter. They never stayed in once place long, living off the spoils taken from the enemy. In those first seven days, they racked up another dozen kills.

A barrel of ale left behind at an abandoned wayhouse capped off the week's work. Blink, it turned out, could cook with the best of them and a bit of grain and some venison had the makings of a hearty stew in his hands. Geth set a watch and let the band indulge that night.

"Got a message from Phelan," Baby told him out of the side of his mouth, stepping across the common room of the place when the bowls were licked clean. They burned no fire, but the heat of many bodies warmed the place.

"I already heard," Geth said.

"You heard he's planning to name his inn after you?"

"He what?"

"He said to tell you that if you get him out, he'll name his inn after you. When he has one, that is."

Geth eyed Baby sideways. "That was his message?"

The green-cloak grinned.

"So why whisper it?"

Baby frowned, rubbed the round belly that had earned him his nickname. "I don't know? He said it was for your ears only."

Geth was still thinking that through when Sweaty came hurrying in his direction.

"What is it?" Geth said, one hand already on his hilt.

"Something strange, sir. A wolf. Circling the shadows outside of camp."

"A wolf?"

"Should we shoot it? He won't leave."

Geth followed the green-cloak back outside and there it was, grey-white and bounding right toward him.

"Eko!" Geth laughed as the animal closed the distance, stretched up on two legs to nuzzle and lick his face. Geth rubbed his head, kissed him back, but Eko dropped down on all four, turning a circle, whining and nudging Geth with his nose.

"Is that the Seer's wolf?" Neary asked, arriving out in front of the wayhouse.

"It is."

"Where is he then?"

Geth looked both ways down the road. "I don't know."

They shared a look, Eko whining and nudging Geth all the while

"Somethings wrong, Neary."

"You think he's in trouble?"

Geth nodded. "Spread the word and gather your things. We're leaving."

Eko led and Geth followed. They left the little valley and the road beside the wayhouse and marched over dark hills to the west. Bare-branched trees cast claw-like moonshadows across their path. At least they had enough light to see by.

They traveled through the cold, without halt, for hours. When Geth did pull them up, the beast whined and turned circles again. Geth looked to Neary. The Umbleman guessed his thoughts.

"You go ahead. I'll stay with the band and make camp here. But take Sweaty so you don't get lost on the way back."

"I'll take Dodger too. He never sleeps. And Kerrel, in case I need a good sword."

"Better take Drayic and his bow too."

With his four men and a minimum of supplies, Geth whistled for the wolfdog, and they set out again. His feet were sore and his eyelids heavy, but one look from the beast was enough to keep him moving. What Eko wanted, Geth couldn't say, but he knew the matter was grave.

Sweaty stopped them at the crest of a hill. "We're near the enemy lines, sir. The siege."

Geth looked down. The first grey light of a new day tinged the eastern sky, to their right. The river wound like a smooth white ribbon below them. Towerrock stood tall and defiant on its island.

"Where are you leading us?" he muttered aloud.

Drayic came to stand at Geth's side. He cleared his throat. "You said this was the Ilar's wolf, sir. Can we trust it?"

"We can trust Agrem." Geth looked to Eko. "And we can trust Eko. Did the Shaper ever make anything so loyal as a dog?"

"I suppose he didn't."

It wasn't much farther. They had to move carefully this close to the Ilar encampments, but when Eko took off at a sprint for a thicket, Geth knew this was it. There among the close-spaced trees, an Ilar tent had been raised. The fire beside it had burned out.

Geth waved his men to a halt at the edge of the trees. "Agrem!" he called, half yell, half whisper.

The tent flap parted, and the Seer appeared, Eko at his side tongue lolling. Agrem's cheeks stretched in a smile, seeing the big warrior, but they were hollow beneath his beard, the lines on his forehead deeper than Geth remembered.

"Smart dog, Eko. Mmmm?"

"Brave too."

Agrem shook his head, patting the beast's side. "And I thought he just ran away."

Geth closed the distance to embrace the tribesman. Agrem waved him toward the remains of his fire. They sat on the ground, hands tucked under their cloaks, not bothering to kindle a flame.

"Well?" Geth asked.

Agrem heaved a sigh. "Iyngaer sent me out. I have nothing. Only enemies."

The defeat in his tone was plain. Geth looked up to find Kerrel, Sweaty and Drayic circled around, looking anxious. They couldn't stay long.

"Are you hungry?"

That got the Seer's attention. He'd never been one to look sideways at a meal.

"Good." Geth rose, reached out a hand to help Agrem up. "I've got a cook that can make crumbs to cutlets, just over the hill."

CHAPTER ELEVEN

Geth got them moving again before cold and weariness could really sink in. Eko trotted contentedly beside his master until they met the rest of the band over and beyond the top of the bluffs overlooking the river valley. After an hour's rest, Geth pushed them all the way to the wayhouse. He collapsed in one of the rooms, Agrem snoring beside him, just like the old days. Eko stretched out in front of the door.

The smell of Blink's cooking woke Geth sometime later. He found Agrem at one of the tables, already on his second helping. Blink hurried over with to set a bowl down for Geth across from the Seer.

"I told you I knew I good cook," Geth said, pulling up a seat.

"Mmmm." The Ilar looked down at his bowl, breathed a sigh. "Thank you. Agrem the Seer, starving in the woods..."

"It's his loss, Agrem. All you want is what's best for Dues. I never liked that ball-scratcher anyway."

"Iyngaer? He is a great man. He wants great things. I stood in the way."

"You can see the future, 'Grem. Can he see anything beyond the tip of his own cock?"

"Mmmm."

"You did what was right for your folk. The tribes weren't starving, you said it yourself. Every man, woman, and child that dies in this war has died because of his greed."

The Seer looked up to meet Geth's eye. "What do I do now?"

"You help stop him."

"I can't fight him."

Geth grimaced. The poor bastard looked about as dejected as a wet cat. "Well—"

"And I can't help you fight him, mmmm? Iyngaer is still my chieftain, the Duei still my people."

"What about Ceter and his lot?"

The Seer blinked. "Ceter. Never liked this...ball-scratch, as you say."

Geth laughed, clapped the Ilar on the back. "Me neither. Let's start there."

The last of the Ilar berry wine washed down Blink's stew. Night fell. Geth took a turn at watch then retired back to the same room he'd shared with Agrem earlier. The Ilar snored softly in his sleep. Eko climbed up on Geth's bed and settled against his leg, head resting over one calf like a huge puppy.

Geth stared up at the ceiling. The sight of Towerrock the day before had stuck in his head, the town of Greenfell half-burned, Ilar tents ringing all of it in. He thought of Iyngaer, of Ceter. The things they'd done to Geth and his friends could never be forgiven.

Hadean and Phelan wriggled in their net even now, subsisting on half-rations less than two months into the siege. How long could they last? How long before the Tooth crumbled from inside out under the weight of starvation and fear?

"We need to do more," Geth told Neary in the common room of the wayhouse.

The Umbelman nodded that grey head. "Been thinking the same thing."

"Every time we pass a burned homestead or village, I wonder if we could have stopped it."

"That's war."

"But what have we accomplished so far?" Geth met his friend's eye. "For Hadean and everyone else? We've let a little blood, that's true. But just a drop compared to the buckets the Ilars have spilled."

"What are you saying?"

"We've been doing things all wrong,"

Neary frowned. "How can we make things level, twenty of us against Iyngaer's thousands?"

"We can't. But what we *can* do is send a message."

"To the Ilars?"

"Towerrock too. Let them know we're out here, getting in a few licks, sticking it to those leather-stinking bastards."

Neary smiled. "So, what's the plan?"

"Well for starters, I reckon we should have left more tribesmen alive after each strike."

"To carry word back. Right."

Geth nodded. "Spread the fear. Let it be known there's a dog in the yard now. Beware or get bit."

"That's something."

"We can't just rely on a rumor though. And then there's the Tooth. We need to show, not tell."

Neary raised an eyebrow.

"It's King Hadean and all his soldiers who really need the message. Phelan too. We need to hit the siege itself, take a bite out of the tribes, beneath the walls for all to see."

They set to work straightaway, allowing one tribesman to escape from each of the next two ambushes they set. A couple of Ilars had managed to survive earlier efforts and Geth reckoned the word of those few would have spread by now as well. He moved his band across the river to the western banks of the river before Iyngaer could retaliate.

That's where he wanted to be anyway. According to the Dozen, the Ilar ranks ringing the great fortress were much thinner in the west since the island sat nearer the opposite bank. They spotted one roving band of Ilars along the way, but between his file and the lot from Stoney, they knew the paths better than any tribesman and arrived unscathed and unseen on a pine-topped hill overlooking the North River's valley.

Geth left the band hidden in the woods and crawled up beside Bird-man that night to get a view.

"Down there," the green-cloak said. He pointed through the trees to a swathe of Ilar tents clustered along the banks of the frozen river. A fresh blanket of snow on the ground amplified the light of a waning moon. Towerrock's five grey spires gleamed ghostly white in the distance.

"We could wait for a darker night," Geth mused aloud. "But every day grinds down the men in the Tooth as much as those bastards down there."

"That's an awful lot of tents," Bird-man said. "I don't know..."

"We need to get closer, have a better look."

Bird-man nodded and they crept carefully downhill until individual tribesmen could be made out, wrapped in cloaks beside their fires, snoozing through their watch, Geth imagined. Not a one of them faced him, eyes trained on the river and the fortress instead. There were sharpened stakes angled that way and a half-height earthwork along a stretch of the banks as well. But not a man so much as took a piss westward, in Geth's direction.

"Easy pickings," he muttered. Except for those few huddled sentinels and a row of men standing guard atop that earthwork, the entire camp slept. His eyes had already moved back to the tents when Bird-man sucked in a breath.

"What is it?" Geth followed the Umbelman's gaze back to the makeshift wall facing the water.

"Those aren't guards on that wall."

"Vorda's dripping slot." Geth's worst curses weren't bad enough. They were corpses.

Bird-man's eyes were sharper than anyone's, but with a closer look, even Geth could see how that row of men atop the earthwork stood too still, too rigid. He swore again, thinking of the heads he'd taken. The Ilars knew how to play that game as well.

"They've impaled 'em," Bird-man said. He swallowed, knobby apple bobbing on his thin neck. "More than a dozen. You think there's a chance they might be Ilar deserters? A message to the others not to try it themselves?"

Geth shook his head. "Those might be deserters. But from the Tooth, not the tribes."

The only thing for it now was to figure how to get even. Geth squinted hard at the scene below. Judging from the tents scattered along a good mile of riverbank, he reckoned the Ilar force at over two thousand fighters—on this side of the water alone. That might be one reason Brant and Towdric hadn't rushed to whip the bastards back to Ilia—or better yet, to Vorda's cold hell. There were probably three or four times as many tribesmen on the eastern bank.

Geth swallowed another curse, studied the markings on shields leaned up against one another outside stretched-hide tents. The antlered hart of the Arnui, others like a badger, a ram, and something resembling a flowing river. He couldn't attribute these to any tribes he knew, but he didn't miss the absence of the bear of Iyngaer's Duei and the fox of Ceter's Thirings.

"No crescent moon for Vriana's folk either," he said aloud. But those shields had given him an idea. He made note of the placement of the Ilar tents, where the horses had been tethered, the position of their wagons and stores. There were several paths in and out.

"Hit and fly," he muttered under his breath. He waved for Bird-man and started back up the hill.

Geth knelt beside a crude map scratched in the mud, crowded around by the band. They'd spent a day resting and were ready for some action. Geth had used that time to fashion a plan that would give it to them.

"So, we sneak in from here," he pointed with a stick, "and ride out like hell from here. Tonight, in the darkest hours."

He looked up and was met by firm nods. They'd been over it enough times. Everyone knew their part.

The idea was simple: kill a few sentinels, burn as much as possible, and ride away. But with only ten horses, a clean execution would be critical. And a clean exit. They'd chosen the only road out that wound *between* the hills, rather than up them. They'd hit the lines of besiegers nearest that route.

A winding retreat set up the possibility of laying an ambush for their pursuers as well. That's where the real bloodletting would happen. Blink and Red had come up with the idea to stretch a rope across the path behind them. In the dark, riding hard, the Ilars would never see it in time. Hidden archers could pick off the downed riders one by one. With any luck, the mere sight of that deathtrap would send any late pursuers back the way they'd come.

Geth assigned the gang from Stoney the archer's job. His Dead-man Dozen would do the rest. Creeping in, they'd slit throats and light fires then ride out on their ten horses. The others would wait along the exit route with their bows, tying up the tripwires once the Dozen passed and sending arrows at anything that came after.

"Remember, it's the fires that will give the Tooth something to see." Geth stood, dusted off his hands. "Torch the wagons first, they'll burn brightest. Forget about the tents."

He left them with orders to take more rest but crawled back over and down the hill to get one last look at the enemy by light of day. It was a jovial bunch the tribes had gathered, frying eggs from chickens they'd filched, drinking from barrels stolen out of Umbel's taverns. Geth's eyes flicked from the impaled Umbelmen on the wall to the wagons of stores he planned to burn, the lines of pinched horses he'd cut loose and scare away. He rested a hand on the hilt of the sword he'd taken in the high country. *Soon*, he told himself.

But first he returned to camp, leaned his round Ilar shield up against a tree. Using a thick finger to smudge wet lime on the hide-covered planks, he drew the crude outline of a dog in white. The tribesmen wouldn't miss that, bouncing on his back as he made his retreat. Neither would the watchmen on the Tooth, if he was lucky. Looking down at the drawing, he smiled. When he turned around, the rest of the band were watching him.

Kerrel reached for the lime. His face screwed up as he copied the symbol on his own shield. The rest followed suit.

"Now we're all one pack," said the lad.

The band grunted their agreement.

The pack. Geth smiled, nodded grimly. Night couldn't come fast enough.

CHAPTER TWELVE

"This is where we split up," Geth said. "Bowmen—"

"And women," said Loura.

"—and women," Geth repeated, "you take the horse and get down to the road. Drayic, you're in charge. Everyone else follow me down the hill, quiet as you can."

Umbel-style salutes of fist to heart answered and Geth waved his group on. He surveyed the moonlit surrounds, the grey shapes of his warriors. Each had that dog-shield, a sword, and a determined look in the eye that made him proud. Under one arm Geth carried a sack with kindling and ten hastily fashioned torches.

He'd assigned each man a target based on his lightness of foot. Bird-man and Kerrel—the fastest—would strike the two furthest wagons. Baby and his sizeable stomach would take the nearest. The last thing they needed was for someone to get killed.

But the closer they sneaked, the more obvious it became how easy the first part would be. Take down one sleepy sentinel, light a torch, and set fire to the nearest wagon. Geth could only hope they'd draw a few Ilars in pursuit. The running away he wouldn't relish, but the killing? Truth be told, it was the only thing he'd ever really been good at.

"Ready, boys?"

He looked to the left and right, met the eyes of each of his fighters. Torches and kindling passed from hand to hand. He motioned to his lips for silence and nodded. Each of them crept off toward his assigned campfire.

Geth hurried behind Bird-man until he was just paces from his target, a blanket wrapped outline seated on a pelt beside a guttering fire. Two strides took him within grasp of the tribesman and his sword slid in and out from between the man's ribs.

That's for the men on spiked on the wall.

A gasp left the Ilar's lips, nothing more, as Geth clutched him by the shoulders, eased him quietly to the ground. Kindling went in amongst the stores in the nearest wagon. Geth's torch set the whole thing alight.

Fires to the left and right sprang up almost in unison. Dark shapes hurried back toward the exit point. A voice in Geth's head urged him to light a few tents on fire and massacre the drowsy bastards that crawled out, but a cry of alarm in the Ilar tongue punctured the still air before he got the chance.

The sound came from somewhere near their path out. "Damn." Geth looked around, eyes landing on a row of tethered horses. With a sawing motion he cut them loose, hopping bareback on the last one, heedless of the noise as he galloped back the way he'd come.

More cries rang out. A leather-and-fur-wrapped figure appeared from a tent off Geth's right. He swerved to chop him down, howled as the ecstasy of battle filled him. Fires licked high into the dark sky ahead and behind, coloring the night a devilish red. He'd reached the last burning wagon when he saw Baby hacking desperately at a pair of tribesmen.

"No!"

Sliding from the back of his mount, Geth swung clear through the parry of the first Ilar, kicking out at the second before he could raise his weapon. A vengeful thrust finished him, but Baby had collapsed into the snow, one hand on his belly.

"Baby!"

"They got me."

Geth hauled the Umbelman to his feet from under the arms, slung him across the back of his stolen horse. More tribesmen had started toward them and Geth turned, pulled the animal by the reins, and ran like hell.

"He's dead."

They stopped for a breather in a stand of evergreens some miles from Towerrock, the night's carnage well behind. Geth lowered Baby's considerable weight down to the ground. He lay there pale and still. Geth had known he was gone a while back but wasn't about to leave a friend behind to end up on that Ilar wall.

The men and women of his band dismounted, wiping sweat from brows, sinking to the ground against tree trunks to sit in the snow. The ropes had worked—the hidden bowmen too. Cutting the tethered horses helped, but plenty of Ilars came after them anyway. Those that did lost their lives, their weapons, and their mounts.

Geth heaved a sigh. They'd killed, burned, taken spoils, and given Towerrock a show. Baby was the only casualty. Perhaps he was a fool to think he could keep the Dozen from Vorda's clutches, but that loss curdled any sense of victory.

Drayic cleared his throat. "Should we bury him here?"

"In the middle of nowhere?" Geth looked around, shook his head. "No. Back to the wayhouse. We make a proper funeral of this."

They traveled for another day, crossing the river and leaving any lingering pursuit behind. Agrem had stayed back and Eko ran out to meet Geth as the wayhouse came within sight. But he slowed, head down as he came near. The beast knew. A dog *always* knows. He wore that sad look only a canine could manage. Whether Agrem had foreseen this or not, the Seer's face mirrored the defeat of everyone else.

"Someone find a shovel." Geth'd spent some months in the company of a gravedigger and he used his sword to test the soil, pick the right spot, then began digging. Dirt and snow flew over his shoulder with each swing.

What had he been thinking? This was the Dead-man Dozen, not a band of war-hardened Mog or Turian clansmen. Good lads, his file, but clumsy as a litter of newborn pups. It had only been a matter of time.

They laid Baby down on a bed of pine boughs, broken arrows at his feet and an empty jug in the crook of his arm.

"He was never far from an ale," Red-eye explained. "When there was ale to be had." The Umbelman started on one of his sneezing fits.

Blink filled in. "And he liked my cooking."

"Everyone likes your cooking," someone said.

Blink smiled. Hack clapped him on the shoulder.

Geth raised his hands to begin the words Gravedigger had taught him, and the band fell silent. "Wise Lady Vorda, Keeper of Souls, welcome Baby to your bosom."

"He was a brave friend," Neary intoned.

"And true," said Kerrel.

"Honest," said Loura.

"Funny."

"Generous."

The accolades rang on until each person had spoken. This was the custom of common folk back in Pellon, but they knew the ritual here in Umbel as well. They'd been through this sort of thing recently after all, be it through war or the Affliction that came before. When it came to Agrem's turn, however, the Seer sang a mournful song in his native tongue. Hack, of all people, started crying. Soon everyone was sniffling. Geth knelt and threw the first handful of dirt over his friend, followed by each member of the pack. Together, they filled the grave.

They retired back inside the wayhouse. "I didn't know you could sing," Geth told Agrem.

"It calls the harrows, this song" Agrem explained. "They have come. He is gone. He rests with the Longfathers now."

Everyone was exhausted, but Dodger offered to take first watch and Blink had already started on a soup. Eko sprawled out between Geth and his master, waiting like everyone else for the meal. When it arrived, Geth just looked down at it.

The Seer watched from across the table. "This is war, mmmm?"

"Who knows it better than me?" Geth lifted his bowl, paused halfway to his lips. "But how can we continue the fight? I mean twenty of us against thousands?"

"Twenty-one."

"Alright, twenty-one. My apologies. But you're no fighter, 'Grem. And you wouldn't fight Iyngaer even if you were."

"I would fight Ceter. With bare hands, if I could catch him."

Geth watched the Seer. There was something in the Ilar's tone beyond the vehemence in his words. "You're trying to tell me something, aren't you? And this is your crazy way of doing it."

Agrem snorted, but Geth knew he wasn't wrong. The Seer nodded finally, spread his hands. "You want to fight, mmmm?"

"Of course."

"You need friends."

"Fighters, you mean? Sure. But I don't see many options. If this were that eastern checkerboard game, I'd say the pieces had been laid."

"Mmmm. But you are forgetting one piece."

"Who is that?"

"I know someone else who would fight Ceter. Someone who is not on this board."

Geth blinked. He could think of only one person. "Vriana."

Agrem nodded.

Of course.

By every indication, Vriana's tribe, the Laeri, had not marched south with the others into Umbel. And if anyone hated Ceter, it was her. But why had she stayed behind? And would she really join the fight now, against her own folk?

"I need to take a piss," Geth lied.

He left his soup and stood. Eko looked to his master, got the nod, and sat up. Geth stalked outside, wolfdog at his heels.

Outside, the band watched him cross toward the east-west cart path that ran beside the wayhouse. He kept going until he reached the second path, a winding course running across it. He stood at the crossroads, gazing north.

"Thram and bloody Awer."

Only four months had passed since his trek into Ilia, a series of beatings, narrow escapes, ending with a trial by ordeal and finally a fight to the death. He didn't have fond memories of the place, even if he'd made it out whole in the end with Hadean alive at his side.

And Vriana's hillfort had been the worst of it. Would she really help? There was always the chance she'd just take him captive again as a good-will gesture to Iyngaer. Or hold him for ransom as she had before. She looked out for her own interest, that woman. Everyone did, except a few dumb, loyal bastards like himself.

And the Dozen. Geth turned back toward the wayhouse. His eyes rested on the fresh turned earth of Baby's grave.

"You know," he told Eko, "I've buried a lot of good men. Good *friends*. Among the Mog, we sang and drank to the memory of the fallen. Same thing among the pit-fighters of Adamar. But is that really the best way, drinking and singing?"

Geth looked down at the wolfdog. The beast met his eyes, licked his chops. Geth smiled.

"No, you're right. It isn't. The best way to mourn a friend is to get even."

Vriana and her swords would give him the means to do that, hit the tribes where it hurt. The added numbers could only help protect his dozen as well. Geth started back across the road.

"Clever sonofabitch, your master." He patted Eko's side as they stepped inside the wayhouse. "Only he would know it was a dog that held the answers."

Agrem looked up from his bowl at Geth's entry. He'd started eating the big warrior's soup, but Geth didn't care.

"You want to go to Ilia?" he said. "Fine. When do we leave?"

CHAPTER THIRTEEN

Geth told Neary the plan the next morning. "I'm only taking Agrem and the wolf. Until I get back, you're in charge."

Neary made a face. "Wasn't Vriana the one that beat you and Phelan and threw you down a hole?"

"I killed a few of her people."

"She gutted Point-fort too, if I remember. Killed just about everyone inside except that lout Gylfric."

"No one's perfect."

"Uh-huh." Neary's breath escaped into the cold morning air in a cloud.

"Look, I know it's a risk. But she's got an army. Think what we could do with just a few dozen of her warriors?"

"Think what we could do if you don't come back. Nothing, that's what."

"Agrem thinks she'll join us. They call him 'The Seer' for a reason."

"So, he said he's foreseen it? I think you would have come out with that first if it was true."

"Well—"

"Why don't we carry on? We've sent the tribes a message now. And we just might dig up other allies if we try hard enough."

Geth didn't know what allies Neary was talking about, but he wasn't about to go begging Brant and Towdric. His eyes wandered north, toward Ilia, before he pulled them back.

"After that last strike, we've got a horse for everyone," he said. "And we've got the bows. But the chieftains know about us by now. With only a handful of fighters, we'll never be more than a biting fly, whatever we paint on our shields."

Neary frowned. "They saw the fires, Geth. In the Tooth. We did it! Hadean and everyone else will know we're out here. It won't fill their bellies maybe, but it will fill their hearts."

"Those hungry bellies will be nipping at the underside of their hearts if we don't bust that siege soon. You know that as well as I."

"You think Vriana's gonna bring enough fighters to bust that siege?"

"Maybe."

Neary shook his head, left it at that. Geth didn't believe it himself, but if she gave him just a dozen fighters, it would be something. He saddled his grey and chose a horse for Agrem. The Ilar had already packed a tent and provisions for the both of them. Within the hour they were ready to set out.

"We'll be there and back in twelve days if all goes well," Geth told the band. "Stay here and keep your heads low until then. Neary's in charge."

Geth saluted with fist to heart and stepped into the saddle. Dodger hurried up before he could flick the reins.

"Captain, I've got a message from Phelan." He looked over both shoulders to make sure no one was listening.

Geth wondered if he wasn't starting to see a pattern. "Alright, let's have it."

"Melagus has a spy roaming the hills. A woman."

"And Phelan said to tell me, right? And no one else?"

Dodger nodded.

"Nothing about being hungry? Or an inn, or ale or whores?"

"Uh, no sir."

It was Geth's turn to nod.

"Do you think he means Vriana, sir?"

Geth didn't know the answer. But he supposed he'd soon find out. With a pat on the back, he thanked Dodger and turned his mount north. Agrem followed, Eko at his side.

The journey to Vriana's hillfort would take five days. Geth couldn't say if there were magicks involved, but they caught neither hair nor hide of any tribesmen between the wayhouse and the edge of the forest. What they *did* see was almost worse, whole villages abandoned and plundered, doors kicked in, chimneys cold.

Snow crunched under hoof as they moved north,. Pines groaned under the weight of it. As soon as they passed under the eaves and into the lands of the tribes, Agrem led the way over the frozen North River to the western side. The eastern bank belonged to Iyngaer, the man who'd exiled him.

"These are Ceter's lands if I remember," Geth said, scanning the trees. "Are we safe? I had to leave in a hurry last time I was here."

Agrem nodded. "Mmmm. But Ceter the Old is in the south. And we have Eko to warn us of danger."

Geth hoped it was true. If he succeeded in convincing Vriana to help, he realized they'd have to cross back this way as well. But as in Umbel, they ran into no Ilars, friend or foe.

The Seer grew chatty on their fourth day out. Geth reckoned they'd left the lands of Ceter's Thirings and arrived in the domain of Vriana and the Laer tribe. Agrem spoke of the Ilar gods, the land itself, and, as always, of good food. With nothing but cold biscuits and dried pork for the journey, Geth didn't want to think about that last.

"You never told me why Vriana didn't join Iyngaer," he said, leading his horse alongside the Ilar down narrow snow-covered trails.

Agrem's boots crunched for several steps before he answered. "Because Ceter joined him first. Ceter attacked her in her own hall, mmmm? A woman never forgets."

"Or could it have been some lover's quarrel with Iyngaer that caused her to stay behind?"

"Ha!" Agrem slapped his thigh. "Iyngaer and Vriana?"

Geth didn't care if the woman had *three* husbands, something about the fact that the tree-top bastard couldn't have her made him smile.

"She promised him not to make trouble, mmmm?" the Seer went on. "Here, in Ilia."

"While he was gone? Trouble for who?"

"Ceter. While he fights in the sunlands"

Of course. Geth nodded, as much to himself as to Agrem. *A truce.* Otherwise, the silver-haired bastard would've had to leave a sizable force behind to cover his flank, protect his holdings.

Geth made the Seer tell him everything he knew about the Chieftess after that. He wasn't surprised to learn she'd come to rule after killing her own brother, though rumors conflicted over who tried to kill who first. She'd already made a name for herself by then, harassing neighboring tribes, raiding for cattle, horses, whatever else they could steal. She had a knack for it by every indication. And Ceter's land had been her favorite hunting ground.

"She hates him," Agrem concluded.

Geth smiled. "Why did I ever doubt you? There's no way Vriana can say no to us. We're giving her exactly what she wants."

"Mmmm."

They crossed the lonely wilds of Laer until Vriana's white-mantled hillfort appeared on its mud-tracked tor, peeking over the trees at the center of a shallow valley. Geth rode with one hand on his hilt despite more of the Seer's carefree banter. Smoke drifted off the scattered longhouses they passed but no one paid them any mind. The gates to the fort stood open and they cantered inside with little more than curious looks from the sentinels on the walls.

"Ehken Laer," Agrem said. "That's what is called Vriana's home. 'Nest of the Laeri.'"

"Nest." Geth repeated. He eyed the rings of longhouses, the high timber walls. "Sounds comfortable. But that's not how I remember it."

A steep-roofed hall crowned the hill, muddy lanes snaking down from it like wild tresses toward gates and guardhouses along the ramparts. Agrem led the way up. A stern-eyed warrior with a yellow ponytail and a horse-face halted them in front of the door.

Agrem motioned the man aside. They exchanged words, including several of the curses Geth had learned on his last visit to the forest. A handful of eager-eyed warriors gathered to back their countryman, but Agrem waved the lot of them aside with a final command.

"What did you tell them?" Geth whispered.

Horse-face glared at the pair of them but pulled the heavy doors open.

The Seer answered over his shoulder as he brushed past. "I told them get out of the way. Or I would turn their grapes into..."

He slowed, frowning, looking to Geth for help.

Geth blinked. It was a moment before he caught on. "Raisins?" He started to laugh, then stopped midway. "Wait, you can do that?"

The Seer marched with purpose toward the great fire burning at the center of the long chamber. Vriana's hall was little more than a smaller version of Iyngaer's or Ceter's, skulls of deer and other creatures nailed above the lintels, high ceiling lit red by the flames. Ilar warriors drank from horns on pelts strewn about the floor as women stitched or tended pots hung over the flames. Other ladies wandering amid their menfolk, sometimes serving, other times chiding. A few of the warriors were women themselves.

Be it man, woman, or child, all fell silent at the sight of Geth and Agrem, watching the entrance of these two outsiders and their wolfdog.

All except Vriana. Seated cross-legged on a luxurious onyx spread on the far side of the fire, she never looked their way, directing an Ilar lad on some errand and sipping casually at her horn.

Agrem stabbed a finger at a pair of tribesmen seated near the chieftess. They scowled but vacated their pelts for Geth and the Seer. Vriana finally flicked them a glance. She sipped at her wine once more and the Ilar lad returned with a steaming plate of what, judging by the delicious smell, could only be lamb.

Vriana took a shank in hand and motioned lazily toward Agrem to speak, the meat her scepter of office.

"O Vriana Govendis," he began.

He spoke at length, his tone firm but absent the few choice words Geth had learned. Vriana bit off mouthfuls as she listened. Geth didn't know what the Seer was saying, but he couldn't take his eyes off her, that juicy lamb, the way she licked the grease off her lips...

She didn't seem inclined to share. No surprise for the sunlander who had escaped from that very hillfort and decapitated one of her men along the way. But she hardly paid the renowned mystic any mind either.

Geth folded his hands. It was all posturing with Vriana. Always was. Who knew what she was actually thinking? Or what the Seer was telling her for that matter. Finely wrought golden honeybee combs held the hair back behind her ears, giving her a potent, queenly air. The sword strapped to her back reminded Geth what she was capable of, the hilt pushing up between a river of gold-flecked locks flowing down to her shoulders.

She looked to Geth finally, raised an eyebrow almost like she'd just noticed him. "Hungry?" With a wave, her serving boy returned with food. This time his platter bore a tangle of cold, stringy meat.

"Probably from one of those queer black squirrels," Geth muttered.

Agrem paused to look down at the meager offering, but Geth tore off a strip and smiled around a mouthful. *Two can play at this game.* He dangled a bite for Eko to snap up, cooed at the beast like a baby.

"Ah, cutlets." He looked up to meet Vriana's eye. "If I'd known how good your cooks were, I would have never left last time I was here."

The chieftess snorted. "Is that why the Seer brought you? To eat and fart under my roof?"

"I think you know why I'm here."

"I should kill you and be done. This I know. I could make powerful friends."

"You don't want those friends. If you did, you would have killed me the first time you had the chance."

Vriana reached for her horn, swirled it once, took a casual sip. "So like a man, to think he knows what a woman wants. I do not make the same mistake, mmmm? Now speak plain. Why are you here?"

"I want you to come south. You and all your fighters."

"You want Vriana to come south?"

Geth nodded.

"Vriana is of the north. And always will be."

"There's a war going on. You should be there."

Vriana wrinkled her lips. "There will be more wars."

"A little dust up at your border over some cows?" Geth laughed. "You call that a war? What's happening to the south is the real thing. *War*, Vriana. The other tribes are all there, each winning glory. And saving none of it for Ehken Laer, her warriors, or her chieftess."

Vriana lifted that lamb shank again and took another bite. "The same thing Iyngaer said. War. Glory." She spoke around a mouthful, waved that meaty length of bone dismissively.

Geth shook his head. "Look at this place. Is this a fortress fitting a warrior like yourself? You deserve more. Your men deserve more."

"We have all that we need. We do not kill for gold."

"All that you need? This shithole?"

A stir passed through the warriors nearby. Apparently the chieftess wasn't the only one who spoke Aturian. But maybe, Geth reckoned, that was his angle.

"What about your men?" He asked. "You don't think they want a share of the spoils?"

Vriana sipped at her cup once more, but a muscle in her jaw twitched. Geth looked to Horse-face, seated behind her. The Ilar wore a frown.

The chieftess directed a reply toward Agrem in their native tongue. He made no reply except to push up to his feet. Geth didn't need a translation. They'd been dismissed.

"What now?" he asked. They started back out the hall, Eko in tow. "Is she coming south or not?"

The Seer looked from Geth to Horse-face and back as he escorted them toward the door. He hummed, shook his head.

This once, Geth had no idea what that meant.

Chapter Fourteen

Horse-face led them to Vriana's 'guesthouse' to take their rest, the very same hovel Geth had been imprisoned in during his last visit to Ehken Laer. A smug curl on the Ilar's lips told him it was no coincidence. Still, there was a tallow candle burning inside the single long room this time and logs stacked for a fire. Pelts had been laid out on the floor. Eko plopped down on one near the low entry as their escort shut the door.

"I guess the chieftess needs time to think," Geth said. He sat, back propped up against the earthen wall.

Agrem knelt with flint and tinder to start a fire. "She hates Ceter. She must remember how much."

"They crossed swords in her hall. That's how Phelan and I managed to escape. But I gather there was bad blood before that."

"Mmmm." Agrem's fire sprang to life. He added kindling and sat against the opposite wall to face Geth. "Ceter turned her brother against her. Vriana became Govendis. She never forgot."

"So, we just need to remind her of that. That shouldn't be too hard. But if she's like everyone else that's ever sat in the big chair, she'll want to make out like it was her idea."

"Kill Ceter. This is what her heart wants. This is what we want, mmmm?"

"That would be a good start."

"More than that." Firelight flickered across the deep wrinkles on the Seer's brow. "Ceter the Old moves the pieces on this board, as you say. Iyngaer is his dragon piece, but this war is Ceter's."

"What are you getting at?" Geth frowned. "If it's really Ceter pulling the strings, you reckon taking him down could be enough to send the tribes back home?"

Agrem hummed.

This time Geth recognized the affirmation in his tone. That frown turned to a smile. He'd come to Ilia hoping to gain allies and bolster his hit and fly campaign. Unless he was mistaken, this could be the beginning of a whole lot more.

With a knock at the door, Horse-face woke Geth the next day, summoning him back up the hill before he had the chance to seek out Vriana himself. Did he dare hope she'd come to the obvious conclusion on her own? He whispered a prayer to Awer the Red. He of all the gods knew the blood they would spill if she came south as planned.

Vriana waited for them beside her central fire, seated straight-backed on a brass-bound chest this time. The same fine combs held her hair, but her sword lay across her lap, bared and gleaming beside the flames. Geth didn't like the look of that. Neither the scores of armed warriors watching intently from the wings. Eko stuck to Geth's leg as he walked, attuned to the tension as only an animal could be.

"Good morning, m'lady." Geth put on his best face. He went so far as to bow. "That's a fine blade you have. I thank you again for allowing me to use it on that bastard Othwid."

Geth didn't have to fake a smile, remembering his final trusla, sword to sword against the chieftain of the Arnus tribe. But Vriana's eyes were as cold and hard as the snow-blown hills outside. She passed the weapon to a woman in waiting, leaned forward to regard him with narrowed eyes. Her fingers drummed against the side of that chest.

Agrem broke the silence. His words flowed meaningless past Geth, rattled out in the Ilar language. Vriana made a curt reply, eyes flicking to the Seer only briefly before coming to rest back on the big warrior, fingers still tapping the seat beneath her.

"Alright, fine," Geth said. "I'll bite. What's in the box?"

"You want to know, mmmm?"

"Don't try to tell me its gold or riches, that you don't need me and my promises of plunder. I know what wealth smells like, and this isn't it."

Vriana raised an eyebrow. "You know many things. But come, take the smell, as you say, and then tell me what's inside."

The chieftess rose from her seat and motioned Geth forward. He hesitated then stepped up beside her, looking down at the low, brass-bound box. She bent to rest a hand on each of its clasps, looked up to make sure he was watching, and pulled the lid open wide.

The most horrible stench of death and decay wafted out. Geth jerked back as if struck. "Thram and bloody Awer..."

Agrem caught the scent a second later. He swore in his own language.

Beside Geth, Vriana's eyes smoldered. "Look!"

Anger came off her in waves. Geth thanked the gods she'd handed her sword away. He covered his nose with one hand and leaned forward far enough to catch a glimpse. Inside the chest, on a bed of pine needles, rested a bald, withered head.

Katáre.

Geth cursed all the gods. He'd killed them man, stolen his head, and even defiled it in revenge. But the gods couldn't let that stand. No, here he was, resurrected, if only in memory, to torment Geth one last time. Down below, in Vorda's cold halls, he imagined the bandy-legged bastard laughing.

And what kind of sick she-devil went through the effort to track down such a thing and then keep it for all these months? From beside him, Vriana's eyes narrowed with indignation. Geth didn't miss her woman inch forward to stand in easy reach with that sword.

His palm itched but he forced it down, away from his hilt. "We're here as allies, not enemies," he said.

"You seek allies." Vriana's voice was tight. She flicked her chin over one shoulder toward Horse-face and a few of her warriors. "But you killed their friend. My friend. Do you remember? And stole his sword."

"Do I remember?" Geth tried to bite his own lip, but as the memories flashed through his mind, his own anger flared to life. "Do I remember his fists and elbows? His piss in my drink? Oh, I remember, Vriana of the gods-forsaken North. And I remember sending him to Vorda's tit, cutting of his head with his own sword, and taking it with me as a souvenir. It was the best part of the whole journey."

Geth leaned over the chest, spit down into it, and slammed the lid closed. The sound echoed with a loud boom under the high ceiling. All went silent for a shocked moment, then tribesmen to either side growled, reached for their swords, crowding forward until Agrem rushed up, arms raised, hissing in their native tongue.

Vriana's eyes never left Geth's. "You come here looking for friends. But you are weak. And your enemies are strong. Why would Vriana want such friends and such enemies, mmmm? You owe a life for this life you took. Maybe I put your head in the box. And maybe I give it as a gift and make new friends."

Geth was already counting the sharps, anticipating the inevitable massacre. Eko growled low and menacing, backed up against Geth's leg. Agrem barked something in the Ilar tongue, though, and whatever he said this time, it struck a chord. Vriana snapped something back.

But the Seer lifted his chin, eyed the warriors circled around. His reply came almost in a whisper and the entire room seemed to shrink back a step. Geth blinked, hand still firmly on his hilt. Agrem softened his stance, stepped toward the chest and Katare's head. He rested a hand on the lid, closed his eyes and uttered something like a prayer. When he looked up, he met Geth's eye.

"She will go to speak to the Fathers. They will give her wisdom."

"Wisdom?"

"To decide. March south, join us. Or join Iyngaer."

Geth watched Ilars hurry off in every direction. Vriana's woman handed her sword back and brought her a cloak and gloves. Agrem motioned Geth to follow as she stalked out the doors of her hall.

"Why are they fetching horses?" Geth asked. "These Fathers don't live in Ehken Laer?"

Agrem pulled his own cloak tighter against the cold. "Mmmm. The Fathers are our ancestors. We go to the great cave, Isa Vlen. The wisdom of the ancestors comes to us there."

"Did you just trick me into another trusla?"

Agrem snorted.

The journey would take less than half a day. Vriana started downhill, boots squelching in the muddy snow as she led her steed as far as the gates. Horse-face and a good twenty grim-eyed warriors saddled up to join them. At least Geth didn't see that brass-bound chest among the baggage.

He mounted alongside the Seer and they set out. Geth's stomach gnawed at his ribs as he rode, but they turned toward a craggy ridge line before long. Eko bounded ahead, down the snow-blanketed track, coming to a halt at a set of rough-hewn steps leading up to a yawning opening in the side of a hill.

Geth slid out of the saddle and pushed up beside the chiestess. "I'm going in too."

Vriana considered him, back to her usual calm and control. Geth flicked a glance toward Agrem. He nodded his approval. The chiestess sniffed but didn't argue. She turned to hand her cloak and sword to her woman and stalked up the steps toward the cave.

Horse-face said something to Agrem. The Seer turned toward Geth. "Give me your weapons."

Geth handed over his sword, belt knife, and cloak just as Vriana had. "What do I do?"

"Go in. Receive wisdom. Come out."

"Right."

Men began pitching tents on a flat patch below the stairs. Campfires were lit and a dozen torches prepared from pitch-soaked rags tied around hacked off pine limbs. When these were ready, Horse-face, Agrem and several other tribesmen led the way under the rock arch and into flame-chased darkness. Eko moved silently at the Seer's side.

A low-ceilinged anteroom of sorts gave way to a much larger chamber further in the cave. Though the mouth was only a few inches above Geth's head, the belly of Isa Vlen stood easily four times a man's height, the walls covered with drawings of limby hunters, game and horses, hand-prints by the score. Red torchlight danced across orange and black and brown figures, gave life to men, women, and deer.

"Well, I wasn't expecting that," Geth muttered.

"Find your longfather," Vriana told him. She stepped up beside a wall to measure her hand against several of the outlined prints. She settled on one that matched the size of her own.

Agrem stepped up beside the big warrior, waving his torch at the painted hands. "The ancestors of all the peoples were here once. The Fathers."

Geth searched for a print to match his own meaty palm, settled for one that was a little small. *Longfathers?* To him, those prints looked more like the marks of a legion of desperate souls trying to claw their way out of Vorda's underworld.

Geth lowered his voice and leaned in toward his friend. "This place is what the diviners back in Pellon call a devil-pit."

"Mmmm?"

"You know the story of Earth's making, how the Almighty first crafted the land as male?"

"A sunlander tale."

"The first child of the Great Eye, the Sun, and Seremone, the Moon, was called Ord. But Ord was an evil bastard. So vile in fact, that the Almighty Shaper killed him, thrusting his hands through Ord's middle and turning him inside-out. From the corpse of dead Ord, he remade the land. Female this time. We call her Earth."

Agrem just listened.

"Well, Ord's flesh still lives, see. Earthmother was made from him. But only in deep places like this do we see the signs. Some say the hatred of Ord seeps through in places like this."

Agrem nodded, reading Geth's concern. "You think Vriana will decide to kill you, mmmm? She will not. I *remember*."

Geth did his best to hide a scowl. *Bloody magicks*. "Let's hope your memory serves."

The tribesmen had each found their 'longfather' by then. One by one they trickled back outside with their torches and the chamber darkened. All except the chieftess and her woman who carried an oil lamp. Agrem squeezed Geth's shoulder and left as well, Eko in tow. Vriana's retainer set two pelts and the lamp down on the floor at the center of the cave.

"Sit," Vriana said.

But as her woman turned to Geth, he caught the gleam of something on her hand. It was a gold ring set with a red stone—the same ring Vriana had stolen from Phelan, the ring they'd meant to give her on their last visit to Ehken Laer.

Geth muttered a curse and settled down cross-legged like the chieftess. He'd thought that gift might curry favor. She'd stolen it to make a point but had given it away just as fast—as good a reminder as any how little he understood her.

"I feel wiser already," he muttered.

Vriana frowned. The soft glow of the lamp twinkled in her eyes, accented her high cheekbones. Maybe it was the lighting, or maybe some magick of that cave, but she looked a rare beauty at that moment. Geth shook his head to dispel the thoughts that tried to creep in. Vriana closed her eyes, exhaled long and slow.

"Be still. Quiet. Or I send you back outside."

Geth grimaced. Evidently the magick didn't run both ways.

He followed Vriana's lead, closed his eyes, breathed deep. A part of him wondered why she trusted him, especially after all she'd done to warrant his wrath. Then again, her warriors were just a shout away. And it was *him* that needed *her*, not the other way around.

Thinking of his friends, under siege to the south, he set his mind to the task at hand. *Wisdom. Fathers*. He had to admit he could use all the help he could get. And if he didn't get this right, he could send another whole tribe of enemies down on Umbel, maybe get himself killed in the process.

Geth opened his eyes. Vriana's were still closed, he lips parted just so.

What did he really know about her? If there was one thing he'd learned, it was that Vriana wasn't afraid to act boldly when it was in her interest. And she never did anything that wasn't. He thought of that ring. He'd gotten it all wrong on his last visit to Ehken Laer.

So how do I get it right?

His eyes had adjusted by then and he watched the soft glow of candlelight play off the hunters and game, the horses and handprints climbing the walls. He thought of everything he'd ever seen or heard about Vriana and her Laeri. He knew she could be a ruthless enemy. She'd somehow breached the defenses of Point-fort and massacred the garrison inside. But she'd also refused to march at Iyngaer's side in this latest campaign. That was a step in the right direction. And he knew she hated Ceter, whatever she might say about cutting off heads and making friends.

Agrem's words, that Ceter had turned Vriana's own brother against her, now that was something new. Her hatred, he reckoned, must have finally boiled over when the old warlock came to ransom himself and Phelan. But why then? She would have profited from the deal and Ceter would have gotten what he wanted: his lover's murderer. A win for each of them. If anything, Geth might have expected a reconciliation.

He blew out a sigh, looked up to the hunters on the wall, some standing tall, others crouched, waiting.

And then he knew.

"Clever woman." He laughed out loud.

Vriana opened her eyes to glare at him.

"You never intended to sell me to Ceter," he told her. "It was a trap. You lured him to Ehken Laer to get even once and for all."

"You talk too much."

Geth just shook his head, grinning under his mustache. No doubt she'd told Iyngaer and whoever else that Ceter had played a part in the fray, but Geth knew with rare certainty that her intent had been to kill the warlock all along.

Only she'd failed.

"If the bastard had turned *my* brother against *me*," Geth said, "I would have tried to gut him too. Only I would have succeeded."

"I should have left you outside."

"It's nothing to be ashamed of. He didn't get so old by being easy to kill."

She pointed toward the cave entrance. "Go. If I call my men, they will break your legs and drag you out."

"Wait! Don't you see? This is the wisdom you were looking for. The wisdom we were both looking for. You want Ceter dead. I'm the one person who can kill him."

"Ha! You think you can kill him? Ceter the Old has strong magick. Maybe he cannot die."

Geth snorted. "He can die. Remember when I fought Othwid, when I turned on Ceter? If he couldn't die, why did he cower back?"

"Mmmm."

"I've felt his magicks too, the fear he sends out. But you were there for that final trusla. He used his fear against me to help Othwid. It didn't work."

"This is your wisdom? These words? Ceter has more than just magic. He has the Thiring tribe. Many thousand spears and swords. Maybe he can die. *Maybe.* But you cannot kill him."

Geth smiled. "Not alone."

CHAPTER FIFTEEN

Night had fallen by the time they emerged from the cave. Vriana left Geth without a word to rejoin her people. He didn't care. The job was done. She hadn't said as much, but a scowl from Horse-face confirmed she would come south.

Eko trotted up to greet Geth as he climbed down the stairs, sliding his head under an outstretched hand. Agrem stood waiting from beside the ring of tents. The big warrior looked back over his shoulder at the mouth of Isa Vlen.

"Maybe there's something to it."

"Mmmm."

"This place, the wisdom, I mean. These Ilar fathers gave me more than my real father ever did."

"That is the magic."

"I don't have to tell you that we did it, do I. She's coming."

They slept there in tents erected beside the cave and set out for Ehken Laer the next morning. Geth wanted to ride straight for Umbel, straight into the ranks of Ceter's fighters with Vriana and her band. But there were preparations to make, warriors to gather. He spurred his mount alongside the chieftess as they wended toward her hillfort.

"Well? How soon can we leave for Umbel?"

Vriana gave him that cool, considering look. "When the horses and men are ready."

"How many?"

"Fifty."

Geth bit down a curse. "You have thousands of warriors, Chieftess. Do you think we can do the job with just fifty?"

"You want me to march thousands down into Umbel?"

Geth blinked. He hadn't thought of it like that. If she did march her whole army south, what was to stop her from joining Iyngaer's campaign once they'd killed Ceter? Best he could tell, it was only the warlock's involvement that had kept her from joining the other tribes in the first place.

But by Agrem's account, Ceter was the linchpin to this whole bloody war. If they succeeded in killing the warlock, it just might be enough to undo the entire alliance of tribes. Worth the risk, by Geth's reckoning, whatever number she could bring.

"So, fifty swords." Geth nodded. "Would be easier with a hundred, but we'll find a way."

Vriana rolled her eyes. "We have fifty horses, and so we bring fifty fighters. When Ceter is dead, we still have to get away, mmmm? We need horses."

"Of course—"

"And we cannot march all my thousands quietly. Ceter would learn of our coming. And Iyngaer would say I had broken my promise not to start trouble."

"I thought you promised not to start trouble in *Ilia*. This would be in Umbel."

Vriana looked at him evenly. "Mmmm."

Geth had to smile. *Coy, this woman.*

He set his mind to the task ahead. The fate of Phelan, Hadean, and the entire kingdom hinged on whether they could pull it off. The original idea had been to convince the chieftess to swarm down with hundreds—if not thousands—to terrorize the other tribes, test their will to hold onto their siege. Or weaken them enough to allow King Hadean's forces to break it themselves by sallying from the gates. Taking down a single chieftain offered a much simpler proposition.

But at the same time, it would be far more challenging. Geth pulled at his mustache as he rode. Any attempt to get at Ceter by penetrating his camp was suicide, even for a man with Geth's sword arm. If they had the time, perhaps Vriana could plant a mole, learn his routines, maybe try a knife in the back, or poison. But wouldn't she have done that already if she thought it might work? And the Tooth might succumb to starvation before they could make it happen.

They had to draw him out. That begged a different question. Geth reined in until he was riding beside Agrem again. "I need to know more about Ceter's magicks."

The Seer frowned into the distance. "Ceter is very old. And he has many magicks, as you call them. You have already felt the fear he breaths."

"That's the one I'm worried about. His fearspell. It stopped me dead in my tracks during the truslas. Can he do that to a whole army?"

Agrem smiled. "No, thank the Fathers."

"But he *can* do it to more than one person at a time."

"Mmmm."

"And he can send it out over the miles. Phelan and I felt that in Ilia. It was weak, but we felt it."

"Yes. When close, he is stronger." Agrem shook his head. "But Ceter has many tricks. In the great battle, he used his fear against your horses."

"Copper Ridge?"

The Seer hummed. "The men were too many. But animals are easier, mmmm? With this he stopped Hadean's horsemen."

"So, he has to get close and he's stronger if he leans on fewer men or on animals." Geth thought that through. "For myself, now that I know what to expect, I think I might be able to resist his spell better than I did when I was fighting Othwid."

Agrem watched him. "What do you plan?"

"Ceter hates me, right? As much as Vriana hates him. I killed his lover after all. If there's any man that can draw him out, it's me."

"Do you hope to fight him?"

"No. I hope to use myself as bait."

Competing ideas wrestled in Geth's mind. They rode back through their own tracks toward the snowy hillfort of Ehken Laer. He reckoned he could lure Ceter out alright. The problem was living to tell the tale.

Their road followed a frozen river, winding through the hills back toward Vriana's stronghold. Maybe it was the cold, but Geth's stomach gnawed at itself. They didn't stop for a meal either. The sun gleamed on the white surrounds, and they only passed one group of tribesmen along the way, four men walking around on the ice as easily as if they stood on sand, working the surface with poles of some sort.

"What are they doing?" Geth asked Agrem.

"Cutting the ice."

"Those are saws?"

The Seer nodded. "Ice-saws."

"And how do they walk so easily out there?"

"Ice-shoes."

"What's the point of cutting the ice? Are they fishing?"

"Mmmm."

"Let me guess. Ice-fish?"

Agrem snorted. "What is an ice-fish?"

The Seer left him, kicking his mount toward the four men. They traded words, laughing and pointing back at Geth. Something changed hands. Agrem returned with several trout.

"Dinner, mmmm?"

At that moment, Geth truly loved the man.

They cooked and ate those fish in Vriana's hall that evening, Geth still chewing over just how they might hit Ceter's force and draw him out. A breakfast followed the next morning and another meal in the evening, a plan taking shape bite by bite. With his belly full, Geth wandered the snowy lanes between longhouses until he came upon the same tribesmen he'd seen fishing out on the river.

Like the ice they worked, his ideas suddenly came solid. He traded a pair of Ilar knives he'd plundered for ice-saws and other supplies. By the following day, the fifty Laeri horsemen had been gathered and they started south.

Agrem eyed those pole-saws but said nothing. Geth kept his idea to himself, poking at it all the long ride through Ilia and into Umbel, searching out a weakness. Five days later they were welcomed back at the wayhouse by Neary and the band.

"What's that I smell cooking?" Geth asked as the grey-haired Umbelman strode out grinning.

Neary embraced him, slapped his shoulder for good measure. "Blink's cooking. He's huffing and puffing in the kitchen, trying to whip up enough to feed Vriana's people. I wouldn't bet against him getting it done."

"I gotta say, I was nervous when we first rode in. I thought you guys might mistake her lot for the enemy and put arrows into a few of them."

Neary waved that off. "Bird-man was posted on lookout. He saw you coming miles away and sent back word."

Vriana's fighters dismounted and started pitching tents. Blink waved them all in and soon everyone was tearing off pieces of venison he and Red-eye and Sweaty had roasting over a coal bed out behind the wayhouse. Geth motioned the chieftess inside where they sank into chairs in the common room.

Vriana ate across from Geth at a table. She licked her fingers when she was done. "When do we fight Ceter?"

"As soon as possible," Geth said.

"He is at the sunlander fortress. On the east side of the river, to the north. My people tell me this."

"I've scouted the area as well, hit the Anui pretty good a few weeks back."

Vriana nodded. "We have heard of the Wolf of the Hills. Even in Laer."

Geth paused, a strip of venison halfway to his mouth. "The who?"

"The Wolf."

His expression must have betrayed his confusion. The chieftess flicked her chin across the room. His shield leaned up against the wall, the crude emblem he'd drawn in lime could still be made out.

"That's a dog," Geth said.

Vriana shrugged.

Geth chewed his meat. If news of their exploits had traveled as far Ilia, Hadean must have known as well. Phelan too.

But there was no point patting himself on the back just yet. "This is what you may *not* have heard," he told Vriana. "Our attack at the siege was on the *west* side of the river. There are less tribesmen there—less of everything. Attacking the east side, that won't be so easy. Not if we want to make a clean escape."

"Mmmm."

She sipped at the ale she'd been served and grimaced. "We can kill him. We know this. But I want to tell my children after how I stood over Ceter's dead body and spit on his face. Another day I can die."

"I'm not ready for a long nap yet either. Don't worry, I've got an idea how to get to Ceter."

Vriana looked dubious. "And live to sing after?"

"Others will sing of it. I'll just be drinking."

The entire company packed up and rode west the next day. It was cold as always, but there was a whiff of spring in the air, and the presence of reinforcements had them all smiling—Geth's pack at least. Vriana's tribesmen looked grim. Maybe they worried, as Geth did, that it would warm enough to melt the river-ice. That would end Geth's plan before it could begin.

They crossed its frozen surface that first evening, circling west and then north of the Anui tribesmen they'd hit some weeks back. They had a horse for each fighter now and by the second day they'd come within a few miles of the siege. Geth left Drayic and Red in charge, taking Birdman, Neary, Vriana and Horse-face to creep back across the river after nightfall for a look at Ceter's forces, arrayed along the riverside and inside the ruins of Greenfell on the east bank, beside Towerrock.

The five towers of the Tooth gleamed pale in the moon-light across the river's hazy surface. Damn but it was cold. Geth and his scouting party crouched in the snow a hun-dred paces from the barrier of sharpened stakes protecting the flank of the Thiring encampment. Smoke rose from wind-tortured campfires, a few miserable sentinels hud-dled beside them.

"He's down there somewhere," Geth said. "We just need to get him to come out."

"How?" Neary asked.

Vriana and Horse-face watched Geth silently. Bird-man's eyes were wide.

"That's where we'll start." Geth pointed back the way they'd come, across the river. "We leave all the horses a few miles north of the Arnui on the west side. We sneak back here, across the ice on foot, and hit Ceter's camp in the darkest hours. We burn and kill everything we can, just like we did the last go around. But this time, we don't cut the tethers on their horses."

Neary opened his mouth, but Vriana spoke first. "You want them to ride after us."

"That's right. We retreat on foot northward, along the riverbank—"

"Not straight back across?" Neary frowned.

"Not at first," Geth said. "We run north, on foot still, make sure they mount up and come after. Only then do we make a left and cross the ice back toward our own horses on the far bank."

"If they're on horse and we're on foot," Neary said, "I can't see how they don't catch us out on the ice."

"We'll have something waiting for them." Geth looked from face to face to make sure everyone was listening. "Before we head out, a couple of our boys will set a trap for Ceter's horse using those ice-saws. As for us, we'll run up *past* the cut section and then turn to cross. But Ceter's riders will try to cut us off. They'll ride straight into the trap."

Vriana translated for Horse-face. The bastard actually smiled.

"With no horse to chase us after that," Geth went on, "we could ride away at a canter if we wanted."

Vriana didn't look so impressed though. "And Ceter?

"As for the Warlock, I'll draw him out. There's no one he hates more than me, I reckon. I'll lag behind as a rear guard, chop down anyone that makes it out of the river. Ceter will hurry forward, try to get as close as he can to throw his fear at me. I might not be able to get at him myself, but with all eyes on this handsome mustache, one good bowman should be able to take him down."

Neary just shook his head. There were plenty of ways it could go wrong, and he knew it. Bird-man had been brought along for his sharp eyes and he shifted them to study the Ilar ranks as soon as Geth looked at him. Vriana relayed the details to her second then turned back to the big warrior.

"You take great risk. Maybe Ceter comes with twenty men. You're good. But you're not this good, mmmm?"

"It's the only way. I've felt his fearspell before, I know how to resist it. If anyone else gets brushed by it, they're as good as dead."

"So, Ceter comes for you and the arrows come for him?"

"That's the plan."

CHAPTER SIXTEEN

They rested all day, honing blades, testing bow-strings. Torches were prepared, maps drawn in the dirt until night finally fell. When they deemed the skies dark enough, Geth started them by faint moonlight down toward the river.

Geth ordered Blink and Red-eye to accompany Agrem and stay with the horses on the west bank. By his reckoning, those two were the most likely to suffer Baby's fate. Vriana assigned one sullen tribesman to keep them company. Red-eye saluted with fist to heart, sneezing halfway through the motion, as the rest of the combined force of Umbelmen and Ilars padded carefully over the river ice to the far side.

Once they'd climbed back up onto snowy land, Geth turned them right and south. Bird-man with his sharp eyes crept forward a few yards ahead. He drew them up a hundred paces from the edge of the Ilar camp, pointing out sentries.

"There, there…and there."

Geth squinted until he could make out each mark. As they had the night before, the Thiring sentinels huddled beside campfires, hardly a care for their duty to keep watch. Did they expect the magicks of their chieftain to protect them, Geth wondered? *So much the better.*

Vriana peered ahead, sword already in hand. Geth drew his own weapon, the one he'd taken as spoils back in the High Country. The sound drew her eye. He gave her a wink, lifted his sword and kissed the blade.

The chieftess shook her head, muttered an Ilar curse.

Without a wave forward, the company advanced, swords held low, first walking, then running at a crouch. Snow crunched beneath their boots, there was no way to stifle it. The first watchman lifted his head, peered through the night straight at them. Geth let out a howl like a wolf's.

"Aaawooooooo!"

The Ilar managed to free his sword, shrieked an alarm, but Geth was on him a half-second later, bowling him over and continuing on. A cry from over the big warrior's shoulder told him someone behind him had finished the tribesman. A dozen more howls echoed as they arrived

among the still tents and feeble campfires of Ceter's Thirings.

More alarm cries answered. A dog started barking somewhere, but Geth didn't wait for the enemy to come to him.
He slashed at the side of the nearest tent, tore a gap, and
leapt inside.

The nearest Ilar died in his bedroll, stabbed through
the sternum. A second reached for his sword, but Geth
stepped on the sheathed blade to trap it, hacking downward at the same time to take the wide-eyed bastard in
the neck. A third enemy was out of his blankets like a
rabbit and halfway through the tent flap when the red tip
of a blade suddenly emerged from his back, halting him
mid-stride. A set of strong arms drove the tribesman back
inside to collapse among the furs. Vriana appeared in the
entry, a twinkle in her eyes.

She turned back the way she'd come, Geth right behind
her. Outside, torches had already been lit, wielded by jeering Laeri and hooting Umbelmen as they spread flames
throughout the camp. A few of Ceter's folk emerged to
offer a fight, but in this part of the camp at least, they were
vastly outnumbered.

"With me!" Vriana yelled, grinning almost from one ear
to the other. Geth followed her deeper among the tents.
Bootless, half-clad Ilars cried out and ran in every direc-

tion, until eventually a handful of armed enemies found them.

"Argghh!" A brown-bearded tribesman with an axe skipped forward to swing at Geth's middle. The big warrior stepped in close to absorb the strike against his dog-marked shield. His sword slid past the iron rim to pierce the Ilar's gut, and he wrenched the blade free to leap back out of reach of that axe, already in search of the next enemy.

Vriana stood over her own dying foe by then. She led them even deeper into the camp until the first half-destroyed buildings of the town of Greenfell loomed just a furlong away. Ceter would be there, Geth supposed, beside a hearth, under a warm roof.

"This way!" Vriana called.

A knot of Thirings with shield and sword had appeared to her right. The chieftess ran straight for them. Geth howled once more, hoping it might reach Ceter's ear, but the noise only sent their quarry running in the opposite direction.

Vriana cursed in her native tongue then switched back to Aturian. "You ruined it."

But plenty of other groups of armed tribesmen roamed between the tents. Too many. "Time to head back," Geth told her.

She scowled. To stay any longer could only end badly though. Running side by side, they managed to hack down one more Thriring each. The rest saw the infamous chieftess of the Laeri and ran the other way. Or perhaps it was Geth and his shield, the Wolf of the Hills.

Sooner than later, he reckoned, they'd find their courage in numbers. Up ahead, Geth spied Kerrel, sword red in his hand, dog emblem lit orange on his shield by the fires all around. Neary and Drayic flanked him. The heat coming off burning tents hit Geth as he drew near, flames clawing at the night sky.

"Neary!" Geth called. "Start the retreat! North along the riverside, like we said. I'll keep the rearguard."

Vriana shouted similar instructions to her people. As quick as they'd come, Laeri and Umbelmen were slipping back out of camp, hooting and spitting curses. Geth looked over his shoulder as he ran. The night was bright with fires, alive with Thirings scurrying to douse them, crying out, running in every direction and stumbling over their own dead. If this didn't get Ceter's attention, nothing would.

Geth reckoned they'd given the Tooth a show as well. He threw his head back and howled once more for joy.

The path of their retreat took them past Vriana's Ilars out on the ice with their saws. Vriana waved them to leave

their work and join the exit before they were seen. Geth
wondered what the hell they were still doing out there. It
was too late to do more than pray it would work.

The sound of horse hooves reached his ear as vengeful
Thirings finally took to their steeds. Geth hollered up the
line. Somewhere ahead, Neary gave the signal, leading the
war band across the ice. Geth stepped onto the slick surface
as well, but lingered in the rear, as close to the sawed ice as
he dared. He looked back. Ceter's pursuit materialized out
of the darkness, tribesmen spurring their horses left, out
onto the river to cut off the escape just as he needed them
to.

Geth crunched down the riverbank, slipped and slid
across the ice, always moving west to draw the riders into
the trap. He waved his sword and shield overhead. "Here I
am you bastards! Come and get me!"

Lips moved as Thirings shouted insults back. All Geth
heard was the tramp of hooves on river ice. He shuffled out
further and further into the center of the frozen water-
course, mouthing curses in broken Ilar, egging them on.
To his right, on the far bank, Vriana's best archer would
be getting into position by now. The rest of the band had
already made it off the ice.

But nothing happened. The Ilar horsemen had fanned
out as they rode, perhaps in fear of breaking the ice, per-

haps to avoid knocking one another over on the slick surface. Either way it dispersed their weight. Geth cursed the Hoarwinds for freezing the river solid until a great resounding crack rent the night, and the first horse and rider went down.

Like a fleet of ships all capsizing at once, great sections of river ice tore loose from each other and tilted up into dark skies, dumping their load of screaming tribesmen and steeds into the frigid water. Some tried to veer left or right. There was nowhere to go. The trap had been sprung, opening a wide hole clear across the river except for one narrow stretch where it either hadn't been cut well or had frozen over again.

Back behind Geth, triumphant cries echoed. Was he mistaken? Or had he heard a cheer from the walls of Towerrock as well? He howled once more. *Hear me, Phelan! Hear me Hadean!*

"I'm *here!*"

A few tribesmen managed to pull up short on the other side of the gap, dismounting to drag their countrymen from the water. Geth chopped at fingers and stepped on helmets to send others back under water from his side of the chasm. Streaming up on foot, Thirings gathered on the far side. Geth hurled every Ilar curse he knew but no one came for him.

He shuffled right, toward the narrow strip of remaining ice, waving his enemies to follow. "C'mon, you bastards!" Still, no one came. The hairs on the back of his neck stirred and then he knew why.

"Waiting for your magicker, eh?"

Geth whispered a prayer to Red Awer. So far, things had gone to plan. But the hardest part was yet to come. He dropped to one knee, reached into a pocket, fumbled until he found a set of metal cleats that he'd traded for back in Ehken Laer. He strapped an ice-shoe onto one boot and then the other.

With Ceter almost arrived, the Ilars came straight across the river to attack him on that narrow patch of ice—like fools. They could have jogged a few hundred yards to circle around behind him. As before, numbers lent them courage. Geth felt the Warlock and his fear closing in, but that only hardened his resolve. This was it—what he'd come here for.

The wave of footmen flowed toward him like the dark water of Vorus to Geth's left and right. He took a risk just standing there and he knew it. What if that little isthmus of ice cracked away as well? But the set-up was too perfect. And the unsuspecting enemy just kept shuffling forward. Geth waited in a rigid stance at the far end of the ice-bridge,

waited until a good many Thrirings had exposed themselves on that narrow path, then charged straight for them.

Gods, how the first bastard's eye's widened as Geth
closed in, blade swung high to clatter the tribesman's
iron-bound helm clear off his head. Dead or not, the bastard went down. It was Geth who was flowing now, blade
sweeping unsteady foes into the icy water, shield bowling
others over. As fast as they'd come, the Ilars backpedaled,
slipping and falling without any help from Geth at all.
That left them vulnerable to a thrust through the back,
a kick across the jaw. It was Awer that had kept that little patch of ice from cracking, Geth was certain. He was
watching close by, in the shape of an owl or a river fish or
some such, reveling at the havoc no one could wreak like
Geth.

The fear struck him with those thoughts still in his
head.

"Thram's balls..." It clutched him, held him fast, sword
half raised above another hapless foe. Ignorant of Geth's
predicament, the lucky tribesman only whined and scrambled back the way he'd come. Geth's eyes followed him,
past the half dozen Ilars marching up in the distance,
landing on Ceter himself, sable furs hanging around his
shoulders like something woven from the dark magicks he
spun.

The warlock's voice rang out, ordering his men forward.

Geth gritted his teeth, forced his thumping heart down, out of his throat. He drew a cold breath. He'd done this before; he could do it again.

He can't hurt you! He's just a man!

Geth's limbs jerked free and he hooted for joy. Another howl left his lips. It was a noise of elation, of the ecstasy of battle, not the wolf's cry. A man with an axe swung for him but he skipped backward to let the strike pass, then sprang forward to thrust home before the Ilar could react. Ceter's disappointment, his outrage, was a palpable thing.

With those cleats catching firm where the enemies' boots betrayed them, nothing about the fight was fair. The tribesmen held the advantage of numbers, but they couldn't come at Geth more than a few at a time in that narrow space. He hacked men down, sent others screaming into the river. He could never kill them all though. Sweat rolled down his side even in the frigid night. He gave ground slowly, sparing glances for the old warlock between strokes.

By then, Ceter had come close enough for Geth to read the strain on his face. The warlock's lips contorted. His brow furrowed. Geth felt the weight of the fearspell heavy in his chest, in his every limb. Somewhere on the west bank, Vriana's bowman would be picking his mark. He managed to fight through the burden with gritted teeth.

But no arrows flew. A knot of fighters surrounded their chieftain, making him a difficult target. Perhaps the bowman didn't want to loose his bolts and reveal himself too soon? Geth cursed. He had to kill more of them, thin Ceter's escort. Or draw the old bastard into the open.

"Remember me, old man? I killed your lover! Come here and let me send you to join him!"

For some damn reason, Ceter only laughed. Geth blinked. He twisted his neck to follow the warlock's eyes into the distance behind him. Hurrying across the ice back there, several tribesmen had finally made the move to flank him.

He was out of time. With a lunge at the enemies ahead of him, Geth drove one over the edge into the water, the others back a few yards. He turned toward the Ilars arriving behind him. Cleated boots launched him faster than they could react, and a hacking blow sent the first stumbling into the second, landing them in a tangle on the ice as their footing gave way. With no time to thrust, Geth chopped at the back of a head, crushing bone. He let the other Ilar scramble in retreat.

Whirling again, he turned toward Ceter and his bodyguards. Several of them had hurried forward onto the isth-

mus of ice, hoping to catch Geth between hammer and
anvil, but he'd already dealt with the hammer. He rushed
with those firm footfalls, used his shield to bowl over first
one, then another into the river to either side. A third Ilar
slipped as he spun in retreat. He went over the edge of his
own accord.

Geth roared in triumph.

Ceter had moved almost onto the isthmus by then himself, urging his fighters forward. His jaw clenched, his voice
reaching Geth as clearly as his own men, booming directly
inside the big warrior's mind.

Kill him!

"Come and try!" Geth shouted out loud.

The warlock had grown careless. A mere handful of
fighters stood between them and Geth lowered his shoulder again, hefted his blade. One good charge would take
him all the way through to the white-haired bastard himself. Tired legs found the strength to launch Geth forward,
but halfway toward the warlock's first guard, one of his
cleat-straps tore loose, sending him face first onto the ice
right at the tribesman's feet.

The Ilar laughed.

There was nowhere for Geth to go, no way to recover
quick enough to avoid the sword that was about to come
down through his neck. He braced himself for the blow,

but a *thunk* sounded above him, and something warm hit the back of his hand rather than the cold blade he'd expected. He looked up just as the Ilar collapsed down in front of him. The Thiring hit the ice, dead eyes level with Geth's own.

Curses flew, and another Ilar fell. Geth scrambled backward, then to his feet. The arrows, finally.

Thank you!. Raised shields surrounded and protected Ceter still, but Geth owed someone his life. He spared a glance far to the right, along the riverbank, for the man.

It was Vriana.

He didn't have time to blink before the weight of Ceter's fear shifted. Across the ice, bow arm still outstretched, Vriana's eyes went round. A knocked arrow tumbled to the riverbank. Ceter's voice rang in Geth's mind once more.

Bring me her head!

A pair of Thirings took off toward Vriana. Geth bent low and gripped his sword, scrambled to rise. But with only one cleated foot and half a dozen fighters still protecting the warlock, there was no way he'd get through to Ceter before his tribesmen reached the chieftess. Geth planted one foot to charge, looked down at the single ice-shoe still strapped to his left boot. His eyes landed on an Ilar axe, the haft tilted just so, offering itself toward him.

It was some kind of madness. Geth almost laughed. But was Ceter that was going to die there, he vowed, not Vriana.

Dropping both his sword and shield, he reached for that axe. Eyes widened among Ilar warriors as they struggled to backpedal off that narrow frozen lane. But Ceter's focus was all on the chieftess. Geth spread his feet wide, lifted the axe overhead, and smashed it down with all his might.

An ear-ringing crack echoed through the frozen air. Before Geth could lift the axe for a second blow, the ice beneath one foot shifted, sending him to his rump, weapon flung from his grip. He twisted and reached for something,—anything—to grab onto. Cold water hit his legs first, climbed all the way up to his chest, driving his breath out in a gasp as the river's frigid fingers clutched him.

Cries and the noise of splashing water sounded all around. A voice rang in Geth's head. *Noooo!*

It was Ceter who felt the fear now, frozen by icy river water as surely as by any spell. But the frigid current had already begun to carry Geth away as well. He reached up with a hand as it tried to pull him under the edge of the ice, caught hold with his fingernails and hooked his chin on the lip, gulping air.

Gods how the water tore at him, how his wet clothes dragged him down. His handhold slipped. Mighty Vorus, river of the north, prevailed, sucked him under. He gasped and closed his mouth as the water went over his head, still clinging with numb fingers to the edge. His eyes rolled up, but his ears registered a high-pitched screech before all went dark. A strong grip caught his hand, hauled him up from the underworld, back among the living.

CHAPTER SEVENTEEN

Geth awoke in a mass of furs inside an Ilar tent. He was alone, but even before memory of the fight came back to him, somehow he knew he was safe. When he did recall that stealthy attack and the trap they laid, he threw off the blankets, sat up, and grinned.

Ceter was dead. Geth hurried to don the Ilar leathers that sat waiting for him, stamping into his still-damp boots. Voices and laughter sounded from outside and he slipped past the flap to join them. It was night, but a dozen fires burned merrily, surrounded by capering warriors.

"Hey!"

"Oye!"

Umbelmen and Ilars alike cheered as Geth joined the nearest throng. Vriana's tribesmen had brought along plenty of that tart berry wine. They shared it around. Hack started in on a song and Horse-face clapped Geth on the back then started off toward a tall pile of firewood, torch in hand.

"Now that you're up," Neary said, face red under his white hair, "we can begin a proper celebration."

Horse-face worked his brand until a bonfire roared to life. Red and Loura skipped around the fire, clapped on by many admirers among the Laeri. Eko slid up beside Geth, mouth agape like a smile, looking up at him with bright eyes. Geth rubbed his ears thoroughly. Agrem waved from across the fire, but it was Vriana that Geth was looking for.

He found her leaned up against a tree just outside the ring of firelight. "You're a damn fine archer," he said, leaving the others to join her. "Saved my skin back there, I have to admit it."

The chieftess nodded. "Twice."

"Twice."

She didn't concede that he'd saved her life as well, but she did pass over a wineskin. Even better.

Geth took a hearty pull. He coughed as hot, dark Ilar liquor burned down his throat. "Thram's balls! That's not wine."

Vriana snickered, honey-brown eyes twinkling.

Geth felt his cheeks stretch in a smile as well. There was a glow to Vriana that told him she was already deep in the drink. Good for her. Maybe that cold river water had taken some of the hard edge off her. Geth reckoned it had taken something out of him as well. He could feel the effects of the liquor after just one drink.

The chieftess took the skin again before he could get another swallow. She downed a mouthful and winced. "Tell me, where did you learn to fight?"

Geth reached for the liquor. "Me? I've been fighting all my life."

"Me too."

He felt her eyes on him as he drank, a mellow half-smile on her mouth. Arms folded under her cloak only accentuated the curve of her breasts, but Geth forced his eyes back on the skin in his hands. He sucked in a swig, handed it back. The chieftess took an impressive pull and the two sat quiet.

Singing and the crackle of that huge fire filled the silence until Vriana loosed a sigh. "Iyngaer will not be happy." She pulled her cloak a bit tighter, tucked her chin under the fringe.

"Iyngaer?" Geth snorted. "Did his happiness ever lead you to yours?"

Her eyes shifted from the fire back to him, but she said nothing.

"You're a great warrior, Vriana. A queen. You deserve more than Iyngaer could ever promise you."

She waved a hand. "Iyngaer means nothing. It is the north. The north is everything."

"Well, the north won't be able to contain your story now. Ceter is gone. You've made yourself a legend."

"You can have the songs. I just wanted him dead."

She looked away, but Geth could see the corners of that smile peeking up from the edge of her cloak. She took another healthy drink and pushed off the tree. Geth accepted the skin, swallowed a gulp himself. His eye slid up and down her form despite himself as she spread open that cloak and resettled it around her shoulders.

"You know—"

The chieftess shushed him with a raised finger. "Be quiet."

She beckoned with the flick of her head. Geth followed her clear around the bonfire until they reached a tent. *Her* tent. She smiled coyly from over one shoulder then ducked inside.

Geth hesitated. He still held the liquor. It seemed as good a time as ever for another pull. He took a long one and slipped in behind her. She was already lying down among the furs, eyes smokey, as the flap closed behind him.

Vriana woke Geth in the very best way the next morning, confirmation the previous night hadn't been a dream. His stomach rumbled, but he didn't dare leave until after the chieftess dressed and marched out ahead of him. Groggy Ilars and Umbelmen hunched around fires, nibbling at whatever they could find, laughing and cursing each other like only sword brothers do.

Neary hailed Geth, waving what looked like a charred sausage on the end of a stick. Vriana was nowhere to be seen. Geth hurried over to join him.

"We did it," he told the lanky Umbleman around a greasy mouthful. "And lived to tell the tale."

Neary nodded. "To a man. A few lads needed stitching up, but no one got it worse than you."

"And Ceter dead too? Victory never tasted so sweet."

"Did you hear them howling from the walls?"

"Towerrock?"

"They saw." Neary beamed. "The first part anyways. And they knew it was you."

Geth reached out a hand to rest it on Neary's shoulder. "It was *us*."

The Umbelman nodded. Members of the pack had already hailed him in ones and twos, but Geth spied Blink wringing his hands, waiting in the wings. Rising, he stepped over toward him.

"One helluva meal, Blink. Yet again. And I see you kept the horses all together yesterday when it mattered."

The Umbelman's face went red. He opened his mouth then closed it again, glancing to either side.

Geth leaned in close. "What have you got?"

"A message," Blink whispered. "From Phelan."

Of course. "Let's have it."

"He said to tell you and only you. He said there's a hoard buried up at Point-fort. Some of the things that have gone missing. And more."

"A hoard?"

"That's what he called it. Does that mean you're rich?"

Geth smiled. "I don't know. It's better than nothing."

He slapped Blink's shoulder, but the Umbelman's eyes had drifted off. Geth followed his stare to a group of Laeri packing up tents. Others loaded saddlebags. Spying Vriana stuffing her own bags, Geth left Blink to join her.

"Breaking camp already?"

"Mmmm."

"What's the plan then? Back to the wayhouse? A proper feast perhaps?"

Vriana never looked up from her baggage, squatting low to roll up pelts and stow them in a leather bag. "Back to Ehken Laer."

Geth's mouth opened and closed. "Oh."

She muttered something under her breath in the Ilar tongue and stood. "Are you angry?"

"Angry? Of course not."

"We have done what we said, mmmm? Ceter is dead."

Geth frowned. "But why leave now? There are more battles to be fought."

"Those are not my battles."

"Well—"

"You are a mighty warrior, Geth et Trusla." She stood, rested a hand on his shoulder. "Someday, I hope we may fight again, side by side."

Geth just stood there. She hefted her bag and strode away, barking orders to her people. *Let her go,* he told himself. It wasn't the first time a woman had left. No doubt she was wiser for it.

Neary was at his elbow before he could think of all the other women that had gone before. "Was that what I think it was?"

Geth grimaced. "They're going home."

At least the lanky Umbelman didn't make any comments. Phelan, no doubt, would have had something to say about Geth's performance the night before. Or the lack thereof. Thinking of his friend only made Geth want to laugh and cry at the same time.

Instead, he stood there with Neary and watched as the chieftess and her fifty swords made their farewells. Agrem and all the band saluted and waved. More than a few tribesmen raised a hand toward Geth, but Vriana only looked back over her shoulder once, met Geth's eye, and rode away.

Agrem stepped over to join them as the last rider disappeared out of sight. "Vriana is wise."

"I'm gonna try not to take that personal," Geth said. By the tone of Agrem's hum, Geth reckoned he didn't understand.

"We took the victory we wanted," said the Seer. "The young king and all his men saw, mmmm?"

Geth considered those words, remembered others Agrem had told him. "Back in Ilia, you said Ceter pulled the strings, that the rest of the chieftains did his dance. Well, we've lost Vriana, but do you reckon we've started the boulder rolling? Ceter's gone after all. Am I crazy to hope that this entire alliance of tribes might crumble away?"

"How far has he gone, mmmm?"

"Ceter? All the way to Vorda's teat."

"You saw this?"

"He hit the water just like me. And from what Vriana said, nobody pulled him out. There's no way he survived."

"Ceter, dead."

"Doesn't seem like you share my optimism."

The Seer frowned. "Mmmm."

CHAPTER EIGHTEEN

Geth wasn't sure what Agrem really meant, but he took the old warlock, along with Bird-man and those sharp eyes, to get another look at Iyngaer's siege. He sent the rest of the company south toward the wayhouse and wound through the hills in the opposite direction for another full day to arrive at the Ilar encampment from the east. With any luck, they'd be packing bags like Vriana had done.

They weren't.

"What do you see, Bird-man?" Geth squinted beside the green-cloak from a copse of trees a good mile outside the half-ruins of Greenfell. The five spires of Towerrock glowed with the inauspicious hue of a red dawn.

"Scorched earth," Bird-man said, "where we burned them up, I guess. And they've added more stakes at the edge of camp, seems like. But I don't see anyone packing anything."

"That's because they've got no horses to carry the stuff off, thanks to us." Geth forced a smile.

But it was a half-hearted expression. A part of him had really believed taking down Ceter might unstitch the entire alliance of tribes. Now that he stood there watching the enemy, something told him it had done the opposite.

Bird-man's eyes went round. Geth followed his gaze, cursed.

"Uro's puckered ass."

"Is that Iyngaer there among the Thirings?" Bird-man asked. "In the white bear furs?"

It had to be. But Geth didn't utter aloud what he reckoned that meant. "Let's go."

Bird-man obliged. Agrem and Eko were still sleeping back at their campsite. Geth woke them and started the party riding straightaway. He told the Seer what they'd seen. His hum only confirmed Geth's fears. By all appearances, they'd just handed the rule of another tribe to Iyngaer.

They rode at pace, south, for the wayhouse. Away from Iyngaer's siege. They'd kicked the hornets' nest good this time. Getting stung wasn't part of the plan.

The wayhouse was almost within sight when something made the hairs on the back of Geth's neck stand up. He pulled them to a halt right there in the middle of the road, one hand on his hilt. Bird-man seemed to feel it too. Eko's ears had gone up, but Agrem only chuckled from his saddle. Before the big warrior could spare him a glance, a woman appeared right in front of him on the road, leaning on a walking stick, riding hood unable to completely cover the huge grey bun on her head.

"Well, aren't you going to introduce us, Seer?"

Geth didn't care for the familiarity, but Agrem's smile stopped him short of lopping the old hag's head off.

"Amalia." The Ilar dipped his head low.

"Who are you, woman?" Geth eyed her up and down. "And what do you want? I'm only going to tell you this once: keep your magicks to yourself, if that's what you're about."

The woman dipped her head. "You must be the Wolf of the Hills. Just the man I'm looking for. I am Amalia. Some call me the Lady of Witchwood."

Bird-man took in a sharp breath.

But the title meant nothing to Geth. "How do you know I'm the wolf?"

"It's right there on your shield." She pointed.

"That's a dog."

Amalia snorted. Eko had wandered toward her, sniffing cautiously. "I suppose that's a dog then too?"

She held out a hand and the beast inched forward, decided he liked her scent, and leaned his big head in for a scratch. The woman rubbed his ears, smiling down and uttering gibberish like he was some huge puppy.

"This one's a darling. What's his name?"

"Eko," Agrem said, teeth bared in a wide smile.

Amalia chortled. "I thought so."

At the Seer's invitation, she retrieved a pack horse from the woods and fell in with them, leading the animal on foot to the wayhouse. She chatted all the while, about birds and trees and other nonsense, the Seer nodding and humming from time to time. Geth let the pair of them lead, keeping her ahead of him where he could see her.

Blink welcomed them when they arrived, and Loura and Drayic took their horses, tack and baggage. Amalia plunked down at a table and, after a whispered word from Bird-man, Neary hurried to provide bowls of hot soup for Geth, Agrem, and also the witch. She complimented Blink on his victuals and uttered more baby-talk toward

Eko between spoonfuls. The fool dog devoured the attention—and got to lick her bowl for his troubles.

Geth just rolled his eyes. "So, you're a witch. I suppose that means you're here because you've heard what we did to Ceter. He's gone now. You're welcome."

Amalia smiled, flicked a knowing glance at Agrem. "I've been sent from Towerrock actually. You've seen how I can move...*carefully,* when I need to."

"Bloody magicks."

"I come bearing a message."

Geth harrumphed. "From Hadean?"

"From Melagus."

Geth blinked. "What could the worm want from me?"

"He needs your help."

"Well, he would. I reckon he's feeling a bit cramped these days."

"It's more than that. A lot more."

Amalia waved for Blink. That motherly smile of hers fetched him instantly. Or maybe it was some kind of charm. Geth tried not to think about it. A cup of steaming hot tea rested in front of each of them in seconds.

He hated tea.

"Hadean is running out of time," Amalia said after a careful sip. "I'm gathering all the allies I can. And you're a man that's proven his loyalty time and time again."

"That's not all though, is it?"

"No."

"Speak plain. I've got a thick skull."

Amalia flicked a glance from side to side, lowered her voice. "The king has enemies. No secret there. But the counselor has learned that some of those enemies may be inside the walls of Towerrock already. What's more, we've received word that a killer has come to these shores on a ship out of Pellon."

Geth clamped his mouth shut, trapped a curse. He took a breath. "And this assassin is in the Tooth?"

"If our information is correct, he didn't make it inside before the siege began. At least we don't think so. But what *is* clear is that someone from within Towerrock has been in touch with the king's enemies."

"So, we have an assassin *and* a spy." Geth's eyes narrowed. "Is someone watching Hadean's back at least?"

"Melagus is with him at all times."

"Is that supposed to make me feel better?"

A chuckle slipped past Amalia's lips before she could catch herself. It didn't allay Geth's fears—far from it—but he really couldn't dislike the woman anymore.

"As I said, I'm rousing all of the king's allies," she told him. "And any could-be allies. On behalf of young Hadean, I ask that you do the same."

"I'm always looking for allies."

"Good. Because as I said before, we're running out of time. Spring is on the doorstep. You're a man of war. I don't need to tell you that it will be impossible for the men inside Towerrock to mount a sally once the river ice has melted."

Quick as she'd come, the Lady of Witchwood loaded up her shaggy packhorse and was leaving again. Dull morning skies hung overhead. Geth watched her from the doorway of the wayhouse.

"I have business further south," she told him. "With the lords Towdric and Brant."

Geth scowled, accepting the reins of her beast as she pulled her hood over that huge beehive on top of her head. "Let me know how that goes."

"Together they lead several thousands."

"You said you were gathering *allies*. From where I'm standing, those two don't qualify."

"'The enemy of my enemy is my friend' as the saying goes. Never forget that."

Neary arrived with a basket from Blink which Amalia accepted with a smile. The old Umbelman blushed and dipped his head. She took the lead and started off with a cheery wave, the other hand plying her walking stick. Geth watched that hooded bun bob over the hills and out of sight, pack animal in tow.

Phelan's message about a woman spy in Umbel's ranks came to mind. No doubt Amalia was the person he'd spoken of. But what about the news she bore?

She hadn't lied about running out of time. Stores would be even lower by now and the winter wouldn't last much longer either. With no food to be had and no way to fight their way out, Hadean would have few options except to surrender. Unless Geth or someone else did something about it.

"You've never heard of her, have you?" Neary said, shaking Geth from his thoughts.

"Can't say I have. Bird-man seemed to know something. And Agrem. From the whispers going around, I'm starting to think I'm the only one who hasn't."

"You probably are." Neary's expression was hard to read, a mix of awe and fear maybe. "She's a witch."

"I gathered that."

"Not just any witch, she's the Witch of the Woods."

Geth thought that through. "You mean the Witchwood, to the north and west."

"That's the one. I've heard tell she's an Ilar, but I reckon that's wrong now that we've met. In any case, they say she's got great powers: the power to heal you or stop your heart where you stand. She protects that wood, or so it's said. And she's about as old as the hills themselves."

"Older than you?"

Neary grinned.

But Geth just shook his head. "A powerful witch, as old as the hills and can stop your heart? I reckon we could have used her help with Ceter."

"Who knew? In the story I heard, she could never leave her woods."

"Guess they got that part wrong too."

Neary shrugged.

Geth turned them back toward the door to the way-house. "Whoever she is, I feel like I've seen her before. The one thing I do know is that she's gonna need a fair bit of magick to sway Towdric and Brant."

Geth pushed through the door and inside the common room to settle in a chair beside the hearth. Neary joined him. He stretched his hands out toward the fire.

"Brant fought with us at Copper Ridge. Some say he saved the king's life, throwing his reserves in at just the right time. Thats gotta mean something."

Geth snorted. "Yeah, but he was the first to desert us after. And Towdric never even answered the call north, bloody coward."

"Oh, he's no coward. He likes to get his hands red, believe me. He spent years fighting the Westings at Autumn Pass and I can tell you, he ties the noose himself when it's time to hang a criminal."

"Whatever he likes or doesn't like, he's no friend of Hadean's. That's for certain."

"So, what do we do?"

Geth just stared at the fire. If Hadean was really under threat inside his own keep and stores were as low as Geth had heard, they certainly had to do something. But what?

He didn't have a chance to scrape together an answer before Sweaty came bounding through the door, face even damper than usual.

"Ilars! Not a mile to the north, Sergeant!"

"How many?"

"All of them!"

CHAPTER NINETEEN

T he pickets had done their job. With an early warning, the band was able to saddle their horses and
escape further south ahead of the approaching tribesmen.
The Ilars would find warm ashes, hastily abandoned food
and supplies, but nothing living to vent their anger on.

Astride the horses they'd taken on their first attack,
Geth's band made good time. A few miles south of the
wayhouse, he turned his pack east. Best he could tell, no
one trailed them. After another handful of miles, he curled
their line back northward.

"Are we headed where I think we're headed?" Neary
asked.

Geth nodded. "Stoney. We lost a lot of supplies. We need
to stock up. I wonder if we might muster up a few more
boys for the cause as well."

"Girls too, if they can work a bow like Red and Loura."

"From your lips to the Red God's ears."

They made the distance in two shivering days. A cold spell had blown down out of the north, but Geth didn't curse the Hoarwinds this time. Amalia's words rang in his ear. They needed it to stay cold. Once the river ice melted, Hadean had no way to mount a sally and aid any attack of their own.

Without the aid of Hadean's force on his river isle, it would be almost impossible to muster the numbers to break the siege. Geth thought of Vriana's departure. How he wished for her fighters now. And for the woman herself.

There was no point dwelling on that though. The way things were going, Hadean would have to surrender and there wouldn't be anyone alive to save. *Just get to Stoney, have a hot meal, and you can give it a good think after that.* Geth nodded to himself as he rode. Neary was quiet along the way as well, no more certain of anything himself, Geth supposed.

They weren't within bow shot of the town when Red-eye came running downhill toward them, tears streaking his cheeks and even more flushed than usual. "Sir!"

Geth pulled the band to a halt. "What is it?"

"The village has been hit, sir! They're all dead! Dead to a man!"

An advanced party, including Drayic, Red and Bird-man inspected the place. Once it was clear the attackers had gone, Geth and the remainder of the band trudged up Stoney's hill and through the unhinged gates. A body full of Ilar-fletched arrows had to be dragged off the threshold. A dozen more were strewn about the muddied lanes of the town, across the green, in the doorways of homes and shops. That scowling old soldier was among them.

"Gods all be damned."

It was Geth's fault, and he knew it. Landren had predicted it. The hornets had left the nest indeed, but it was Stoney that felt the sting.

"Not everyone is dead, mmmm?"

Geth turned to find Agrem pointing toward the back of the village where Drayic squatted low, studying the ground. The Umbelman's face was etched with anger and grief. This had been his home after all.

Eko slid up against Geth's leg, looked up to meet his eye, licked his hand.

"Thanks, boy." Geth rubbed the beast's head, heaved a sigh.

"They made it out," Drayic said, looking up.

"How many?"

The bowman shook his head, uncertain. "Some."

"Some." Geth cast a glance around, noting the details this time. There certainly weren't enough bodies to account for the entire village. But the Ilars weren't shy about taking prisoners as slaves either.

And there was always the chance Iyngaer had marched the rest of the villagers to the Tooth to execute them there, for all to see. It was a tactic many a general had used before. Geth kept the possibility to himself, though Neary still wore that pensive expression, prompting him to wonder if the Umbelman wasn't thinking the same thing.

"Start looking for some shovels," he told Drayic. "I'll find a place to dig."

The heroes of Stoney were buried, the words spoken, and a fire lit in the hearth of the Goose and Gander. Geth reckoned it a blessing the tribesmen had only ransacked the inn, left it otherwise whole. It was clear they'd been moving at speed, hoping to catch the wolf unaware.

They hadn't, which only left Geth alive and gnashing his teeth those that had been massacred in his stead. Neary and Agrem took over, leading the search for supplies. But

Eko never left the big warrior's side. Geth stared at the flames, burning with his own need for vengeance, frustrated by the inability to strike back.

Bird-man cleared his throat from the common room doorway.

Geth couldn't hide the bitterness in his reply. "What?"

The Umbelman saluted with fist to heart. "Got a message, sir."

"From Phelan, right?"

Bird-man's big eyes went a little rounder. By now the formula was clear to Geth, even if the seven men sent bearing those messages had no idea how Phelan had put each of them to use. Geth waited.

Bird-man swallowed, apple bobbing on his long neck. "It's not good I'm afraid. And I'm sorry I didn't deliver it sooner."

Geth nodded. "Well, you had to deliver it secretly, I'd imagine."

"That's right."

"And?"

"It's Towdric. Phelan said I should remind you that Towdric has plenty of allies. Even inside the Tooth."

Geth muttered a curse. Did that mean it was Towdric's people spying on behalf of the Ilars? Was that what Amalia had meant? Geth sighed. There was no way to be sure.

The Umbelman's message begged another question as well. "Tell me something, Bird-man. How does Phelan know all this? Jailers talk, but even they can only know so much."

"Well, he's not in his cell all the time."

Geth blinked. "He what?"

"They let him out to have walks, play a round of dice and the like."

"They let him out of his cell?"

"Well, they did when we were still there. Plenty of times."

"What if he escaped?"

Bird-man gave rueful smile.

Geth laughed at himself. "I'm a fool, aren't I? They're under siege, where's he gonna go?"

"Just so long as Melagus isn't around to see, the boys don't mind if he stretches his legs. At least they didn't. You've still got friends in there, sir. And they all know he's your man."

They shared another smile. Geth followed Bird-man back outside. No sooner had Bird-man left than Sweaty came strolling up, casting a glance over both shoulders.

"Got a message for me from Phelan, have you?" Geth asked.

Sweaty stopped dead in his tracks.

"It's alright, the secret is safe."

The Umbelman exhaled. Geth steeled himself, but Sweaty stood too loose to be carrying anything serious. "Phelan says you're buying him a woman first thing when this siege is busted."

"That's his message? He wasted one seventh of his messengers on that?"

"Uh..." Sweaty looked confused. "Maybe it's a code?"

Geth just shook his head. "But why wait 'til now to deliver the message, Sweaty?"

"Well, uh..."

"Never mind. I do have one question though, seeing as Phelan's in want of a tumble. I hear he has free run of the Tooth, right? Didn't any of the working ladies of Greenfell make it inside the fortress?"

"They did." Sweaty grinned. "But they don't work for free."

Geth laughed. A cold wind hit him and wiped that expression from his face, but he took it as a wake-up rather than any ill omen. Phelan's message as well. Geth breathed the chill air. The Hoarwinds were on his side, at least for now. He just had to think of some way to bring the fight to Iyngaer before winds from the south turned the tide.

But how to crack the tribes apart, break their siege? The thought of Phelan, sneaking out of his cell to play dice and tell lies with the other soldiers provided the answer. "I'm a bloody fool." If Phelan could make friends of his jailers, couldn't Geth make a few friends as well?

Wandering the town, he searched out Neary. He found him up on the ramparts, cloak tight about him, facing south.

"I reckon you're thinking what I'm thinking," Geth said.

Neary turned to watch as the big warrior climbed a ladder to join him. "I don't know about that."

"We need allies. That's what the witch said, right?"

"She did."

"Well, the enemy of my enemy just might be my friend after all."

Neary's eyes narrowed.

"I'm talking about Towdric and Brant. Everyone stands to lose if Iyngaer has his way, right? He's our true enemy."

"That's right. But I reckon those two are just fine with Iyngaer having his way for now. You said it yourself, that's their plan. Let the tribes handle Hadean, then deal with Iyngaer after."

"Then we've got to convince them that won't work."

Neary looked dubious but held his tongue. Truth be told, Geth had no idea how to pull that off either. He paced the rampart several times before turning back.

"This whole time I've been trying to get the Ilars to turn on Iyngaer, split them at the seams. But the truth is, it's Umbel that's come undone. Melagus said a long time ago that it was division among the tribes that defeated them. It seems to me it's the Kingdom of Umbel that's divided now."

"What are you thinking?"

"It's time to march south, Neary. All the way to Waterset. We need to patch over Umbel's cracks before we do anything else."

"That won't be easy."

The big warrior sighed. "No, but it's something we've known all along. Between Towdric, Brant, and Hadean's force inside Towerrock, we've got the men to break the siege. We've just got to get everyone on the same side again. And we've got to do it quick."

The journey to Waterset took three days. The sun peeked out and the weather warmed, but that only reminded Geth of Amalia's warning. Behind him came the entire band in a long meandering line, loaded up with as many provisions as they could carry. He was all in.

Bird-man spied the first scout ahead before the man saw him, but Geth marched them straight down the River Road. Dog-emblazoned shields hung across their backs. He wasn't trying to hide. The nocked arrows and drawn swords that greeted them a few miles up, however, weren't the welcome he'd expected.

"Who are you?" a ruddy-faced green-cloak snapped from the front of a company of footmen arrayed across the road. "Hands away from your arms. State your business!"

"I think you know who we are," Geth said, kicking his mount forward. "And you know our business well enough."

"Can't say that I do."

"Killing Ilars. And if you really don't know who I am, they've put the wrong man in charge."

The Umbelman's mouth went tight—his face couldn't go any redder. He gestured with his sword toward Agrem. "If you're such a great killer, how did an Ilar sneak right onto the saddle behind you?"

Geth opened his mouth, but Eko slid out from between the horses, teeth bared, growling low from his throat. The Seer sat stiffly on his mount. Ruddy hadn't noticed the animal before he'd approached but he hurried to backtrack now.

"Arrows!" he cried.

"Wait!" Geth slid out of the saddle, arms upraised. "We're all friends here. Brothers, really. That's what the green cloak means. We've come to join forces. To make friends, not enemies."

"A bit late to be joining the war now, isn't it?"

Geth bit down a sharp reply about who was joining late. But letting Ruddy have the last word seemed to work. He sheathed his weapon, gestured toward the big warrior's hilt.

"I'll have that. Same goes for all of you. Until we sort out who's really friend and foe."

Geth worked his buckle and handed the whole sword belt over. "Take it. Now, can we ride, or do you want the shorts off my ass too?"

Ruddy didn't laugh. He sent his men to collect weapons up and down the column then waived the group forward. "Take them to lord Brant."

Geth didn't know whether to thank the gods or curse them. As much bad news as he'd heard about Towdric, it was Brant who knew how close Geth was to Hadean. And it wouldn't help that he'd killed the man's father either.

CHAPTER TWENTY

T he town of Waterset crowned the bluffs on the east bank of the river, encircled by squarish stone ramparts. It guarded over snowy fields spreading from the base of the bluffs down to the river's edge. Down there on the flood plain, rows of tents sprawled out behind a half-hearted barrier of sharpened stakes, not unlike those tilted toward Hadean's position in the Tooth. Men in Umbel green milled about campfires or wandered in groups up and down the road climbing toward Waterset, but Geth supposed the bulk of the soldiers must have been housed among the thatched rooftops up the hill. A dozen guardsmen watched as they passed, posted beside a yard full of over-stuffed wagons. The only sign of anything amiss was a body hanging from a lonely oak halfway up to the town.

"Deserter," Geth told Neary as they followed Ruddy uphill.

The white-haired Umbelman frowned. "Or a thief. You see all those supplies back there?"

"These boys are living better than we were, that's for sure."

The green-cloaks they passed along the way didn't look happy, despite the largess. A few eyed Geth's dog shields, but most looked disinterested. He knew low morale when he saw it. That explained the deserter hanging in the tree. And the need to make an example of him.

Through the gates and into town, Ruddy led them eventually to a citadel of sorts. A walled-in yard surrounded a sturdy keep, more supplies piled to either side. The doors to a feasting hall swung open to admit them and delicious smells wafted out to Geth's nose.

"Gods but I'm hungry," he muttered.

Only Geth was allowed inside, his people made to wait in the yard. A scattering of green-cloaks and other denizens mixed among the tables and benches, but Brant sat alone at the furthest table, an empty chair across from him. He flicked a glance at Ruddy and Geth was ushered toward it.

Brant lifted an empty cup, watching Geth's approach, and a lad hurried to fill it. The lord didn't rise as Geth joined him. "You must be hungry." His smile was mere formality. "I've ordered you a soup."

Geth took the chair he was offered and the same lad returned to set a lukewarm bowl in front of him. Thin as it appeared, it took all Geth's will not to attack that soup. Something about the line of Brant's mouth made him feel that to accept it was to acknowledge defeat. *He* had come to Brant. *He* needed something.

Geth cleared his throat to buy time, studied the man across from him.

He was handsome, Brant, of a similar age as Geth, fine-featured with the same dark hair as his cousin Hadean, the same straight shoulders. He wore a sword, but it didn't hang easy at his side. And he didn't rush to anger, despite reasons in plenty to hate Geth. No, he was nothing like Gylfric, Wayan, or even his father, Lord Eldric, other traitors Geth had crossed since his arrival.

Well, I don't need this gods-be-damned soup anyway.

"You have come," Brant said finally. "Is there something you wish to say to me?"

Geth's jaw clenched and unclenched. He composed and discarded several quips before managing a half-civil reply. "There's a war going on. I invite you to join me in fighting it."

Brant snorted a half-laugh. He reached for his wine, took a sip, set it back down. "Yes. The war."

Geth might have known what to say next if the man *had* been more like hot-headed Wayan, Gylfric the braggart, or Eldric with his schemes. But he wasn't. He just sat there coolly, watching, waiting. Geth reminded himself that this was the man that had saved the king at Copper Ridge—friend not foe. *If he can bottle it up, so can I.*

"We both serve the realm," Geth said at last. "If we wait until the army inside Towerrock surrenders, we both lose."

"We do indeed both serve," Brant nodded, "but I fear that's something that may not seem clear from where you sit."

"I heard what you did back at Copper Ridge, throwing in your reserves in the nick of time."

"It was a great victory."

"That's not how I remember it, but we didn't lose."

Brant grunted. "As I said, the view from your seat is much different than mine. For you, Copper Ridge seemed like a battle we could win. Because you don't realize it's a battle that we never should have risked fighting at all."

"Four tribes marched into your kingdom. Did you want to sit and watch?"

"The Ilars wage war against each other for fun. How could our half-trained conscripts ever match up against born killers? How could we hope to win a battle against them, in the field, on even ground? Believe me, for everyone in the war room the night before the battle, surviving was victory in itself. Everyone except Hadean, that is."

"*King* Hadean," Geth said.

Brant dipped his head, then smiled down into his cup and took a sip. "I know my cousin was loath to cede the northern reaches so easily, but you see it happened anyway."

"That sounds like something your father said."

Brant's eyes went narrow, but Geth hurried on before he could speak.

"But you aren't him, are you? No, you're your own man. A hero even, maybe. You saved your cousin's life at Copper Ridge, didn't you? So why leave him to die now?"

"Because I'm guarding the south." Brant set the wine down. "Hadean is holding out just fine. But do you know how much damage Iyngaer could do with a handful of raids downriver?"

Geth pushed his soup aside and leaned both forearms against the table. "With one good push we could drive the Ilars so far north they'll be tickling the back of the Hoarwinds' throats."

"When you're a hammer everything looks like a nail, doesn't it?"

"And when you're a snake, everything looks like a hole where you can slither away and hide."

Brant's voice went low. "Speak plain, Paellian, if you have something to say."

"You made sure to leave before the siege came in, didn't you? And now you won't go back. From where I'm sitting, it looks like you're scared."

Brant's stare wasn't so cool anymore. For Geth's part, the hammer felt like he was looking at a nail as well. No doubt it showed in his face—Geth's temper wasn't a secret to anyone in Umbel. Hostile mutters sounded from the green-cloaks behind the big warrior. Across the table, the lord's fist flexed around his wine cup. He opened his mouth, perhaps to order Geth beaten or hauled away, but a booming voice rang from the doorway before he could speak.

"The Wolf of the Hills!"

Geth turned to find a bald-headed barrel of a man striding toward him, one hand casual on the hilt of his sword, a broad smile beneath his grey mustache. Mud splattered a fine cloak and mail. By every description Geth had heard, this was Lord Towdric.

Except for the smile.

"My lord." Rising, the big warrior forced himself to bow.

Brant rose stiffly. "Lord Uncle."

Towdric pulled over a chair, clapped at a servant for a drink. He settled to his rump with a sigh, motioned Geth back into his own seat. "The Wolf! We are honored by the visit! Tell me, what brings you from the field?"

"I'm looking for men to join me," Geth said. "To take the war to the Ilars with more than just my file. I've heard you, my lord, and the lord Brant here, are just such men."

"That we are, isn't that right, my lord?"

Brant offered a perfunctory smile.

But there was more at play here than whether they'd march or not. Geth flicked a glance from one lord to the other. Unless he was mistaken, there was as much tension between those two as there had been between Brant and his father.

Geth wasn't fooled by Towdric's niceties either.

"It's no easy you task you've done here, guarding the south from Iyngaer's horde," he told the man, happy enough to play along for now. "Everyone knows it. But as Lord Brant and I were just discussing, the time's come to tighten the noose on the tribes."

Towdric nodded. "It's past time."

"So, you'll join me, march north to fight the Ilars?"

"I've just got word from our scouts that there are Ilars not a half day's ride from here as we speak. Perhaps we might ride out, sing the sword songs together, eh?"

"Uh…" Geth would have pinched himself if he could have done it without being seen. "I'd call that a good start, my lord."

"Of course you would! But where is your sword? Gods all be damned, someone get this man his weapons! Is this how we treat a hero of the realm?"

CHAPTER TWENTY-ONE

G eth didn't know what the hell was happening. Neary and his men had already been fed and boarded and he joined them at an inn called the Hook and Net. Their horses had been stabled. Everyone but Agrem and Neary were already sacked out.

"Well?" the Umbelman asked, propped up on one elbow in his bedroll as Geth crept in.

"He agreed."

"Brant?"

"No, Towdric."

Neary scowled. "Agreed to do what? Jail the lot of us?"

"I asked for help fighting the Ilars, to march north. He said his scouts have their eyes on a party of tribesmen just upriver from here. We're headed after them at dawn."

Neary rolled on his back, looked up at the ceiling, thinking that through, evidently.

Agrem hummed beside him, one hand stroking Eko's neck. "Towdric is no fool. If he fights tomorrow, he has some reason."

"You don't think it's a set up? To kill me, perhaps? Take the wolf down?"

Neary turned back to Geth. "Do they need to be sneaky about that? I mean, no offense, but being a foreigner, I reckon they could just make up any manner of lie and sentence you to death."

"I guess that's true," Geth said. "Been through as much already. Only Hadean saved me."

Neary shook his head, frowning. "So, what could Towdric want?"

"Thram and bloody Awer, I just don't know."

Agrem hummed. "One thing you can do, mmmm?" He raised a finger. "Go with him and find out."

A runner arrived to fetch Geth some time before dawn. More than a few of the men looked up, concerned, but he motioned them to stay, leaving Neary in charge. Geth didn't really expect Brant and Towdric to betray him out there. And he didn't want to risk any of his own men if he didn't have to, especially when he wasn't in charge. Gods bless them, but they weren't called the Dead-man Dozen for nothing.

As expected, the runner led him to a force gathered in the square beside Waterset's gate. The sounds of whetstones on steel echoed across the cobbles as final preparations were made.

Geth studied the fifty-odd fighters the lords had assembled— hard men by the look of it, battle-tested. Geth nodded to himself. He'd made the right decision in leaving his band behind. If some thick-skulled captain expected Blink or Bird-man to pull the same weight as this lot, most of his dozen would be dead men indeed.

"Here he is!" That voice turned Geth. Towdric marched toward him, barrel chest puffed, arms swinging at his sides.

"Here to send us off, my lord?"

That smile split Towdric's grey beard. "Ha! Do you think I'd miss out on such a day? I'll be having a bit of action myself. And I'll get to watch the Wolf on the hunt as well."

Towdric's smile went even broader.

But Geth didn't trust him for a minute. He managed to show his teeth in reply. *We need this bastard,* he reminded himself. *Hadean and Phelan need him.*

Feet went in stirrups, shields were slung over backs, and the troop rode out the gates, down across the whitened flood plain, and eventually back up into snowy, leafless hills of oak and scattered pine. Brant hadn't joined them, but Ruddy was there with a contingent of warriors. Geth soon recognized a symbol like three hills on the shields of Towdric's men, a wavy river emblem on Brant's. The two parties rode a little apart. Geth made note of that as well.

It wasn't long before a scout returned from further afield with news. He rattled off his report with a salute of fist to heart. Towdric waved Geth forward when the man had gone.

"Did you hear that? Ilars, right in our front yard. We'll meet them just over the next hill. They've settled in a homestead. A couple dozen, not more."

Geth frowned. "Awful bold of them, twenty or more Ilars within a half day's ride of Waterset."

"They've been there for days. I've had my eye on them the whole while."

"Could it be a trap?"

Towdric waved that off. "They're bold alright, these snow-sucking bastards. Bold enough to ride out from under their forests and try for a slice of southern lands, but too blind to see the axe over their heads. We'll teach them something today—this pack of strays anyway."

Geth clenched his mouth shut. No wonder the tribes had grown bold, with the two lords at Waterset sitting on their hands. The shout of a captain with bushy eye-brows and the same barrel-chested strut as Towdric turned Geth's thoughts back to the fight ahead. The order came to dismount.

Towdric's kinsman arrayed them in a loose line atop a hill looking down on the homestead. Ruddy fanned his men out to the right in similar fashion. The advantage of attacking on horseback had been deemed less useful than the advantage of surprise, Geth supposed. Down below, a dozen of the shaggy horses the tribesmen favored clustered in the space between houses and barns, smoke drifting from the chimneys. They wouldn't be facing any riders either.

Bushy-brows walked up and down the line giving in-structions. "They won't be expecting us," he told Geth and the men around him, "but Awer will have to be smil-ing pretty hard for us to make it all the way down without someone crying the alarm. So be ready. We'll be in too close for arrows by then. It's numbers we're betting on. Protect the man to your left and your right. We move in as quick and quiet as we can. Chop down anybody on the outside and burn up anyone hiding inside."

Geth hadn't noticed torches and fuel among the bag-gage, but they came out now. He couldn't find fault with the approach. It relied on superior numbers and competent swordsmanship, luxuries he'd never had while leading his own campaign. Such a plan would very likely result in losses though, something else Geth couldn't abide with his own meager band.

"Let's see if the Wolf's got any teeth," someone muttered, somewhere to the right. Another soldier snorted in reply.

Geth didn't even turn. His eyes were on the compound down below, looking for the odd dog, a man wandering out for a piss, a sentinel hidden amongst the undergrowth. He found none, but it didn't mean they weren't there. With a nod from Towdric, they started down the hill, boots sliding on snowy ground, breath huffing out into the cold air in clouds. The brawny bastard was really smiling now.

An Ilar cried out and an alarm went up before they'd come halfway. Geth didn't see where it came from, but the tribesmen knew they were there. A war cry answered from the green-cloaks to either side of him. Half-dressed tribesmen piled out the doors to meet them. A patchy shield wall came together at the bottom of the hill and Towdric's men were forced to slow down and form up as well.

"Beside me!" Towdric called.

Moving in lockstep, shields overlapping, they advanced. Curses flew back and forth. Geth spit a few of his own as the thrill of battle pumped through his veins. Leaning into the last few yards, he hefted his sword and slammed his shield into the bristling wall of tribesmen ahead.

The clang and clamor of battle shook winter-quiet hills as swords hacked down against iron-rimmed shields. Up close, Geth uttered every Ilar curse he knew, pushing and stabbing, vying for leverage. The tribesmen had chosen a space between buildings to form up, negating Towdric's numerical advantage. But men would be sent circling around to flank the enemy. Geth couldn't see over the shields ahead of him to see if any had yet arrived.

He wasn't going to wait to find out. Heaving with all his strength, he created a space between himself and his enemy, used it to dart a thrust between shields. A man screamed and went down. The Ilars behind the man dragged him back, but Geth swung for his countryman to the left next, exposed for a brief instant, and a second tribesman fell.

The green-cloak to Geth's right leapt forward at just the right moment to widen the breach. Others piled in behind him, pushing, grunting, trying to swing over his head. The Ilar line bent, threatened to break. It stood only a few men deep. The tribesmen didn't have the numbers for more.

Geth heaved again, battering at swords and helms to make more space for the men behind him to fill. The Ilar shield wall ahead caved in finally and parted.

"For Umbel!" someone shouted.

The slaughter was about to begin. Geth heard an Ilar cry out the word 'Eko,' wondering if they recognized him, but just then the green-cloak to his right groaned and went down to one knee. Raising his weapon, Geth skipped forward, driving a ratty-bearded Ilar back before he could finish the Umbelman. Someone behind Geth hauled the injured warrior back from the front line and Geth let out a wolf-howl, smashing his sword against his own shield, challenging the enemy to try and follow after.

They knew that call. Smoke reached Geth's nose as the first thatched rooftop took flame. But the Ilars were already in retreat. The back ranks hopped on horseback and tried hacking through Towdric's flanking maneuver. Those in the front were too busy being cut down.

A handful of riders escaped, not more. As quickly as it had begun, it was over. But more than the battle had ended for several of the Umbelmen that had ridden out with them that day. Geth turned to check on the man who'd fought at his right. They'd sat him up against the bowl of a tree where he clutched at a gash in his hip that had cut clear through his ring mail. He stripped off his helmet at Geth's approach to reveal a familiar red face.

"Help me up." Ruddy stretched out a hand. Geth took it, hauled the Umbelman to his feet. Ruddy winced but stood, sweat rolling down his temples despite the cold.

"You alright?" Geth asked.

"Better than them."

He flicked his chin toward several slain Umbelmen, lying still on the red-flecked snow. Others took water and consolation from their fellows, but Geth could smell death on them already. He mouthed a curse almost at the same time as Ruddy

The Umbelman waved Geth closer to lean on him like a crutch as they waited for men to fetch their horses down from atop the hill.

"You're gonna need some stitches," Geth told him. "At the very least."

"Lord Brant has a healer woman," Ruddy grunted. "She'll patch me up."

The horses arrived, the dead men were slung over their saddles. The living had already picked through the fallen Ilar's belongings, but Towdric hadn't given any orders to burn or bury them.

"The Wolf's snout can do more than just howl," Ruddy said. "There's more than one that's denied it, but now I've seen for myself."

Geth looked up from the dead men to face him. "The longer we allowed that shield wall to stand, the more horses would be carrying dead men on their backs."

Ruddy looked like he might start in on the curses again, but Towdric appeared from around the side of an outbuilding, an Ilar head dangling from his grasp.

"There he is, the Wolf!" Towdric raised the severed head and grinned through his beard. "This bastard gutted one of our boys. I'm taking his head as payment. Take them all, in fact! Let it be known among those pine-stinking bastards that to leave the forests is to leave them for good!"

CHAPTER TWENTY-TWO

B loody heads topped spears and bobbed from saddles as Towdric's war party made the journey home. The sun had dipped by the time they climbed to Waterset's height, but Geth was assured that fire and cheer awaited in Lord Brant's hall. A good thing too—Towdric added another full mile to the journey, parading those Ilar heads all through town before turning for the keep.

It had the effect he was after, best Geth could tell. Men and women alike shouted and shook fists from windows and doorways. Soldiers saluted with fist to heart. On the cold lawn outside Brant's hall, the delicious smells of a pig roasting over a bed of coals greeted them when they finally arrived.

"We've earned as much," Geth told Ruddy. Horse grooms took their reins and they slid from saddles. "But I didn't expect Lord Brant would be the one to feast us."

Ruddy snorted. "This is Towdric's doing, make no mistake. And it's no mistake that he's done it here either."

A woman came around with cloth and water to wash away the grime before Geth could reply. He took a damp rag. Ruddy waved her off, limping in the direction of the keep with a grimace.

Geth still had plenty of questions, but he let the man hobble off in search of treatment. The smell of sizzling meat tickled the inside of Geth's nose, turned his stomach in flips. No injury could have kept him from the table at that moment. When the great doors to the hall came open, a throng of highborns welcomed him and all the rest with hearty cheers.

"We've done it." A hand came to rest on Geth's shoulder. He turned to find Towdric grinning at his side. There was evil in that grin and Geth knew it. But the joy on his face was just as real.

"We've done *something*."

"Smell that pig?" Towdric took an exaggerated whiff. "You've gone without such comforts these past months, I'm sure. Well, you'll eat like the cook himself tonight."

"I'm not the only one that's gone without," Geth said.

Towdric's eyes narrowed, a hint of the devil in him, but Geth explained before he could draw the wrong conclusion.

"My file. My whole band, in fact."

"Ah!" That grin again. "They must join us!"

Ahead of them, Brant rose from his customary seat to wave them forward. Towdric walked Geth all the way to a chair reserved for him, just to the side of lord's table. His hand never left Geth's shoulder, smiling at beringed men and jeweled ladies along the way. Important people, Geth was sure. He hadn't quite figured out why Towdric needed to show off his pet wolf, but the trays of bread and cheese on the tables pushed that from his thoughts.

He plopped down in his seat and gathered a share of each. Warriors patted his back in passing, knuckled their brows, or just nodded. A stuffed mouth helped him avoid conversation. He'd spent weeks cursing this lot for cowards anyway. Agrem and Neary arrived to save him, taking the chairs to either side.

"There you are," Geth said.

Neary reached for a wedge of cheese and spoke out of the corner of his mouth for only Geth to hear. "We saw the heads. I think Agrem might have known some of them."

Geth turned to find the Seer tearing his bread into little shreds. Geth gave the Seer the wine out of his own hand and called for two more. The rest of the file were seated at the far end of the hall, near the door with the lowest ranks. At least they would eat and drink.

"So, what do you make of it?" Neary asked. "Has Towdric had a change of heart?"

Geth frowned. "I don't know. He's not shy about wading into a fight, that's for sure. And it's clear he wants everyone in Waterset to know he's spilled enemy blood."

"Whatever he's up to, you've finally spurred him to action."

Neary drained his cup and waved in vain for more. The pork came around, as fatty and delicious as Geth had imagined. He ate until he was full, chewing over Towdric, his play, his motives, at the same time. Perhaps it was an over-stuffed belly, but something didn't sit right.

"We took losses today," he told Neary, sipping at his wine, "losses that could have been avoided."

The Umbelman just listened.

"We might not have come back with quite as many heads, but we could have still killed a few tribesmen and driven the rest off without so much as a scratch."

"This isn't your band, Geth."

"You're right about that. We didn't have lives to spare, did we? We needed everyone to come out in one piece."

"And we gave a shit." Neary lifted his cup, spilled a portion. "Rest in peace, Baby."

Agrem hummed his agreement, the first noise he'd made.

Geth turned in that direction. "What do you make of it, 'Grem?"

Agrem sighed. "Towdric has a problem, mmmm?"

Geth frowned, unsure what he meant.

"The man in the tree. He was not the first to try to leave."

"The hanged man?"

Neary leaned in from the other side. "We didn't waste the day while you were gone. It seems there was a wave of desertions before that man died. Towdric hates deserters. He thinks of it as a personal betrayal."

"Personal betrayal?" Geth snorted. "More than a little irony in that."

"There's more." Neary opened his mouth to continue but Hack, Blink, and a third green-cloak Geth didn't recognize interrupted arrived, saluting, each in turn.

"What is it, men?" Geth asked. "Did you get your fill?"

"Yes, sir!" Hack thumped his fist against his chest as if eating the pork had been an urgent mission. He flicked a glance at the third man, opened and closed his mouth until Blink spoke for him.

"This is Ratcher, sir." Blink nodded toward the fellow they'd brought along. "He's asked to join the file. We could use a man to fill in for Baby."

Geth looked the newcomer up and down, wondering if he'd volunteered just to get in on the feast. A blocky head with pudgy cheeks sat atop a frame that reminded Geth of a baker more than any kind of soldier. The man would fit right in with his dozen.

"Well, Ratcher? You want in? We could use a good man."

Ratcher saluted Umbel-style, face screwed up all serious. "I just arrived from downriver. Don't have a sergeant or a lord or anything. Suppose I need one."

"Just came up all by yourself?"

"Got no family, sir. Just a dead brother. The Affliction, sir. Nothing holding me back."

"I see you've got a sword and a cloak. If you're not afraid to continue the march north, then welcome to the file." *If you don't disappear later tonight, once you've had your fill of meat and drink...*

But Ratcher smiled, revealing a nice set of choppers. As far as Geth could tell, he was still smiling when the trio rejoined the rest of the band. From Geth's side, Agrem wore that faraway look again, but Neary watched the boys lead the new recruit back toward their seats.

"What do you think, a drunk?" he asked. "A gambler maybe?"

"Either he'll stick with us," Geth said, "or he won't. In the meantime, it's Towdric I'm thinking of."

As the soldiers got deeper into their cups, the singing began. Geth didn't join in. He downed his wine, kicked his chair back, and headed behind the head table toward Towdric and Brant. Before he could open his mouth, Towdric rose to hail him.

"The Wolf! Well fought today!"

"Thank you, my lord."

Towdric kept on before he could say more, turning toward Brant. "This man cracked the enemy shield wall almost by himself. Saved a fair few lives in doing it."

"I'm ready to do it again. Only bigger this time."

Brant offered that polite, meaningless smile again, but Towdric's grin did more to convince. "I wager you are!"

"We need to march north, my lord. That's why I've come. The king needs our help."

"We shall, sir, we shall." Towdric wrapped a thick arm across Geth's shoulder and lifted his voice so those sitting nearby couldn't help but overhear. "We shall drive the Ilars back under their trees! These tribesmen won't be leaving without some encouragement, will they? Believe me when I tell you we've just gotten started!"

"The sooner the better, my lord," Geth said. "The king is running short on supplies already."

"Just as soon as preparations can be made, we'll march forth with the fury of Red Awer. In the meantime, drink!" He raised that cup again, shouting in earnest this time. "To the Wolf!"

Geth was no fool. Towdric's game had become clear. The big warrior returned to his seat between Neary and Agrem and downed his wine with a curse.

"We're not heading north, are we?" Neary said.

"It's all just for show. That's what the smiling sono-fabitch is about. He's just wasting time, using me to add some glitter to his own sword. There was never any plan to go to war."

"That's about what I'd expect, given the rumors that are floating about."

Geth looked to his friend.

"He's got a strong claim to the throne," Neary explained. "He was first cousin to King Aeldan, Hadean's father. That's means he's got an equal claim as lord Brant himself. And that makes one of the two the heir to the kingdom, should Hadean die without a child."

Geth whistled. The tension between the two lords made perfect sense now. He flicked a glance back up to their table, watched Towdric clutch at the arm of another high-born, laughing all the while. Brant faced the other way, in some discussion of his own with Captain Ruddy.

"Towdric's got to be after it for himself," Geth said. "As for Brant, if he had wanted Hadean's crown, he could have left him to die at Copper Ridge. His father would have become king and himself after."

"But is he willing to hand the crown to Towdric?" Neary asked.

"I don't get the feeling he loves the man."

The Umbelman snorted. "No one loves Towdric. Not those who know him anyway."

"Seems a likable bastard though."

"As long as you don't cross him. He'll hit you with the smile first, but if that doesn't work, it's an iron fist that follows. Hanged about fifty suspected highwaymen without so much as a trial some years back."

Geth frowned. He knew the type: quick to laugh, just as quick to anger. That was the short of it.

But he reckoned he knew Towdric's long game as well. The attack that morning, the parade through town...it was all part of his campaign to build support, become king. Brant didn't seem likely to stand in his way either.

And Geth's arrival had played right into the bastard's hands. "Gods all be damned."

Neary rested a hand on his arm. "It's plain Towdric's trying to make friends, but believe me, he's got staunch enemies out there as well."

"Tell me something good, Neary. I need to hear it."

"The Aldwood."

Geth's eyes narrowed. The grim look Neary wore made it hard to believe he had something positive to say but the big warrior held his tongue. "I'm listening."

"You've heard the Aldwood is filled with brigands, right? That's why there's few travelers that will risk that stretch of the King's Passage anymore. We skirted 'round ourselves on the way back from Pellon."

"I remember."

"Well, the men I mentioned—the ones that Towdric hanged—most of those weren't highwaymen at all. Their only crime was being the brothers or fathers or sons of the Aldwood's thieves. That was Towdric's way of getting back at Crookbow and his lot. No one hates the bastard more than he does."

"Crookbow?"

"The man that leads the Aldwood thieves." Neary nodded. "I want your permission to go there and try to win him over."

"You think this Crookbow scratch might hate Towdric enough to help take him down?"

"I know he does."

"How?"

"I used to be his partner."

CHAPTER TWENTY-THREE

"I t's risky."

The feast was over. After a night of fitful sleep, Geth stood beside Neary outside the inn, breath rising like misty apparitions into the frigid morning air. The idea of enlisting the thieves of Aldwood still hung there between them.

"It won't stay this cold for long," Neary said. "Once the river ice melts, Hadean will be stuck fast. He'll have no choice but to surrender or starve. They'll have eaten everything down to the rats by then."

Geth muttered a curse but didn't answer one way or the other. So many questions—Neary's full history with Crookbow not least among them.

He left the Umbelman at the inn, ambling through Waterset's streets until he reached the ramparts guarding the town. A ladder took him up to parapets that watched over the frozen trail of mighty Vorus, river of the north, and the bleak grey hills beyond. Nowhere better to have a think than the heights.

"Thram and bloody Awer."

Things were always simpler when there was an enemy position to charge. Geth rested a hand on the cold stones and grimaced into the wind. He needed Towdric and Brant, that much was clear. Their soldiers anyway. But murdering the bastards wasn't going to work this time.

Then seek allies. Geth turned to peer back down at snow-topped roofs of Waterset. *That's what the witch said.*

No sooner had he reminded himself than his eyes landed on Ruddy, walking with a crutch just below him on the street.

"Well, there's an ally..." He trailed off as he recognized the woman at his elbow. "Awer's bloody cock!"

Further along the wall, a sentinel eyed Geth sideways, but the big warrior was too shocked to care. There was no mistaking the witch, Pythelle. The hairs on the back of Geth's neck went up.

What the hell was she doing here? He'd never really understood her motives back in Towerrock, except that she'd been in bed, literally, with the traitor Eldric. It was her witchcraft that helped coordinate Hadean's betrayal in

Ilia. And if it hadn't been for himself and Agrem, the lad would have died there.

Feet started moving on their own, a low growl leaving Geth's lips, but he managed to rein himself in. The last thing he needed was to land himself in another trial for murder.

What to do then? He breathed the cold air, turned his eyes out over the folds of the land, northward. Agrem would know.

He found the warlock back at the inn, picking at a plate of cold meats. "Upset, mmmm?"

"You would be too if you knew who I just ran into."

The Seer kept on eating. Geth had the feeling he already knew.

"Pythelle."

"Mmmm."

"You don't look surprised. Course not, you're the Seer. Tell me then, what the hell is she doing here?"

"Bad things." Agrem looked up from his plate. "Don't need the Sight to know this, mmmm?"

"She was with one of Brant's men. A captain. He mentioned earlier the lord had a healer. Do you reckon she's attached herself to the son the same way she did with the father?"

"Attached?" the Seer raised an eyebrow.

"You know what I mean," Geth snatched a slice of ham off Agrem's plate.

That earned him a frown.

"Well? Could *she* be the one influencing Brant, keeping him at Towdric's side? And keeping him from marching against the Ilars? She needs them, after all. One of them at least. King Hadean knows her part in the betrayal."

"Mmmm."

"Or could she be feeding information to the tribes by way of her magicks? I suppose it could be she's done both. Anything to make sure Hadean doesn't come out on top and hang her for treason."

Agrem shook his head, swallowing down a shred of meat. "Power. This is what she wants."

Geth met his eye. "Survival."

"Mmmm."

No doubt Pythelle had hoped to profit from Eldric's rise, pulling the string of the man she'd helped put on the throne. But Geth had pissed on that parade before it began by killing the traitor. She'd gone from predator to prey. If she wanted to survive, her first order of business would be to dethrone King Hadean.

Geth nodded. But none of that made the way forward any clearer. "So, what do we do? Can't you use your magicks or something?"

"Against Pythelle?"

"Who else?"

"I already am. If she tries to take the Paths, I will know. If she seeks to speak across the miles, I will know. But I do not have the magicks, as you say it, to turn Brant to join us."

"We need friends. That's what Amalia said."

"She is wise."

"Well, can't you summon a spirit or roll some bones or something? Where do we find them?"

"You already know."

By the look in his eye, Geth reckoned he was serious. Perhaps he'd even seen as much, predicted this conversation. For the big warrior, however, his earlier conversation with Neary was the only thing that came to mind.

Crookbow.

"Thram's balls." It was worth a shot. A few dozen thieves were hardly an army, but he wasn't in the position to turn away a eunuch with a sharp stick if he wanted to join up. Geth left the Seer to search for Neary. When he found the Umbelman, his things were already packed.

"Agrem," Neary explained, fastening the last buckle on his saddle bags. "He knew you'd say yes."

Of course he did. "But are you sure these brigands won't nail your hide to the nearest tree?"

"There's an honesty among thieves. That's how the saying goes."

Geth scowled. "I'm not sure I can attest to that."

"He's a wily sonofabitch, Crookbow. But he hates Towdric. And that makes him our friend."

"For now."

"For now," Neary agreed.

"You'll need a good horse. I've got one in mind."

"That grey?"

Geth smiled. "I call him Palladine."

It would take at least five days for Neary to ride to the Aldwood, win Crookbow over, and make the return journey. Geth uttered a prayer, watched the lanky oldster ride out. Only after he'd disappeared downhill into the east did Geth turn back toward the Hook and Net.

In the meantime, he needed to keep busy. "But doing what?" he muttered aloud. The answer was obvious. *Undermining that bastard Towdric, what else?*

Geth wrapped his cloak about himself as he strode the cold, cobbled lanes. Towdric had at least one weakness he knew of: a problem with the rank and file. That deserter hanging in the tree made it clear. So too the need to give the soldiers a victory with the previous day's attack, parading those heads about, the feast afterwards, and all the rest.

But Geth wondered if the lord hadn't lost face among the highborn as well. Why else show off his dog of war, another beast in his kennel? Geth wondered if he hadn't fallen right into the bastard's plot. He'd given Towdric the battle he needed. As far as the other lords knew, he'd thrown in his lot with the traitor as well.

"Thram's hairy...."

An idea came to him before he could finish. The wolf-pack was the only resource he had. They didn't have the sharpest bite, his lot, but they could chew the fat with the best of them.

He took his men aside in threes and fours so as not to draw attention. "Alright soldiers, some of you boys were farmers before this war, right? Well, I need some seeds sown and I need them to sprout tall and thick."

Inevitably there were confused looks.

"It's simple," he explained. "The idea is to rile up Tow-dric's ranks. He's had a problem with deserters in the past and we want to give his lads even more reason to leave out. Start the whispers. Like, 'the supplies are drying up, we'll soon be on half-rations.' 'The army's about to move north to the boundaries, into the cold.' 'There's a grippe going around that'll swell your balls up—whatever you can think of to make 'em itch to be gone."

"What about Brant's men?" Drayic asked. He was no dummy. "Perhaps we should start a rumor that his ranks are getting a bigger share of the rations? Or that they won't have to march north. Something like that."

Loura nodded. "Jealousy works wonders with you men-folk."

"I like it." Geth offered a nod. "Anything we can do to tip the scales against Towdric."

Neary wasn't there to assign the specifics, but Geth did his best to play to the strengths of each member of the band.

"Blink," he said. "You told me you planned to become an acolyte of Thram before this war began. There's gotta be a shrine to the Hunter here in Waterset. And I wager some of Towdric's men make visits. See if you can get our news in the ear of the local robes, let them do the work for us. Bird-man, you go with him. I reckon you've got a solemn look about you without even trying."

Bird-man's stork-like neck bobbed as he knuckled his brow.

"Red-eye, they say you know every inn and tavern from Umbel City up to Greenfell. Find out where Towdric's lads get their drink. That's your playground. Take Dodger along in case your hay fever chokes you up. He's got Se-lel's own luck. Might come in handy if you sneeze on the wrong man's collar.

"Sweaty, you grew up in a soldiering family," Geth went on. "Take Kerrel with you and drift about among the ranks. They'll recognize a couple tried and true green-cloaks. And with any luck they'll buy what you're selling."

"What about me?"

Geth looked over to find Hack frowning. The crater-faced Umbelman considered himself the best swordsman of the lot. And he was, after young Kerrel. But he was also about as blunt as a hammer.

"Keep watch over Agrem," Geth said, thinking on his feet. "There's no love lost for Ilars in this war camp. And keep an eye on Eko as well."

Hack saluted gravely and Geth was surprised to find Ratcher still around and eager to follow along toward the Seer's room. Drayic helped assign tasks for the folk from Stoney and the work began. Geth nodded to himself. Towdric had played him like a fiddle thus far. But Geth reckoned he could play a few notes himself.

By the third day after Neary's departure, evidence of their work could be heard at watering holes and vendors stalls anywhere in Waterset. The stores had nearly run out. A new Affliction had begun taking its toll. Geth even overheard one green-cloak tell another that a powerful Ilar curse had landed on the camp and they'd all break out in boils unless they made the proper sacrifices. Or better yet, packed up and left.

Geth wasn't sure if they'd overshot the mark, but the band had certainly lived up to expectations this time. A good thing too; the sun gleamed high and bright overhead, a mild wind hinting at spring. The river ice wouldn't last much longer.

At least a few of Towdric's men heeded the rumors and broke camp. Some of Brant's men as well. Brows were furrowed at the head table when Geth supped in the lord's hall that evening. Towdric's smile had deserted him for once. Geth chuckled down into his bowl every time he saw the bastard stride past.

"What are you thinking?" he asked Agrem on the evening of the fifth day since Neary left. Geth had hoped Neary might be back by then, to no avail. The Seer just stared up at the ceiling, Eko curled up at the foot of the bed.

"Just thinking."

"Fine, don't tell me." Geth plunked down on his own straw pallet.

"You are thinking too, mmmm?"

"Have we accomplished anything? With all these lies and rumors, I mean. Other than annoying the dear Lord Towdric? Have we done anything to prod these soldiers further north?"

"We have started a boulder rolling, as you say. A dangerous boulder, perhaps, but it is something, not nothing."

"For Thram's sake though, all we've really done is encourage our own warriors to leave camp. Not to mention this whole business with Neary and Crookbow. Assuming he does sign on, what the hell are we gonna do with the scratch? We can't march him into Towdric's camp. There won't be enough trees to hang them all."

Eko stretched, slid down from the bed and came to rest against Geth's leg. Geth obliged with a half-hearted scratch behind the ears. The Seer's expression was unreadable.

"Mmmm."

"You're gonna have to tell me what that means this time."

"Brant."

"Brant?"

"We need Brant. Towdric can be hurt or killed. But he cannot be turned. His roads lead away from peace, not toward it."

Geth didn't ask, but by Agrem's tone, he knew he had *seen* it. The big warrior looked down at Eko, eyes bright but serious. A dog always knew. A wolf. Whatever.

"You're right," Geth said. "Both of you. I need to talk to Brant."

He left for the keep without waiting for a reply. The hour was late, the streets dark and chill. Torchlight welcomed him when he reached the hall, but only a few servants moved about, gathering up table linens and tin plates. A hound looked up from beneath one of the tables, jowls drooping, forlorn. Geth wandered the corridors until he found Brant in his war room, just Ruddy and a cup of wine for company.

"My lord." Geth saluted Umbel-style with fist to heart. "I was hoping for a word. In private."

Brant exchanged looks with his captain. Ruddy considered Geth for a moment, bowed, and left.

"Speak your piece," Brant said.

Geth exhaled. "You need to pick a side. We're running out of time. March north to Hadean, or hand Towdric the crown and watch him rule over Umbel's final days."

Brant scowled.

"Look what I've done with just a tiny force," Geth said. "We've hit the tribes, even taken down one of their chieftains. We can win this war."

"You are very brave." Brant said. "And very foolish."

"It only seems that way because you're scared."

"If Iyngaer marches south—"

"Then march north first! Draw first blood. Once the river ice melts, Hadean and all his fighters will be stranded. And it won't take more than a few hundred tribesmen to keep them hemmed in, freeing up Iyngaer to bring his horde here and burn this city to the ground."

Brant's mouth opened and closed. There really was fear in the man's eyes. And Geth reckoned he knew why.

"This is the witch Pythelle's doing."

"The *Lady* Pythelle."

"And why in Vorda's name is she here?"

"She is a healer. Did you know that? She may also, at time, use her arts to provide valuable information."

"Did you know she used those same arts to help the tribes ambush Hadean?"

Brant's eyes narrowed. "Have you any proof?"

"She showed me how she…" Geth struggled for the words, "*spoke…* to a woman in Ilia. Later, I met this woman. She was the witch of the Chieftain Othwid. Agrem can tell you as much."

Brant snorted. "And why would she show you such a thing? Why would she betray the realm in the first place?"

"Not the realm." Geth softened his tone. "Just King Hadean. She was with your father before she came south to Umbel City. And after. She was his mistress."

Brant's face went red. Geth wondered if he hadn't slept with the woman indeed. Whatever the case, something seemed to struck a chord with him now.

"My father." He shook his head, lifted his cup and drained it before looking back to Geth. "He got what he deserved, didn't he? He was greedy man, always wanted more. Did you know that? From his wife, from his son. From the realm."

Geth opened his mouth and closed it again.

"But he was smart." Brant grimaced. "Careful. Even if he failed to acknowledge the same qualities in those around him, he was certainly smart otherwise."

"Maybe a little too smart," Geth said. "And not careful enou—"

The door to the war room burst open to admit a half dozen armed warriors led by Towdric himself. "Not careful enough indeed."

CHAPTER TWENTY-FOUR

"What is this?" Brant demanded.

Towdric ignored him, gesturing at Geth with his sword. "Ask the Wolf. The *dog*, I should say. Isn't that the truth of it?"

"What do you want?" Geth circled beside Brant, behind the heavy oak table at the center of the room. He didn't yet reach for his blade. He eyed Towdric's men as the fanned out to either side. Brant stood red-faced, indignant, but rooted in place.

"You think you're pretty clever, don't you, Paellian." Towdric's eyes gleamed evilly. "Did you think I wouldn't find out?"

"Find out about what?" said Brant.

Towdric ignored that, gesturing toward Geth. "Take him."

"You can try," Geth growled.

One hand floated toward his hilt, the menace in his voice freezing the six guardsmen where they stood. But their lord just laughed. He turned toward the open door behind him and waved at someone in the hall. Another pair of guardsmen came in after, dragging Agrem between them, face bloodied, head loose on his neck like a drunk's.

"You bastards." Geth's hand moved from his hilt to the edge of the table, ready to hurl it at his enemies.

But Agrem raised his eyes, shook his head ever so slightly. Geth clamped his mouth shut, exhaled through his nose long and slow.

"It's alright," Towdric told his men. "He won't resist. To the dungeons with him."

Brant uttered more questions, but Geth was already out in the hall, ushered along at sword point. He craned his neck to see Agrem hauled out in his wake. Towdric had found his smile again, but that evil glint hadn't left his eye.

"Is somebody going to tell me what this is all about?" Geth asked. "Am I being charged with something?"

"Aiding a deserter." Towdric said. "Your friend, the grey-haired fellow. Not to mention all the others who believed your lies."

"Has someone deserted?"

They took Geth down a set of stairs, arriving in a low-ceilinged hallway lined with heavy timber doors. The tip of a sword between the shoulder blades prodded Geth toward the furthest one. He whirled to face Towdric before they could throw him in.

But the bastard had pulled the Seer up close, his sword draped across his neck. "Get inside."

Geth raised his hands. "Hang on! Even if I did send my man away from the camp, is this how you treat a loyal hero of the realm?"

"This is how I treat a foreign sellsword playing at green-cloak."

"You think you can get back at the king by hanging his man? Or hanging me? Like you hung all those innocent people to get back at Crookbow?"

Towdric just smiled. "Don't worry. This time there's going to be a trial."

By the noises coming in through the barred window in the door, Geth reckoned Agrem had been stowed in the cell next to him. "You alright, 'Grem?"

"Alright? Mmmm."

Geth snorted a bitter laugh. He thought of the king, of Phelan, of the band. Of all the people counting on him. A noise sounded from down the hall, and he braced himself.

The new recruit, Ratcher, wasn't the person Geth had expected to see.

"Is that you, Captain?" The blocky headed green-cloak squinted through the bars set in the door.

"Ratcher? Can you break us out of here?"

"Afraid not, sir."

"I figured as much. I won't ask how you got down here in the first place."

"Just came to check in on you."

"I need you to carry a message to the band, Ratcher. Tell them to get out of camp, back to the hills. Before Towdric comes for them."

"I can do that."

They faced each other silently through the bars for a long moment. Geth waited. Had Towdric sent the man, promised some reward if he could get Geth to reveal something or other?

But the Umbelman asked no questions. "I respect you," he said. "Whatever happens, I just want you to know that. And I'll get your boys out safe."

"Good man."

A noise echoed down the hall. Ratcher frowned, turned back to Geth. "Sorry they've got you. But it could have been worse."

It was Geth's turn to frown. The green-cloak hurried out the way he'd come before he could speak. Towdric came the other way. Geth stared daggers at him through the bars, but Brant stepped up beside the treacherous bastard before the big warrior could say his piece.

"Serious accusations have been levelled at you, Master Geth," said Brant. "We've had a wave of desertions. It seems you've been stirring up false claims, though I can't understand why. Do you deny it?"

"Did I order my man to leave the camp? The answer is yes. On an errand for the war. He's my man, not either of yours. And he's not a deserter. As for stirring up trouble, where's the proof? I've hardly spoken to anyone outside of my band for the last five days. How can I be charged with stirring up trouble?"

"You ask for proof?" Towdric's mouth curled. "I have it from several of my soldiers that it was one of your men, or women, who first mentioned a new Affliction in the camp or a dearth of supplies. These are exactly the sort of reasons a soldier will forsake his duty, and you know it! As for your man and this 'errand,' pray tell, where *did* you send him?"

"None of your business."

"Ha!" Towdric looked at Brant like he'd extracted an admission of guilt.

The younger lord just rubbed his beard. "Is that it? This is the reason we've jailed a lauded warrior?"

"Jail is where this man belongs." Towdric spoke slow, like he was talking to a child. "He is a criminal. Why else would he leave his home? But that's a tale of its own, I'm sure."

"I won't hold a man prisoner for no other reason than he left his home."

Geth smiled through the bars at Towdric. The lord ignored him, dipping his head at Brant.

"Don't worry, there's more." Towdric looked back the way they'd come. The sound of soft footfalls echoed in Geth's ears as a third person joined them. Geth smelled her before he saw her, perfumed with rosewater or the like. There was only one woman it could be.

"He's been communicating with the tribes," said Pythelle. "Through his Ilar warlock, Agrem. The Seer is well known as Iyngaer's personal sorcerer. Do you deny it, Seer?"

From the next cell over, Agrem cursed her roundly in the Ilar tongue.

But Pythelle just shook her head, expression grave. Geth watched Brant. She had the poor bastard.

"You may keep him here," he said finally. "Until the trial."

He started back the way he'd come, trailed by the witch. Towdric stayed behind, eying Geth through the bars.

"You here to gloat?" said Geth. "I thought mighty lords had better things to do. Like driving invaders out of their kingdom."

Towdric loosed an exaggerated sigh. "It didn't have to be this way. Whatever Hadean's paying, I could have matched it. I would have paid more even. I've seen what you can do in the field."

"Hadean's not *paying* me," Geth spat.

"Well, that was a mistake. Among others." Towdric's face came close to the bars. "You see, some of us have grown tired of the boy and his antics. He's had his chance to rule. Where has it gotten him? Trapped within a fortress and starving, surrounded by enemies. While the country-side burns."

"No one would be trapped, and nothing would have burned if his friends—"

"Friends? You think you know something about friends? You think your dear little king knows something? Ha! Friendship requires give *and* take. Listening to the counsel of your elders. Offering something in return."

Geth gripped the bars. "Counsel? You never even an-swered the muster. You didn't stand at Copper Ridge. But maybe that's because you weren't *offered* anything, as you say. Loyalty can't be bought you sonofabitch."

"Not blind loyalty, no. That's a thing that resides only in the heart of a fool. Friendship on the other hand, that's another matter. You must *give* before you can take."

He turned on his heels, left Geth in the darkness, pacing his tiny cell, cursing all the gods. What the hell did all that mean? And what exactly did he intend to give? Whatever it was, Geth didn't like the sound of it.

Brant didn't delay. In the morning, Geth was taken upstairs to the lord's hall, shackled at wrist and ankle. He craned his neck to find Agrem hauled up behind him.

"Gods but I hate a trial." Geth muttered.

All except the head table had been cleared and dozens of spectators packed the hall. They parted for the accused men to pass, some watching smugly, others solemn-eyed. Geth didn't look for the faces of his band. With any luck they'd already slipped out of camp. Even with Drayic and his bows, they hadn't a chance of breaking him free anyway.

Brant, it seemed, would preside over the trial. For that, Geth was grateful. Ample space stood clear before the head table where the lord occupied his customary place, flanked by Captain Ruddy—whose real name Geth still didn't know—and Pythelle. The witch seemed to be standing in as a scribe if the pen and ledger in front of her meant anything.

Towdric cleared his throat to address the head table, and indeed the entire chamber, with his booming voice. "These men, Geth of Pellon and Agrem of Dues, are charged with betraying the Sworn Realm of Umbel. They aided the desertion of a soldier called Neary. If he is here, let him show himself. If not, let it be agreed he has fled."

"He didn't flee," Geth said. "I sent him on an errand."

Brant raised a hand. "You shall have your turn to speak. For now, let the charges be laid and the evidence presented."

Towdric laughed. "It's alright, let the man speak if he has nothing to hide."

All eyes turned to Geth, and the big warrior nodded. "Neary is gone, it's true. You won't find him here. I sent him on an errand as I said. I am no traitor. Any man that fought with me a few days ago or stood beside me at Copper Ridge can attest to that."

"But you sent a soldier of the realm out of camp?" Towdric raised a thick finger. "And if the rumors are any indication, your men encouraged plenty of others to flee as well."

"I told you, Neary didn't flee."

"Then where did you send him?"

"To visit his sick mother."

A murmur passed through the crowd. And more than a few snickers.

But Towdric smiled as well. "Won't tell, eh? Are you sure it wasn't north, to Iyngaer, chieftain of the Duei?"

"You're an ass."

"And you're a traitor. Which brings us to the other charges."

Brant frowned. "Which are...?"

"That this Paellian, and his Ilar friend here have used witchcraft and sorcery to communicate vital information with our enemies, the tribes. Is this man not called Agrem the Seer, famous henchman of Iyngaer himself?"

Geth opened his mouth, but Towdric boomed over him before he could speak.

"Hasn't he used his sorcery to betray our secrets?"

"What secrets?" Geth snorted.

"The chieftain could gain much from knowledge of our numbers, our whereabouts. Our intent."

"Ha! Iyngaer has nothing to fear from you. You won't march within a hundred miles of him. And as for 'Grem, yes, he is the fabled Seer. But he's Iyngaer's man no longer. He wants the tribes out of Umbel as much as we do."

Towdric pointed his finger at the Ilar, opened his mouth.

But Brant spoke first. "To be clear, Master Geth, you are charged with aiding a deserter. But you say the man, Neary, was ordered to leave—"

"On a mission for Umbel, my lord. He's not off wenching at some tavern."

Brant grimaced and shook his head. "The second charge is that you have used your Ilar friend's powers to communicate with the enemy to the north. Can this be proved?"

Towdric dipped his head. "Well, the Lady Pythelle is known to have special talents herself. It is she who first uncovered the plot. I for one take her word for it."

Brant looked to his right. Pythelle nodded then scribbled something in her ledger.

Geth snorted. "So, that's it?" He stared daggers at the witch. "It's her word against mine? Well, I'll tell you an easier way to get to the truth of it. March your armies north and ask Iyngaer himself."

Jeers sounded from some, but an appreciative murmur rose from others. This camp of Towdric and Brant's was two separate camps indeed. Up at the head table, Ruddy had leaned close to whisper something in his lord's ear. Brant nodded, let out a sigh.

"I've heard enough. If there is no more testimony to be given, I have come to a decision."

Geth shot a glance at Towdric. Could that really be it? No one wanted this trial to be over faster than him, but even a gutterborn sellsword knew a quick deliberation couldn't bode well.

Brant stood, raised both hands for silence. "Geth of Pellon, I strike down the charges of treason against you. It may be true that your man is gone, but I accept your explanation. As for the accusation that you encouraged others to flee, I won't hang a man on hearsay."

Geth let out a breath.

"Your final and most grievous charge, that of communicating with the enemy, is a difficult one." Brant flicked a glance to Pythelle. "While I accept the word of the Lady Pythelle, could it not be that the Ilar, Agrem, has taken such actions on his own? The answer isn't clear. And given your service to the realm, I find it unseemly to hold you on such grounds. Therefore, Geth of Pellon, I release you at this time, immediately."

Catcalls followed, but there were cheers as well. One of the guards holding Geth clapped him on the back. Up at the head table, Pythelle didn't look pleased. Geth flicked a glance to Towdric. The bastard had found that gods-be-damned smile again.

"Apologies, apologies," he boomed. "Perhaps it was all for nothing. It seems I did not have sufficient evidence to sentence this Paellian. But as it happens, someone else does."

That smile nearly split Towdric's fat head. Another murmur passed through the assemblage, one of confusion. Geth braced himself.

"You see," Towdric said. "The mercenary Geth has already been sentenced in another court. Back home in Pellon."

Geth's eyes widened. Brant frowned, peering over the heads of the crowd as the doors to his hall groaned open.

"You may release him, Lord Brant," Towdric said. "But it is your duty to hand him back to our sworn allies. And here is the Captain Palladine now."

CHAPTER TWENTY-FIVE

"T hram and *bloody* Awer."

"I told you this man fled his homeland as a criminal!" Towdric was actually shouting now, "and here are King Elius's own emissaries, arrived to collect the fugitive! Let us hand over his custody to their keeping, that he may face his crimes! The bonds of the Sworn Realms can never be forgotten after all. It is an ancient friendship. I'm sure Lord Brant must agree."

Geth struggled to collect himself. How long had Towdric known? Had he been planning this all along, or had Palladine just turned up at the right time? *Gods but I really am a fool.*

"As for the warlock," Towdric jabbed a finger in Agrem's direction. "Can he really be allowed to roam free with the accusations against him still unanswered? No, he must be held. In the meantime, I promise you, I shall get to the truth of it."

Towdric strode over to smirk down at the Seer.

Out of nowhere a low shape appeared, teeth flashing, sending the lord backpedaling.

"Eko!" Geth cried.

No sooner had the beast appeared than Palladine's men raised their slings and let fly, the same twins that helped capture Geth months before. The poor animal yipped and went down as the stones struck. Towdric stepped in between before more could follow.

"Wait! Treat an animal with mercy." He lifted his head to meet Geth's eye first, then Agrem's, as he drew his sword. "Put this poor creature out of its misery."

Geth's eyes went wide. "No!"

But the sword lashed out, quick and lethal. Eko yipped once more, went still. Visions of blood filled Geth's head, and he lunged after Towdric.

Chains at Geth's feet made him stumble and the guards behind him caught him from behind. A good thing too, truth be told. Towdric still held that sword, the point dripping red. Geth dragged the two guards forward as far as he could until a couple of Palladine's brutes joined in with clubs to batter him to his knees. Geth raised his arms to protect his head, looking back to see Agrem down as well, cradling his dead companion. The big warrior howled his fury until a blow across the back of his head jarred his vision and sent him face first into a puddle of Eko's blood.

The subterranean jail of Brant's keep wasn't as dark as the Tower of the Moon, but still Geth had never felt lower. A hundred miles to the north, Hadean and Phelan would soon starve or surrender and meet the sword. His band had landed themselves gods only knew where, leaderless, surrounded by enemies. And Neary hadn't yet returned, which could only mean something had gone wrong.

Then there was Towdric. *Gods but I can't die while that bastard yet lives. Not after all he's done.*

Geth pushed himself up, so his mouth was near the tiny, barred window in his door. "Agrem, you there? I won't ask if you're alright this time."

He forced a laugh, but no one answered anyway. They'd stowed the Seer in the cell beside him, he was certain. He just didn't know if the man was alive.

The silence stretched on. It was hard for Geth not to imagine all the ways he might kill Towdric, but the sound of bootheels on worn stone eventually distracted him. The steady, even clip of that stride could only belong to one man.

Palladine's icy blue eyes met Geth's through the bars. "I'm taking you back to Pellon. Alive if I can, dead if needs be."

"Towdric's got a new pet, eh? Well, whatever you think of me, believe it when I tell you he's a traitor to his king. Hadean sits under siege and that bastard holds phony trials and laughs like a blasting forge down here in the south. If you truly are an emissary of Umbel's sworn ally, then you should do something about it."

"I didn't come all this way for Towdric. Or for Hadean."

"No, you came for me."

Palladine's mouth was a flat white line, but his eyes flickered with triumph. "And now I have you."

"You want me to come peacefully back to Pellon? I will, I swear it. But only if you'll throw your support in with the true king, Hadean, Aeldan's son."

"I have been acquainted with King Hadean, but I'm told his position is untenable. Even should the armies here march north, he cannot be saved. Towdric is next in line to be king."

"It's your duty to aid Pellon's sworn ally!" Geth smacked the frame of his little barred window. "And that means Hadean! He's not done. He's got half an army with him right now. And he's protecting half the countryside as well. If not for that, he could weather a siege the whole damn year."

Palladine sniffed. "Perhaps he should have sent his people south. Letting them inside the fortress was a mistake. Not the first, they say."

"Uro's puckered ass, aren't you the hand of justice? Isn't it your job to right wrongs?"

"It's not my responsibility to be concerned with the business of the Kingdom of Umbel. I came here for you and for no other reason. Now it's Lord Towdric that has given me what I want, and for that I am grateful. If he has asked for aid in his war, it is not my decision whether he gets it or not. But I will gladly relay the message to King Elius."

Geth swore, remembering all Towdric had said of friendship, of give and take. The bellowing bastard was a lot smarter than Geth had given him credit for.

"So, you'll throw Pellon's lot in with Towdric? Hand him the crown while the tribes take down the true king? You of all people, a man sworn to uphold the rule of law?"

Palladine's face held no expression. "Count yourself lucky. You should have been dead by now. Instead, you leave this gods-forsaken country in the morning. At least you'll spend your final days in civilized lands."

It was over. Geth knew he could cooperate until he was blue in the face, but Palladine would tell Elius whatever he wanted. Towdric would become king, Iyngaer would eventually destroy him, and Geth's friends and the entire Kingdom of Umbel would collapse under sword and fire. Even after all he'd done.

Maybe because of it.

Damn you, Awer!

It was always the anger, Geth mused, the vengeance that ruined things. If he hadn't gone out of his way to burn down Palladine's manse, would the bastard really have trekked all this way just to nab a fugitive? Brant had been about to grant a pardon, that was clear. He seemed ready to pull away from Pythelle and Towdric. With any luck, they could have been marching north by now.

But anger and vengeance was all Geth had ever been good at. It surged through his veins right there in his cell. He slammed the bars of his doors with both hands.

"It's not over until I say it's over!"

He racked his mind for a way to escape. Maybe it was all for nothing. Maybe his friends would all die upriver, and he and Agrem would die right there, but that anger was a fuel that demanded to be spent. *Bribe the guards. No, wrap these chains around someone's neck and hold them hostage. Something. Anything! There must be a way!*

"Damn it all!" He half-expected to hear an admonishing hum from the cell next to him, but another sound reached his ear instead. Was that *singing?* A woman's voice, enthralling as a siren's, floated through the air, getting closer, if Geth wasn't mistaken. A door scraped open down the hall. Geth froze where he stood, time gone thick and hazy. And then his own door creaked ajar.

"Come out."

"Amalia."

The torchlight stuck to her like stardust. She hummed as she worked a set of keys on the shackles at Geth's wrists and ankles. Restraints fell away and he followed her out into the hallway, watching her in a strange daze as she opened Agrem's door next. Only when she disappeared inside could Geth's shake his head clear.

"Help me," she called. "He needs you."

Geth stepped through the doorway to join her, and his mind went foggy once more.

"Oh, for the love of the woods."

Amalia touched a hand to Geth's cheek. It was as if a shroud came off his head. "What the hell?"

The witch smiled. "Do you like my song?"

She turned her attention back to Agrem. Even by dim torchlight, the bruises and dried blood on the Seer's face were obvious.

"Gods all be damned," Geth shook his head. "He never hurt anyone."

Amalia raised an eyebrow. "Two of those lilies won't be returning to Pellon. That wasn't your doing."

Bending, Geth lifted the Ilar into his arms, carried him like a child back out into the hallway. Amalia led the way upstairs and out into the ward. Right past the guards. She sang, low but sweet. Not a head turned in their direction.

There were plenty of other noises to distract the keep's soldiers and denizens as they wended through the town toward the gates. Troops rushed past them, first in one direction and then in the other. None so much as glanced at them. From the track running down the snowy hill toward the river, Geth spied fires burning down below.

"What the hell happened?"

Amalia continued her song until yet another throng of soldiers hustled past. "Your dozen. And the rest. They've provided a distraction."

Geth felt his eyes go misty. "More than one it seems." Damn those ugly bastards but he loved them.

Their distractions couldn't last long though. Amalia led them downhill at a brisk pace. On the flats below, she took them off the road, boots crunching through snow. Geth was relieved when he saw a wagon waiting for them, horse already hitched. He laid Agrem down as gently as his tired arms could manage, wrapped him in blankets, and joined Amalia on the bench.

"Where to?" he asked.

"Away. You both need healing, but I can't help you here."

"What about the band?"

"They'll be alright. You don't give them enough credit."

Amalia flicked the reins. The cart started rolling. Geth turned for one last look at Waterset up on the heights, Towdric's camped army below it. He'd be back. To kill Towdric if nothing else.

He must have fallen asleep. When Geth awoke, they'd reached an abandoned cottage. Amalia started a fire while he carried Agrem inside and settled him on a straw pallet. The mice didn't appreciate it, but the Ilar clutched weakly at Geth's hand in thanks.

Outside, Amalia walked the perimeter, muttering to herself. The same sort of thing Geth'd seen Agrem do back in Ilia an age ago. Wards of some sort, he reckoned. He busied himself with the horse and baggage and left her to it. He didn't mind the magicks this once.

"You should rest too," she said when she found him inside staring into the fire.

"He played me."

"Towdric?"

Geth prodded the fire a little too hard, sending a puff of embers up into the air. "First, he used me to boost his own status. Then he traded me to Palladine in return for Pellon's allegiance. He's going to use the Paellians in his bid to overthrow King Hadean. All because of me."

Amalia laughed. "Towdric doesn't have to overthrow young Hadean. He's happy to let the Ilars get rid of him. But when the ice melts, he'll find he's got another problem altogether. Iyngaer wants all of Umbel, not just the north."

"I know it. I thought I was getting through to Brant. But now, if King Elius sides with Towdric, I just don't know. Brant doesn't seem the sort who likes risks."

Amalia stepped closer to lay a hand on Geth's shoulder. "Don't worry about all that. Sleep. Heal."

She moved her hands to the center of his back, ran them over his shoulders. He didn't feel anything aside from her touch, but he knew she was using her magicks. Years before, Geth had known a woman with a similar talent, had loved her even. He closed his eyes. He couldn't dwell on the past. Not with the future hanging over him like the headsman's axe

CHAPTER TWENTY-SIX

Whether from Amalia's healing touch or just a good night's sleep, Geth felt a new man in the morning. He didn't remember laying down beside Agrem on the straw pallet, but when he awoke the Ilar was snoring heartily beside him. The Seer's eye was still purple but at least there was color in his face again.

Slumped over in a chair, Amalia snored softly as well. Geth rose as quiet as he could and pulled the blankets back up to her chin. Not for the first time, he thanked the gods for his friends. Without them he'd have been dead a dozen times over.

That brought to mind his file, and the rest of the band. Had they made a clean escape? Were they looking for him even now? And what of Neary?

Towdric will pay, by all the gods! In blood and little bits of bone and skin and brains.

But not yet.

"How do you feel?"

Geth turned to find Amalia sat up, stretching. There were circles under her eyes, but she smiled as always.

"Mad as hell," he told her. "And hungry."

"I've got a few road biscuits." She rose, rummaged through her things. "Some chamomile here. A sip of tea would do us all some good."

Geth lent a hand, and they shared a simple but sufficient breakfast. He threw another log on the fire, piled more to one side. Agrem kept snoring.

"You're leaving," Amalia said, inspecting the store of fuel he'd left beside the hearth.

"My men will be looking for me."

"Maybe. But how will you find them?"

"Well, I know where one of them is and it's a den of vipers I've sent him into."

"Neary? The man they say deserted?"

Geth gave her a flat look. "I sent him away."

Amalia giggled. That beehive bun on her head shook.

"Yes, Neary. I reckon he should've been back by now. That can't bode well. I figure we're only a couple days ride from Aldwood, assuming you'll lend me your horse."

"You sent him to the Aldwood? Whatever for?"

"To enlist the help of a scratch named Crookbow. I'm told he's got a whole band of thieves that might be partial to joining the cause."

"Thieves?" Amalia frowned. "That sounds desperate."

"Hey, it was your idea to look for allies." Geth turned his eyes to the Seer, snoring away on the pallet. "He looks better already, but I trust you'll look after him until I'm back."

The witch nodded. "Spring is on the way. We're running out of time."

Geth threw his cloak over his shoulders and stepped toward the door. He had no sword, but Amalia filled his saddlebags with food for the journey. He didn't need much. He had his anger to fuel him.

In two days' time, the grey tangle of the Aldwood appeared on the eastern horizon. Geth patted Amalia's horse, no racer, but a sturdy, steadfast beast. He shook off the memory of Eko's murder and spurred the steed forward. Eko was gone but there was one friend he could still save.

Neary was in trouble, Geth was certain of it. He knew how vindictive a criminal could be, and no matter what the grey-headed Umbelman said, he didn't imagine anyone with the word 'crook' in his name might be any different. The two had history, Neary and this lord of thieves. Still, Geth wished for about the hundredth time he'd had time to find a new sword before setting out for his lair.

The Aldwood swallowed Geth and his mount. Even after several miles, he saw no sign of any brigands.. Of course not. They'd want to lull their prey to sleep and only hit them once their guard was down. That's what Geth imagined until he finally did come across first sign of Crookbow's band.

"Thram and Awer."

He pulled up in the middle of the road, staring into the trees. There, in a crude wooden cage, sat the bloated, crow-pecked corpse of a woman. Only by the long grey braid did he recognize Landren, the lady of Stoney.

"That's what happens to intruders."

Geth whirled to find a brawny man with sand-brown hair and a gap between his teeth striding toward him, the hilt of a broadsword poking up from a sheath across his back. He stopped a few paces off, hands on his hips, eyeing Geth up and down.

"I have business with Crookbow," Geth said.

"Watch your tone—"

"I see your bowmen," Geth lied. "You think this is my first march into a forest? Tell them to stand down. I have business with your betters. The king's man Neary hasn't returned so I've been sent to sweeten the deal."

Gap-tooth looked like he wanted to try something foolish, but Geth reckoned mention of Neary and promise of a deal might be enough to keep him from ordering death on the spot. He hoped it was.

"I'd take your weapons, but it looks like you showed up with nothing but your dick," the man said finally. He waved Geth to follow and started off the road into the woods. "Crookbow will have a listen to this deal of yours. And if it don't favor, I've got another gibbet with your name on it. One for that sellout, Neary, as well."

One look at Crookbow's compound made Geth whistle. A timber stronghouse, a stable, and several other homes and outbuildings circled a green of trampled snow, populated by a folk that could have passed for normal villagers except for all the bows and swords. There were women among the thieves as well, armed as the others and just as watchful at Geth's arrival.

Snow lay heavy on the thatch, but woody smoke drifted out of chimneys. Whatever Gap-tooth claimed, Geth saw no more gibbets. When the doors to Crookbow's stronghouse came open, however, the dozens of folk bound to-gether to either side drew out a curse. Back in Stoney, he'd been relieved to learn that most of the village had escaped. Evidently, they hadn't got far.

"Is this the man who claims to have a deal for me?" a voice called from somewhere in the dim interior.

Geth straightened his shoulders, forced his hand away from a weaponless hip to stride in. The captives watched him wide-eyed, their captors through narrow slits. Gods but they could kill him in there in a matter of seconds.

Geth choked down any fear before it could rise. "I have an offer for you, straight from King Hadean." He marched in the direction of the voice until his eyes adjusted enough to find the source. A lanky man with a fur cap on his head slouched lazily back in a chair at the head of a long, rough-hewn table. Gap-tooth sauntered over to seat him-self on the right. Neary sat stiffly to the left.

Stiffly, but alive!

A wave of relief washed over Geth at the sight of him. He hadn't realized he'd expected anything less—maybe he hadn't let himself think on it. But after poor Eko, he didn't know what he would have done if things had turned out otherwise.

"An offer from the king?" Crookbow's voice refocused Geth's attention. The old thief jabbed a thumb in the direction of Neary. "That's about what he said. Worst case, I could ransom the both of you I suppose."

"That's not the worst case." Gap-tooth grinned.

Geth hated him more by the minute. "I won't waste your time," he said, turning back to Crookbow. "And I won't be leaving without my friend. But I'll deliver the offer. You decide what to do with it."

Geth paused, pretending to loosen his cloak in the warm air under Crookbow's roof. He made a quick study of this lord of thieves—and the thieves themselves. More than a few of them leaned forward to hear his words. Crookbow's ear was cocked, lazy slouch or no.

"Full pardons," Geth lied, meeting every eye he could throughout the chamber. "For every man that takes on the green."

Silence met those words, followed by laughter. "Full pardons?" Gap-tooth slapped his knee.

"And," Geth raised a finger, looked to either side, "a boundary fort. All its lands and the captaincy for Master Crookbow."

The lanky thief pursed his lips but said nothing.

Geth flicked a glance to Neary. The Umbelman sat stock-still, yet another prisoner no doubt, even if his hands weren't bound.

To the right, however, Gap-tooth sat shaking his head. "It's *Captain* Crookbow. You can't give a man what he already has. Who's to say you have the power to give such things anyway?"

Curses and noises of accord rang out from more than a few thieves. Others cackled like drunken sailors. But a fair number watched in silence. They almost dared to believe.

Crookbow sat up finally, shaking his head. "Gods, man. You're a better liar than me. Cald makes a good point though. How do we know you haven't been sent with the sole purpose of drawing us out? I hear a couple lordlings have got an army set up at Waterset. Who's to say they haven't got the hangmen waiting for us as we speak?"

"Him." Geth pointed at Neary. "Neary may march at my side these days, but he'd be dead already if you didn't trust his word."

A murmur passed through the listening thieves. A few tried to laugh that off, but they were the minority. Neary still did have some status here, Geth reckoned, otherwise he really would have been dead.

Crookbow scratched his chin. "But this deal of yours, it stinks like a scavenger's breath. That boy Hadean's a rule-rider. Everybody knows it. And how in wide Eria could you have gotten such an offer from the lad when he's locked up in the Tooth?"

Geth forced a smile. "Ever heard of a pigeon, friend? This offer is a good one. I suggest you take it."

Crookbow rose from his seat, stepped around the table to come eye to eye with Geth, leaning forward, hands on hips. "And all we gotta do is put on a green cloak?"

"You're no fool, Captain." Geth looked past Crookbow, toward Gap-tooth and the others. "You know you'll have to fight. But let's be honest, you're not afraid of that. And this war is bad for business anyway. If the Ilars win, there won't be any caravans carting goods to Turia, will there?"

"Those savages won't win!" someone shouted.

"Leather-stinking whoresons!"

Geth shook his head, turned from Crookbow to address them. "But they *are* winning, the boss just said it himself. Hadean's locked up in Towerrock. And the only man that can come to his aid is a certain scratch called Towdric. You may have heard of the bastard."

A collective growl rumbled through the hall. Neary hadn't exaggerated when he said this lot hated Turey Hill's lord.

Crookbow cleared his throat, raised a hand for silence. "You're saying Hadean needs Towdric to help break the siege?"

Geth nodded.

"Then he's a dead man."

The curses rang out with renewed vehemence, enough to make the captives from Stoney hunker down even further. Crookbow started back toward his seat.

"Hear me out!" Geth cried.

Crookbow turned, halfway to his seat. "Hear what? You can't offer up the promises of a king who's already done for."

"And who becomes king once Hadean's gone? Towdric, that's who. What deal do you think *he's* likely to offer?"

The chamber fell silent. Geth flicked a glance at Neary. For the first time, he thought he spied a measure of hope in those eyes.

"Lying foreign bastard." Crookbow shook his head.

"That's no lie. Every man here knows it. Brant's got a claim to the throne, true enough, but Towdric will make short work of him if he gets in the way. I don't need to tell you how ruthless he can be."

"Well—"

"Hadean's your only choice. Help him. And leave the past behind, under these trees."

Crookbow said nothing, watching Geth, looking for tells, he was sure.

But Geth hadn't lied. Not really. Whatever he promised, he'd see to it Hadean delivered. The boy had it in him to forgive. No one knew better than him.

"See these?" Geth raised both hands, balled them up. "These are the fists of a criminal. They killed a man right beneath the bloody Oathstone, down south. But Hadean pardoned me, gave me this green cloak. And with it a fresh start. He can do the same for you too, Crookbow. For all of you."

"Who says we want a fresh start?"

That came from Gap-tooth, who stood up from his seat. More than a few men grunted their agreement. Others shook their heads. Crookbow wandered back to his chair, frowning under that fur cap, leaving Geth to answer the brawny bastard.

"You're telling me you'd take these woods over taverns and whores? Over a chance to visit your kin, a fresh cooked meal at the village inn, maybe even a wife to go home to? You telling me you'd rather look over your shoulder every day, living in fear of the hangman?"

Gap-tooth banged the table with a fist. "Around here, it's us that tie the noose! Tell that to Towdric *and* your boy-king."

Those words filled in all the missing pieces.

Geth met Gap-tooth's eye, matched his hateful stare. This was the man responsible for Landren's death. Neary's capture as well. If the old Umbelman's account was true,

Crookbow himself might jump at a pardon. But the bastard to his right was a criminal through and through.

"Seems this house is of two minds." Geth turned to meet the eyes of several of the theives. A woman with a hat like her captain's nodded grimly.

"But we won't split," Crookbow said. "You try that game in here and you'll find yourself strung up indeed."

"By your order? Or someone else's?"

"Geth—" Neary started to rise from his seat. Geth waved him off.

"If any man in this hall wants a pardon, that's what I'm offering. You gonna let this bastard tell you what you can or can't do?"

Crookbow opened his mouth, but Geth's finger was pointed at Gap-tooth. A ruckus started, men cursing each other, waving fists, shouting threats at Geth, or at each other. Crookbow had lost them. He waved his cap and hollared to no avail. It was looking more like Gap-tooth's band than his.

"How does this bastard just walk into our woods anyway?" the brute said. "White-head's got a few friends here I reckon, but who is *he*?"

Voices in accord cursed Geth. A few grumbled in protest, but only Neary shouted loud enough to be heard. "What are you saying, Cald?"

"I'm saying this whoreson—" he stepped around the table toward Geth "—is fair game."

It seemed like the entire chamber leaned in toward Geth, jeering, practically salivating. Gods but he wished for his sword. Only Crookbow himself saved him from an epic brawl, shouting and waving, moving to stand in the middle of the room beside the big warrior.

"Alright, that's enough! That's enough! I say this man's a guest. Some of you disagree. How we gonna settle this?"

Many a brutal suggestion followed, plenty of coarse laughter too. The poor folk from Stoney looked like they'd about shit themselves, but the thieves watched their fur-capped leader. Geth trained his eyes on Gap-tooth.

That ugly smile parted again as the brawny bastard met his stare. "A duel," he said. "I'll fight this foreign dog myself. To the winner goes the spoils."

CHAPTER TWENTY-SEVEN

"I make the rules here!" Crookbow hollered, throwing down that fur cap. "It's a fight off the log, not a duel! We'll not spill our own blood on account of this."

"His is the only blood that'll be spilled," Gap-tooth said.

"Careful what you wish for, Cald."

Geth supposed they might not have heard of his deeds here, but maybe Crookbow knew the look of a real warrior. And Geth knew the look of a killer. By his reckoning, the brute named Cald had bled plenty of men himself.

And women, he reminded himself. "So be it," Geth said finally.

Cald smiled, made a show of rolling out his shoulders. "Off the log then. And I take whatever I want when I win. Including a life."

"That's not—" Crookbow started, but Geth cut him off.

"And I take the folk of Stoney if *I* win."

Crookbow threw up his hands.

"He won't win." Cald cocked his head back to look down his nose at Geth. "Let him ask for the moon."

Judging from the noises throughout the room, the matter was settled. A few opportunistic bastards yelled to begin the wagers and Crookbow sank back into his seat.

"First thing in the morning, boys. Light's already gone. And I'm tired now anyway."

Night had indeed fallen outside. Geth felt the weariness of the road creeping up on him. He accepted a flagon from one of the men that had shouted in his favor but refused the pallet they offered.

"I always sleep with my horse," he said.

"He sleeps with his mount," someone snickered. "Show him to the stables, horse-humping bastard."

Geth ignored that but Neary wore a look of concern as he sidled up to join him outside. "Sleep with your horse?" He spoke through the side of his mouth. "What the hell is this all about?"

"Just trust me, brother."

"Do you even know what fighting off the log is? It's not as easy as it sounds."

Geth turned to take his friend at arm's length, looked him up and down. "Gods, but it's good to see you."

Neary blinked. "Oh boy. What's happened?"

Geth just patted his arm and left him at the stable door. Accepting a lantern from one of the friendlies, he settled down in the stall beside Amalia's horse. The animal had already dropped a few lumps and the place stank, but it was the most defensible position he could think of.

Gap-tooth would be coming for him, of that Geth was sure. Or one of his lackeys. He laughed grimly to himself, shuttered the lantern. More likely two or three. At least this way he picked the arena himself.

Using his baggage as a human dummy, Geth spread his blanket over the top in semblance of a sleeping form. It was the oldest trick in the book, but it would buy him a few precious moments if nothing else. A pitchfork leaned up against a stall would have to serve in place of a sword. With a fond stroke for Amalia's horse, Geth crept back out of the stall to settle in a dark corner across the aisle.

They took their time, but they came alright. Geth had nodded off, the sound of curses startling him awake as his attackers found his blankets empty. They turned at the same time, two of them armed with daggers. Geth hurled his pitchfork like a javelin straight at the first man's chest.

From three yards away, the bastard had no time to react. The pitchfork pierced his ribcage with a sickening squelch. The second attacker's eyes went wide, and he shoved his comrade's convulsing form out of the way in an attempt to flee. Geth dove after, dragging him down from behind. He landed on top of the man's back, pressed him into the manure-stinking floor.

"Wait! Wait!"

With one hand Geth yanked an arm back, barring it up at the elbow. With the other he smashed his attacker's face into the ground. The man groaned, dropped his dagger to clutch at his busted teeth. Geth snatched the weapon up just as fast, sawing the edge across the bastard's neck to bleed his life out.

The commotion brought company. Several more thieves, including Neary and Crookbow himself, rushed in with lanterns and weapons. Geth stood, wiping off the blood from his new dagger on the dead man's shirt.

"What in Vorda's black name is going on in here?" Crookbow demanded.

"Someone tried to rob me," Geth said. "What happened to the old saying 'there's an honesty among thieves,' eh?"

"You're no thief," someone spat.

He wasn't. But just to prove them wrong, Geth tucked the dagger through his belt then made a show of rummaging the pockets of the dead men. Crookbow didn't try to stop him.

"He needs protection, Captain," Neary said. "It's only right. You can't leave him in here alone."

"By my reckoning," Crookbow said, glowering down at the bodies, "he's not the one who needs protecting. But let's get him inside the house before anyone else trips and falls on a blade."

They made a space for Geth in the stronghouse. Dark looks followed Geth from a good many of Crookbow's men. Others cursed his assailants and vowed to keep watch over the big warrior for the rest of the night. In the morning, he'd fight Cald. By all accounts, he'd need his strength.

Neary settled down beside Geth. "It's not going to be as easy as you think," he said, speaking freely now that they were surrounded by those who clearly hoped Geth would win. "Fighting off the log is something unto itself."

Geth leaned in despite the newfound allies all around. "They haven't heard anything about me here, have they? Otherwise, that fool would never have challenged me to any kind of duel."

"That's what I'm trying to tell you. It wouldn't matter if they had. Fighting off the log is something different. It takes practice. Balance. This lot knows all about it, it's Crookbow's way of settling matters without drawing blood or letting the biggest meanest bastard bully the rest."

"But this scratch, Cald—"

"I know, he's just that sort. As it happens, he's the best off the log as well. He whipped me already."

"Well, let's see if he can whip me too then."

"He just might."

"It's the only way, Neary."

The Umbelman scowled.

"Seems you weren't wrong about Crookbow wanting out of the business," Geth told him. "Problem is, about half his gang aren't so sure."

"Cald's half."

"They can't split though, can they? The ones that stuck to thieving could never abide the others walking away, knowing their methods, their whereabouts."

"Knowing too much for Cald's liking."

Geth slept without incident, watched over by friendlies. Amalia's biscuits broke his fast and by midmorning Crookbow had led the entire band plus their captives all the way back to the road where the gibbet hung in its tree.

"All right, boys," he said. "Have one down."

Axes worked a thick tree bole until it collapsed right across the road. Neary came to stand beside Geth. Cald's followers crowded at his back. Crookbow's men cleared a few side limbs, and the captain climbed up on top of the felled tree, arms raised above them all.

"You know what this is," he said, walking its length. "Our old friend Neary has invited this guest to join us. A king's man. Cald says he's not welcome. What do we do about it? Whatever the case, whatever we decide to do, we do it together."

"We take what we want." Cald spit. He was rolling out his shoulders again, his neck too this time. "Just like always. Once I drop this yapping ox into the dirt, it'll be settled."

Crookbow nodded. "We decide now, fighting off the log."

Neary cleared his throat pointedly, flicked a look from Crookbow to Geth and back. "The rules?"

"Ah, right." The captain nodded. "Go ahead and tell him."

Neary spoke loud enough for all to hear, but to Geth it was clear this speech was for him. "Here's the rules. You fight off the log. Three falls takes it. No sharps. No blood if you can manage it. And no clutching."

"Clutching?"

"If you start to fall, you can't clutch your opponent and pull him down with you. That's the rule."

"Simple enough."

A pair of hickory wasters came out and Cald and Geth each took a wooden sword. Neary offered a hand as Geth climbed up on top of the felled tree bole. It flexed and creaked, resting on crushed branches on the one end, a splintered stump on the other. But it didn't roll.

Geth waved his waster about, loosening his shoulders and doing his best to look unfamiliar with a weapon in hand. In truth, he'd trained with such a blade thousands of times. At the other end, beyond Crookbow, Cald swung his blade in elaborate arcs. Geth wanted to laugh.

Neary grimaced from down on the ground. "Watch yourself, Geth. It's all about balance, not swordplay. Don't forget that you can't move side to side. Not even a little."

"I see that, Neary."

"He's got a lot of tricks. Beware!"

Crookbow still stood at the center of the log, his balance impressive for a man that had to be older than Neary. He raised both hands and the gathering fell silent, the last wagers placed. "Three falls wins," he said. "Have at it!"

Neary moved forward to offer a hand and the captain hopped to the ground. Cald sauntered down the length of the log, wooden blade tilted at Geth's chest. They met in the center. Swords touched once, as was custom, and the big brute came at Geth swinging.

Hickory clacked against hickory. The onlookers howled as gap-toothed Cald beat at Geth's guard to send him backpedaling on the log. Moving backward, where he couldn't see each step, the heel of one boot skidded and slid. Geth felt himself teetering. He had no choice but to hop down off the log.

"That's one fall!" Crookbow shouted.

Thieves hooted and cursed. From up on his perch, Cald smirked at Geth, arms folded across his chest. The big thief strode back to his end and Geth climbed back on the log with a curse of his own.

He didn't wait for the gap-toothed bastard this time. As soon as they'd touched swords, Geth aimed a mighty swing at Cald, knocking his waster aside. The brute's eyes went round as Geth skipped forward into the space, shoulder down.

But Cald absorbed the blow on his own shoulder, feet up off the log to hop back safely. The thieves hollered. Neary shouted something about feet, but Geth couldn't hear him over the din.

The two fighters separated, eyed each other over the tips of blades. They came together once more, trading blows back and forth. Geth found himself matched in strength by his adversary, the inability to move side to side negating the speed that often surprised his enemies as well. With a great push, he managed a deflected blow across Cald's shoulder, but in this contest the touch counted for nothing.

"Watch his feet!" Neary shouted.

The Umbelman must have seen it coming, but Geth didn't. Cald jumped in place to shake the entire log, leaving the big warrior no choice but to throw his hands out for balance. Cald hooted as he swung a rib-breaker at Geth's middle.

Hopping backward, Geth dodged the blow, but his boot slipped off the edge and dirty snow and dry leaves rushed up to meet him. Curses and jeers echoed in his ears. The lone thief who'd bet on Geth grumbled and cursed him as well. An old woman among the captives from Stoney quailed.

Geth looked up toward the gibbet where Landren's corpse slouched, eyes long pecked from their sockets. One more fall and it was all over. He cursed Vorda, keeper of the dead. "Not today you bitch."

"That's two falls!" Crookbow held up his fingers. Geth couldn't tell if he looked disappointed or relieved. Dusting dirt and leaves from his shoulder, he rose and climbed back up on the log again.

"Got a few tricks, have you?" Geth stared daggers at Cald. "Well, this dog's learned a few tricks too."

With a twirl of his sword, Geth switched the weapon from his right hand to his left, turning his stance to match. A murmur swept through the onlookers. The one lone thief that had cursed him before now laughed in triumph.

Cald wasn't deterred. He came forward slowly, then hopped several times on the log to send a vibration through it, darting a thrust at Geth as he came within reach. But Geth had taken Neary's advice, watching the bastard's feet, crouching to absorb the shake. He parried the strike and leaned in to jab Cald in the sternum.

On the battlefield, at full stretch, that blow wouldn't have been more than a scratch. But it was enough to surprise Cald. A grunt escaped his lips. Geth sprang forward to follow up with a side kick. Cald's flailing return whacked Geth good across the thigh but his boot did enough to send the bastard teetering off the log.

"Ha!"

Cald cursed from the forest floor, leaves in that sandy hair, cheek grimed. Neary punched the air. A furious argument broke out among the gamblers—evidently Geth hadn't been expected to win a single fall. Crookbow wrangled them finally with a series of threats and Cald clambered back up on the log.

"Sneaky Paellian mutt!"

"Two falls to one!" Crookbow yelled.

Geth tried to capitalize on Cald's anger, rushing forward with a series of cuts before the man could clear his head. The big thief parried evenly, copying the same shoulder barge Geth had used to nullify his advance. The big warrior backed off and they squared themselves once more. Watching Cald down the length of his sword, however, another idea came to Geth.

Those short swords were made for thrusting, not slashing, and as such, the crosspiece was little more than a knob. And yet fighting off the log favored wide swings and the crossing of blades. Geth feigned just such a strike, drawing a block from Cald, but turned his wrist at the last moment so wood slid down wood until his waster scraped over the knobby base to clip the knuckles of the thief's sword-hand.

That blow, on the battlefield, would have taken off fingers. Cald only cursed and dropped his sword. "Bloody bastard!"

Geth sprang toward him with a mind to break bones, but Cald hopped down from the log of his own accord, conceding the fall as he landed cat-like in a three-point stance.

"Two a piece!"

If the last fall had caused a ruckus, this nearly started a war. More than a few fists were thrown. Neary's friends may not have bet with Geth, but they believed in him now. Crookbow hollered for order. It was a good while before Geth faced Cald again down the length of the log.

The gap-toothed brute eyed him warily. Both hands clenched the hilt of his weapon, and his fingers bled. But the set of Cald's mouth told Geth there was nothing wrong with his grip.

Geth returned that wary stare. The malice on Cald's face reminded the big warrior that this was the same man that had sent that pair of knifemen to kill him the night before. He had something nasty in mind, Geth was sure of it. That awkward, two-handed grip gave it away.

But there was more than just malice in those cold eyes. It took Geth a moment to figure out just what.

Desperation.

Geth braced himself. If Cald figured he might lose, he'd try anything. Geth's eyes flicked to Landren unconsciously, dead in that tree. He almost didn't close them in time when Cald's hand flung forward to spray him with snow and dirt.

"Ha!"

Backpedaling as fast as he could, Geth spit mud from his mouth, eyes still closed, waster raised. He opened one just in time to half-parry a blow. The brunt of it caught him across the shoulder, upset his balance. He teetered, began to fall, but not before dropping his weapon to clutch Cald with both hands.

They went down in a tangle of limbs, thudding into the cold dirt with matching grunts. Geth rolled, sprang to his feet, fists up. Cald cursed him roundly, waster raised.

"You clutched!" He came at Geth before the big warrior could so much as speak, slashing with that wooden sword.

But here on solid ground, it didn't matter that Geth held no weapon. He could use his speed.

Backpedaling and twisting, he dodged Cald's first two swipes then swatted a straight thrust aside with the palm of his hand to step inside the bastard's swing and grab him with both hands. They grappled, cursed, and pushed. Geth heaved just hard enough to make Cald heave back then ducked, wrapped both arms around his waist, and arched his back to fling the bastard overhead with his own momentum, a classic wrestler's toss.

Cald hit the ground with an audible thud, but Geth had already rolled back to all fours. He scrambled toward the big brute, climbed on top to unleash a flurry of blows at his face. Cald landed a punch of his own that loosened Geth's jaw, knocked him clear off.

"Filthy whore!"

But Geth had landed more than just one. As Cald struggled to rise, panting on all fours, Geth staggered to his feet. Before Cald could recover, he swung a kick up under his midsection to crumple him back down to the snow. Geth raised that boot again, this time straight up, and brought it crashing down on the back of Cald's neck.

CHAPTER TWENTY-EIGHT

T he sound of bones breaking was unmistakable. Cald lay motionless in the snow at Geth's feet. The big warrior bent at the waist, sucked in cold air to regain his breath.

The shouts all around went quiet. Crookbow rushed over to check on his man. He looked up with wide eyes. "He's dead."

"Of course he is." Geth straightened, spit blood on a patch of white snow. "I guess that means I win."

That got them all shouting again.

"He cheated!"

"The bastard clutched!"

"Cald cheated first!"

Swords left sheaths.

Thank the gods for Neary. The Umbelman and several friendlies crowded around Geth before anyone could get to him. Crookbow climbed up on the log again, waving that fur cap. It took a while before he had everyone's attention.

"All bets are off! That's the first order of business for you greedy bastards. So down with the sharps."

A few of his thieves still grumbled, but daggers, knives and swords went back into sheaths. Crookbow's eye trained on Cald, rolled over by his fellows, hands composed across his chest. Crookbow shook his head, but Geth leapt up onto the log beside him before he could speak.

"To the victor goes the spoils," he said. "You all know who cheated first, but it doesn't matter now. It's over."

Crookbow shushed Cald's muttering lot. "He hasn't lied. That wasn't sporting what Cald did with the dirt. And he came at the Paellian on the ground. The rules of the log don't stick on the dirt. Every man has a right to defend himself."

No one could argue with that. But what came next? The woman-thief with the cap like Crookbow's voiced what all of them must have been thinking.

"What about the king's offer then? And what about Towdric?"

Geth answered before Crookbow had a chance. "What about *her*?" He pointed at Landren's corpse. "You ask about Towdric? Well, he's got bodies just like that hanging from his own trees."

No one cursed him this time. Geth flicked a glance toward the rest of Stoney's folk. They looked hopeful.

"But I reckon I know whose idea it was to string up an old woman." Geth spat in Cald's direction. "And he's dead. As for King Hadean, the offer stands. So, look on Towdric's way of doing things and think hard on who you chose."

"Enough." Crookbow pushed Geth toward the end of the log. "It's time for drink, not talk. We're headed back. Take the log, boys. And someone get Cald."

Geth stopped the captain there, pointing up in the trees. "Landren comes down as well. And to the victor goes the spoils, right? All those prisoners are mine."

The log was trimmed and sawed with practiced efficiency. Soon, the entire contingent, plus a load of fresh timber marched back to Crookbow's little village. It was a clever system Crookbow had come up with. Some stacked wood while others prepared food and drink. The bonds came off Stoney's folk and they crowded Geth, hugged him, praised his name. It was all pretty uncomfortable, given he'd probably incited the Ilar's wrath on their town in the first place.

"Get me a shovel," he said.

He dug the grave for Landren himself. Cold breath came out in misty huffs with each thrust of the shovel, but the effort warmed him. He'd taken Cald's sword. He left whatever else the man possessed to his friends. They laid their dead fellow to rest as well, but not before divvying it all up. Words were uttered and by the time a meal of venison and moonshine went around, nerves had cooled.

Crookbow found Geth among Neary and the friendlies, the glow of his fires warming the hall. He sat beside the big warrior, refilled his cup from a flagon he carried around.

"That was an impressive fight." He took a pull directly from the jug. "Even though you cheated."

Geth took a drink himself. "I'm new at this."

"But you're not new at swinging a sword." Crookbow regarded him with a level eye. "I've heard of you, Wolf of the Hills. Even if I didn't tell Cald."

"You didn't? Then why did he send those knives for me in the stable?"

"Because he was an onery sonofabitch."

"You sure you didn't tell him?"

Crookbow snorted. "Sometimes a captain must know a lot but tell only a little."

"You want this deal." Geth said. It wasn't a question. "And well you should. It's a good one."

"That may be true, if it's for real."

"Why would I lie? You know Hadean needs allies."

"And what happens when he doesn't need us anymore? You cheated Cald off the log, maybe you plan to cheat me too."

Geth spit. "I just dug a grave for an old woman, murdered by a bunch of thieves. And *you* want to question *my* virtues?"

"That's not an answer."

"Listen, I wasn't lying when I said I killed a man under the Oathstone. Hadean gave me a second chance. He'll forget it all, I promise, if you serve him and serve him well."

Crookbow swirled that jug unconsciously. He wanted the pardon, that was clear. The hook was in his mouth, Geth reckoned. But it needed a special kind of jerk to set the line.

"I'm not going to tell you I've never killed a man," Geth said. "Of course, I have. But I never killed an old woman. You're not wrong to wonder if you can ever be forgiven. I wondered the same. But this is for real. It may be your only chance."

"Hadean that desperate, is he?"

"He is. And you better hope he comes out on top. I wasn't lying when I said Towdric has dead men in the trees at his camp."

Crookbow breathed a sigh, topped off Geth's cup again, then took a long pull himself. "That wasn't my doing, the old lady. But there's more cutthroats in this band than just Cald. They'll make trouble for me, by and by. Even if I do take your offer."

"*The king's* offer," Geth said. "But never mind them. Take the offer while you can. Sometimes clutching at something is a good thing."

The food and drink came and went. Crookbow's little banquet wound down. By the captain's resigned manner, Geth knew it was done. So did everyone else, judging by the calm among the thieves, the relieved faces of Stoney's folk.

Neary took the cup from Geth's hand and replaced it with a full one. "Well? You ready to tell me what happened?"

"What do you mean?"

"Back at Waterset."

Geth blew out a sigh to match Crookbow's. "Towdric had me and Agrem arrested. They killed Eko."

Geth relayed the details of Brant's trial, Amalia's aid in their escape, and the file's disappearance. Neary lifted his cup when he was done.

"To the fallen." He blinked, then stood and raised his cup and his voice. "To the fallen!"

Drinks went up all throughout the room. The Umbelman stepped on Geth's foot under the table until he raised his cup as well. Perhaps that soothed Cald's friends a hair.

They slept without fear that night. Geth packed up in the morning. He found Crookbow outside under a bright, inauspicious sun.

"Leaving so soon?" the captain asked.

Geth nodded. "I was under the impression you were coming with me."

"I've got more than fifty men here, not to mention your townsfolk. You think we can just pick up and leave in an afternoon?"

"We're running out of time. If the river ice melts, Hadean's fighters will be trapped in the Tooth. We've got to hit the Ilar siege before it's too late."

"And you really think we can break it with a few dozen thieves? What happens if your king loses?"

"We can't let that happen."

Crookbow snorted. "Towdric takes over, that's what happens. And we end up dangling from his trees, right alongside the others."

"That would have happened anyway. But we aren't going to lose. And Towdric isn't hanging anyone."

"How do you know that?"

"Because he can't kill you if he's dead."

If Geth was going to keep any of the promises he'd made to Crookbow, he could only start one place. *Towdric.* And if he was honest, he knew he couldn't stand to let the man live after what he'd done to Agrem and Eko anyway. What's more, he doubted Brant could be spurred to action with Towdric pulling in the other direction alongside Pythelle. It had to start with Towdric.

"So that's your next move?" Neary said when Geth told him.

"That's right. I don't expect you've got any objections."

Neary rubbed his grey beard, thinking. "Alright, I'm betting you plan on Amalia sneaking you in and out. Even so, is it worth the risk?"

"Do we have any other choice? Towdric's got his hand around Brant's balls. I was just getting through to him too. It's that bellowing bastard that's the problem. We aren't marching north with anybody until Towdric's in the dirt."

Neary nodded. He rubbed his beard, thinking some more, but this once, Geth's need for vengeance matched up with what had to be done. The Umbelman didn't argue against it.

Neary looked back toward Crookbow's stronghouse, sighed. "You saved my skin. I want you to know I'm grateful."

Geth smacked his arm before he could get all sentimental. "Didn't you break me out of the tower back in Pellon?"

"Well—"

"Enough said." But it was Geth's turn to look at the thief's den. "You don't think this bastard will back out, do you?"

"Crookbow? I'll see that he doesn't." Neary forced a smile.

Geth couldn't worry about that now anyway. They agreed on a meeting place halfway between Waterset and the Tooth, where the Umbelman, along with Crookbow and his band, could join them up. Climbing onto Amalia's horse, Geth saluted and set out. The sun on his face only made him kick the poor beast harder.

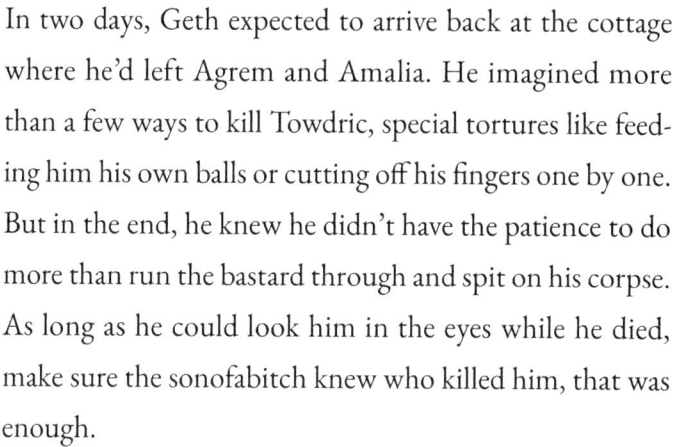

In two days, Geth expected to arrive back at the cottage where he'd left Agrem and Amalia. He imagined more than a few ways to kill Towdric, special tortures like feeding him his own balls or cutting off his fingers one by one. But in the end, he knew he didn't have the patience to do more than run the bastard through and spit on his corpse. As long as he could look him in the eyes while he died, make sure the sonofabitch knew who killed him, that was enough.

Not all Geth's thoughts were bloody. He thought of Vriana. What he would give for her sword by his side, her warriors as well. That wasn't the only reason he wanted her back, but he knew when a woman was done with him.

He thought of his band, the wolf pack some called it. And especially the dozen. Amalia seemed to think they'd escaped just as he had. Did that mean they were out there, looking for him? Should *he* be looking for *them*?

The shouts of a green-cloak that suddenly appeared in the road ahead scattered his thoughts.

"Captain! Captain Geth!"

Geth squinted, shielded his eyes until he recognized that blocky head. "Ratcher?"

"It's me, Captain!"

"It is, isn't it?" Geth slid out of the saddle to stretch his back.

"Whew! We've been looking for you for days. Hack's sure gonna be mad I found you first. An touchy scratch if ever there was such a thing."

Geth offered a half a smile.

But something had the hairs on the back of his neck standing up. His eyes scanned the snowy trees to either side all the way past the paunchy green-cloak down the road. "Where is everybody?"

"We split up to cover more ground. But seeing as Neary had gone to the Aldwood, I camped out here in hopes of catching you on the way in or out. I knew I'd find you."

"The Aldwood? I didn't tell—"

Ratcher's hand went back and Geth had just enough time see a cloud of dust flung at him before he closed his eyes and threw up a hand to protect his face. Blowing hard lest he inhale the stuff, Geth backpedaled, drew Cald's sword. His cheeks burned already, but by the luck of the gods themselves, Ratcher's throw seemed to have blown back at least partially into his own face. Geth heard the sonofabitch curse. When the big warrior tried to open his eyes, however, a pain like fire made him shut them just as fast.

"I knew it!" Geth laid back and forth with his sword to keep his enemy at bay.

"You didn't know a damn thing," Ratcher scoffed.

But by the sound of it, the treacherous bastard had backed away himself. His voice was strained. His ploy had backfired alright, Geth reckoned, even more than he'd first thought.

"I really am sorry," Ratcher went on. "It's a lot easier when you don't like the man that's been marked. But I've been paid. I can't rest until you're dead."

Geth swore. *The Paellian Assassin.* It was only then Geth realized he'd called Hack a 'scratch' a few moments earlier, like only a Paellian would.

"Uro's puckered ass." He really hadn't seen that coming, not from this paunchy lump. Geth strained his ear, listening for the crunch of boots, the huff of breaths. His mind worked together the pieces.

"I reckon they paid you for Hadean first, didn't they? But failing that, you set your eyes on me."

"Hadean?" Ratcher laughed.

He used the noise to try to cover the sound of a sword coming out of its sheath, but Geth didn't miss it.

"Gods no, not Hadean. Heard about that, though. Amateur stuff. Believe me, if the king had been my mark, he would have been—"

Ratcher swung for him.

But Geth hadn't let the small talk distract him the way Ratcher probably hoped. He lifted Cald's blade toward the swoosh of his enemy's, felt the satisfying shock up his arm as it struck dead center and bounced off. A second swing came at Geth's knee, but it was basic sword-yard stuff, the obvious play. He sprang back to let the blade whistle past.

"Well done," Ratcher said. "It's only a matter of time though."

"Maybe."

Ratcher was bluffing, stalling for time. A practiced assassin would have already bled him, Geth reckoned. They were both fighting blind, or near enough.

But the Tower of the Moon had taught Geth a thing or two about that. He moved as quiet as he could, lifting his boots high with each step, uncertain of the terrain under foot. Other than that, the key was to keep the bastard talking, hone in on his voice.

"What's he paying?" Geth asked, ear cocked all the while. "Whatever it is, I can pay double."

"Ha!" Ratcher was well out of reach, circling slowly toward Geth's left. "I really doubt that. He's got the weight of the Golden City behind him."

"Palladine." It had to be. "Bloody bastard."

"Look, if there was any other way, I'd drop the job. I've been watching you for a while now. Your men love you, otherwise I could have finished the job a long time ago. But they hardly let you out of their sight. You're a savage, a lowly whoreson, that's for sure, but you really do give a damn about those ugly bastards. I'll give you that."

"Lowly? So says the rat himself."

Ratcher snickered. "I may sneak like a rat, but I'm an honest rat. If I take payment, a man dies."

Geth was the one to press this time. With a skip forward, he lunged to send a straight thrust where he thought Ratcher's middle must be. A parry knocked his blade aside, but Geth saw the movements clearly in his mind, followed up with a waist high slash Ratcher somehow blocked as well. Geth sprang back, swearing under his breath. Whatever the bastard had done to himself with that powder, either he still had some measure of sight—more than Geth had—or it had begun to wear off.

Geth risked opening one watery eye and caught the shadowy form of his enemy crouched in a perfect swordsman stance for a split second before the pain forced the eyelid closed again. Given the fact that he could see even briefly, he reckoned the effects of Ratcher's throw had, indeed, begun to fade. He just needed more time.

"You said yourself the men love me," Geth said. "How about we join forces, take Palladine down? Hell, we've already been on the same side for a while now, apart from this little disagreement."

Ratcher chuckled again. "What would happen to my reputation if it got around that I don't finish my contracts? And you've seen my face. I'm in a bit of a spot here."

"Alright, that may be so. But explain one thing. You've been with my file since before Palladine arrived. And it sounds like you've been on my tail even longer. How's that?"

"He's a clever scratch, Palladine. That's how."

Geth could hear Ratcher creeping forward. A quick thrust backed him up again. "You were saying?"

"He contracted me long before you ever arrived back in Umbel," Ratcher said. "From the first moment you broke loose of the tower in fact. You'd slipped through his grasp twice already.

"I've been tracking you since before you left Pellon," he went on. "I was within striking distance by the time you reached Stoney, but Palladine stayed my hand. The greedy ball-scratch wanted to take you in alive."

Geth snorted. "That's obvious,"

"He knew he might have to settle for bringing you in cold though. And he was willing to pay a fortune for it. I wasn't trekking out here to Umbel for anything less, was I?"

"You sure there's no buying my way out of this? What kind of Paellian are you?"

Ratcher clicked his tongue. "Already told you, I've got a reputation to uphold. And you've seen my face."

Geth cracked an eye. It hurt, but he could see. Some. He watched Ratcher take a tentative step toward his left this time. By the man's own logic, he'd have to kill all the file, all the band really. They'd seen him too, after all.

Geth couldn't let that stand. He watched Ratcher's slow arc toward his unprotected side but stood still himself. He swung tentatively through the air in front of himself, a ruse. Best Geth could tell, Ratcher bought it. He let the bastard take another half step toward his flank before springing toward him with a furious assault.

Steel rang off steel. Ratcher parried a diagonal cut, a backhand slash the other way, and a thrust at his sternum. Paunchy or not, that gut didn't slow him down. A part of Geth's mind wished he could still have such a swordsman in the band when it was all said and done.

"I guess it's me that can't let you leave now either," Geth said.

Ratcher looked over his shoulder, for a way out, Geth presumed.

"You're thinking of you men," the Paellian said. "You always are. They're safe. As long as they don't know anything. Plus, I'm not killing a whole troop for free. Now, if you were to tell them, I'd have no choice."

"What makes you think you're leaving here alive?"

"Experience."

Ratcher darted forward with a thrust, flinging that damn powder yet again. Geth swore as it caught him in the nose and face, but he launched himself after his enemy in a blind counter. Ratcher parried the first swing, stumbled under the second. The third found its target.

"Ahhh!"

"Ha!" Geth couldn't see, but a cry like that couldn't be faked. The big warrior shook his head, clicked his tongue the way Ratcher had done. "That'll be the death of you I'm afraid."

"Just a flesh wound."

Geth couldn't see, but by the sound of it, Ratcher had managed to back well away. "I know a healer. Give me your word you'll drop the contract, and I'll take you to her."

Ratcher's chuckle had Geth wondering if he'd stabbed the man or not. "I've said you're a decent fellow, but nobody's *that* decent. I'll take my chances."

"Then you'll die."

The sound of boots crunching into the distance was the only answer at first. But somewhere down the road, Ratcher must have turned. "See you around, Wolf. Really wish I didn't have to say that, but I do."

CHAPTER TWENTY-NINE

I t took a good hour for Geth's eyes to stop burning. Rubbing snow in them helped, but he could only pray Ratcher's dust hadn't done any lasting damage. It made sense that it wouldn't, given how easily the bastard had blinded himself with the stuff.

Geth started after him as soon as he could see, tracking his steps easily enough until he found a place where a mount had been tethered. His quarry had taken to horseback.

Geth turned his eyes to a bright sun overhead and cursed. It was pointless. What good to finish off the assassin only to fail Hadean and Phelan?

"Treacherous bastard." He'd have to wait for Ratcher to find *him*, not a prospect any sane man would relish.

Wheeling Amalia's horse around, Geth rode straight through the night until he reached the cottage where he'd left the witch and warlock. Amalia stood waiting for Geth in the doorway when he arrived, extending a mug of hot tea like somebody's grandma.

"Well?" she asked.

Geth took the tea with a grunt in thanks. "Neary's alive. And the thieves are with us."

She ushered him inside. Agrem rose unsteadily but his embrace was firm. Geth settled in a chair with a sigh and told them all that had happened in the Aldwood over a meal of the witch's road biscuits. Agrem nodded and hummed. Amalia looked thoughtful.

"Did you come across any of your men?" she asked.

Ratcher's threat against the dozen echoed in Geth's ear. "No."

"What will you do now?"

"I—"

"He will go to Towdric, mmmm?"

Geth looked to the Seer, shook his head. *Bloody magicks.*

"That's right. Not just for revenge though. I reckon we haven't got a chance of budging the force at Waterset. Not so long as Towdric lives. But once Brant's free of the bastard, we just might be able to shake his armies loose."

"So, you intend to kill him?" Amalia frowned. "How will you get close enough to do that?"

Agrem snorted a laugh, looked toward the witch.

Amalia looked back, blinked. "Oh."

"Will you do it?" Geth asked. "Will you sing?"

Amalia frowned. The wheels were turning behind her eyes. She muttered something under her breath, and sighed. Geth had no idea what to make of it.

"All you have to do is sneak me inside," he said. "Just like you sneaked me out."

"I know. It will be riskier this time though. Pythelle will be watching for me."

Agrem hummed.

The witch looked from Geth to the Seer and back. "There's no other way, is there?" She pursed her lips and nodded one last time. "I'll do it. Come what may."

Geth rested a hand on her shoulder. Tired as he was, he went outside to gather firewood for Agrem. He'd need it while they were gone.

The witch followed him out, a dark and starless sky overhead. "This won't be easy," she said.

Geth ignored that. "Will he be safe?" He flicked a glance toward the cottage.

"No one can find this place. Except *her*. But I doubt the spider will wander so far from her web."

"Pythelle?"

Amalia nodded. "Worry for yourself. For both of us. It will be dangerous, Geth of Pellon. Very."

"You know something, don't you?"

"Nothing is certain. It never is. But Agrem isn't the only one who can see."

Geth's eyes narrowed. "If you've had a vison, spit it out."

"Towdric must die." There was nothing grandmotherly in her tone now. "By whatever means. Promise me you'll kill him."

"I won't stop til he's dead."

"Good. Because otherwise, it's all for nothing."

The scent of fresh-baked biscuits roused Geth a few hours later. After devouring his breakfast and stacking more wood for the Seer, he joined Amalia in front of the cottage. She assured him that Agrem would only grow stronger. He'd need to. Geth had plans for him.

"Can you send for the band?" he asked when Agrem stepped out to see them off. "Like you and Eko sent for me?"

Agrem nodded. "There are ways."

"Good. Neary and Crookbow should meet us within a few days. When you add our lot to theirs, and most of them on horse, that's a decent war party."

The Seer hummed.

They clasped hands and the big warrior started off, Amalia right beside him. They left her mount with Agrem, just in case, setting out south toward Waterset with their supplies on their backs. The witch led the way with a grim urgency. By nightfall, the chimney smoke of Waterset hit their noses and Amalia began humming her tune.

A touch of her hand cleared the fog from Geth's eyes and he took the lead from there. Down below the town, Towdric's army camped. Geth didn't bother looking for the lord there. They strode past sleepy sentinels wrapped in blankets beside their campfires until they reached the road leading uphill to the walled town. Geth growled a curse as they passed the tree with the hanged deserter in it. Two new corpses hung beside the first crow-pecked cadaver.

But those dead men served a potent reminder of what lay ahead. It was only then that Geth really considered the danger he was walking into. *Bloody fool*. Towdric wanted him dead, Brant wasn't about to stand in the way, and Palladine had tortures of his own in mind.

He didn't miss the resignation in Amalia's movements either. For now, at least, her singing dazed any passersby they came across, albeit few at this late hour. The gates to Waterset weren't shut either. Why would they be? Towdric and Brant's refusal to aid Hadean made them allies of Iyngaer more than enemies.

When Geth led them under that arch, however, Amalia sucked in a breath.

"What is it?" he asked.

Amalia's face was as steely as her grey bun. "We must hurry."

Resuming her song, she took the lead, straight toward Brant's keep where Towdric would have taken rooms. Geth loosened Cald's sword in its sheath. They reached the heavy doors to the citadel, passed the two foggy-eyed guardsmen like they weren't there. Geth pushed the doors to the hall open and Amalia gasped. The witch Pythelle and a half dozen soldiers stood waiting for them inside.

Pythelle lifted a finger toward them, but Amalia's song turned to some whispered utterance. The younger witch recoiled as if struck. Her soldiers were still shaking their heads to clear the song-spell as Geth rushed, knocking the first man out with a right hook. He doubled a second over with a kick to the gut and drew his blade to face a third, Towdric's young captain, Bushy-brows. The clatter of more men and weapons arriving turned them both before they could cross swords.

"Stop!"

Brant strode into the room from the back of the hall, blade drawn, crowded around by his own fighters. Geth flicked a glance over his shoulder toward the door but the two guards from outside rushed in to bar it closed. In front of them, Amalia had collapsed to one knee, eyes smoldering. Behind Bushy and his men, Pythelle lay sprawled out on the floor.

"It's the Paellian!" Bushy-brows said. As if everyone couldn't see for themselves. "We've got him! Take him to Lord Towdric."

"Sheathe your swords." Brant spoke with all the confidence of the master of the keep. "He's mine."

Bushy-brows opened his mouth. "Lord Towdric—"

Ruddy, Brant's man, stepped in front of Geth to stare Bushy-brows down. "Off with you! You heard the Lord of Waterset!"

Towdric's man muttered a curse but jogged off, his soldiers dragging the fellow Geth had punched up to his feet.

In search of Uncle Ball-scratch, no doubt. Geth would have cursed aloud, but Brant came to stand in front of him, hands on hips.

"Well? What am I to do with you?"

"Nothing, lord. Just stay out of my way."

"And?"

"And let me kill Towdric."

A murmur passed through the soldiers. Ruddy turned a stare on their direction to silence them. Brant eyed Geth with a frown.

"You really expect I would stand aside and let you kill a lord of the realm? An ally?"

"A lord of *half* a realm. The other half belongs to Iyn-gaer. In no small part because of this *ally* of yours."

Brant opened his mouth, but Geth didn't have time to spare.

"I don't expect you to thank me, but I'd be doing you a favor. We all know Towdric will never march north to Hadean's aid. And if he won't aid the crowned king of Umbel, then it goes to figure he wants the crown for himself. Once he's got that, do you think he'll stand by while a man with equal claim to the kingship yet lives?"

Brant's eyebrows went up. "That's a bold claim you make, Master Geth."

"You're no half-wit. You know it's true."

Brant could only lick his lips. He flicked a glance down the hall where Bushy-brows had disappeared. Ruddy watched his lord as intently as Geth.

"You want me to march north against the Ilars," Brant said finally. "Against a barbarian horde with twice our numbers."

"That's right."

"Of course it is. Whatever you say about Lord Towdric, you have designs of your own. Stirring this army has always been your aim. His mistreatment of you and the Seer is nothing more than a convenience, isn't it? By and by, you always wanted him dead."

Geth gave a grim nod. "You of all people know what I think of traitors. And you forgave me. I—*we*—need him dead in order to help our friend, King Hadean. You helped him once yourself, remember? You saved his life at Copper Ridge. I was there. If we're being honest, you saved the whole battle that day."

Brant's soldiers puffed up at that, looked from one to another with pride. Amalia had regained her feet as well. She came to stand beside Geth.

But the lord sighed, shook his head. "Did you actually think you could get all the way inside here, kill the man, and escape? That's suicide. Was it worth the risk?"

"For my friends?" Geth frowned. "I'd die for them. And they for me. A braver lot you'll never find than these friends I've made in Umbel."

Brant blinked. Geth followed his eyes as they flicked to Pythelle, laid out on the floor still, but stirring. His face went dark. Whatever he was thinking, the sound of footfalls approaching turned them all to the far end of the hall.

"What's this?"

Towdric came in with a bellow, as always. His sword was drawn, as were those of a good dozen of his men. Geth reached for his own, but Brant yanked him back behind his soldiers. Torchlight gleamed off bared steel on both sides. Amalia squeezed in beside the big warrior. Gathering her voice, Geth hoped.

"Ah, there he is!" Towdric smiled. "Well done! Caught the scoundrel sneaking into the keep in the dark of night, did you?"

Brant said nothing. Something in his look stalled Towdric halfway across the room. Smile or no, the tension in the little anteroom was like the air before a storm.

"This man bears a message from the king," Brant said finally. "An order, in fact."

Towdric's smile took on the curl of a snarl. "Is that so?"

"We are ordered to march north to his aid at Towerrock. To break the siege. And to drive the armies of the Chieftain Iyngaer and his allies out of these lands. Or off this world if we can."

Geth felt Ruddy quiver beside him. "That's right!"

"March north?" Towdric feigned confusion. "Why would the king throw us needlessly against a superior force when he sits safely behind the walls of Towerrock? Grinding the tribesmen down as we always have? Why risk the lives of our men now, before the Ilars have been softened, before the weather turns and the fighting season arrives?"

Geth spat over Brant's soldiers. "You know Hadean will be starved into surrender by then!"

"And who are you to open your snout here?" Towdric snapped back. "A foreign sellsword? A fugitive? In these lands, the hand wields the tool, not the other way 'round, Paellian."

"This foreign tool has bled more enemies in this war than you've even laid eyes on. You should kneel at the feet of Lord Brant, do whatever it is he asks. If not for him, you'd already be dead."

"Whoreson foreign—!"

Ruddy grabbed hold of Geth and Brant stepped in between the two sets of fighters, hands raised. "Peace, men of Umbel! There will be no blood on my floor tonight! Foreign or otherwise. In the morning, we're marching north."

"Are we?" Towdric turned an evil eye on his nephew.

"I'm giving you one hour to make your decision. Rouse your troops and join us, Uncle. Or leave Waterset."

CHAPTER THIRTY

Towdric exited the way he'd come. A single, white-cloaked figure came the other way, down the hallway. Torchlight gleamed red off his shaved head, but his eyes were as cold and blue as ever.

He trained them on Brant. "So, you side with the sellsword?"

"I side with the rightful king. The station of the man who serves him bravely is of no consequence."

"Your king has backed himself into a corner in the north." Palladine's tone was even, deliberate. "Think of the future, Lord Brant. And choose your next steps carefully."

"I already have."

Geth couldn't help but puff with triumph. It didn't matter what Palladine said. Brant was not his father; he'd shown that already. Hot purpose coursed through Geth, through all the men around him. He could *feel* it.

A tiny frown from Palladine was his only show of disappointment. He turned those cold eyes on Geth. "This changes nothing. On your feet or across the back of a horse, you're coming home with me."

Geth wanted to laugh, tell the man his assassin was dead. But he let the bastard have the last word instead. Palladine's ignorance bought time if not satisfaction.

That white cloak flashed in the torchlight as he turned to follow in Towdric's wake. Ruddy's hold on the big warrior became a celebratory hug as Palladine disappeared down the hall. Amalia looked at him with wary eyes, however, her mouth a tight white line.

"Pythelle," she said.

Geth looked to where the woman had fallen but she was gone.

If Brant noticed, he only seemed the happier for it. "It will take a day to gather supplies," he told Geth, rubbing his hands together. "But we'll march as soon as we are able."

"The sooner the better. Send a pigeon ahead. We need Hadean's aid from Towerrock. The weather has begun to turn already. He won't be able to sally if the river ice has already melted."

"Then we have no time to waste."

Brant invited Geth to rest among his men. The first run-
ners went out with orders to begin loading wagons and
sharpening steel. It wasn't over though, not entirely. Messengers came from Towdric and went back the other way
several times.

"What's he got to say now?" Geth asked Ruddy.

"Same thing he's been saying all along: that Hadean's
proved his inability to rule. That if he released all the
townsfolk from Towerrock—or hadn't let them in the
Tooth in the first place—he never would have been in this
situation. He also says we don't stand a chance against the
Ilars."

"Bloody coward."

Ruddy shook his head. "We could have marched out a
month ago. I don't know why we didn't."

Geth reckoned he knew why. He couldn't believe they'd
seen the last of Pythelle either.

Towdric and his army packed up and left the very next day. Of course they did. All the traitor had to do now was sit back and wait for Iyngaer to defeat Hadean. By Geth's reckoning, his retreat already halved the numbers the chieftain would need to face. Towdric would like his odds, treacherous bastard.

But Geth had plans of his own. He waved Amalia aside where no one could hear. "If I get you a horse, can you ride north and get inside Towerrock?"

Amalia smiled patiently. "I got out, didn't I?"

"Good. Tell the king to be ready. We're coming." He reached into his pocket and drew out the one cleat that remained from his fight with the Thirings on the ice. "And give him this. If they can craft even a dozen pairs, it could make all the difference when they come across the river."

The witch looked down at the spiked metal in her hand and smiled. "Ice shoes. Clever."

"And Amalia—" Geth touched her shoulder. "Thank you."

She loosed that giggle of hers, beehive shaking on her head. Geth found himself smiling as well.

His smile lingered after she'd gone. It was contagious. *Bloody magicks*. Brant's men saluted and grinned in passing. Geth thought of his band, the last trick up his sleeve.

The addition of Crookbow's thieves to his own pack would have swollen their numbers to nearly a hundred.

Yet in the end, it still amounted to thousands less than the force Towdric had marched away with. Geth looked to the sun. Normally a bright sky would have given him reason to smile. On this day, he cursed. From the heights of Waterset, he could see the frozen course of the river. Unless he was mistaken, there was a gleam on the surface that hadn't been there a few days before.

They set out the day after that, a long train of men, horses, and wagons. An *army,* gods be praised. Axels groaned, saddles creaked, armor and weapons clinked and clanged. It was music to Geth's ears.

And Agrem will have gathered the band by now as well. Despite their shortcomings, the thought gave him comfort. He occupied his mind with where to deploy his pack, how they might help most without being sent into undue danger. Gods willing, they all survived.

The miles passed until Brant ordered the army to make camp at nightfall. There was no way to hide so many men, so they'd taken the fastest route, the River Road. Iyngaer's scouts had likely begun the race back to the chieftain already bearing news of their approach. That tree-top bastard would be laughing. It didn't take a scholar to count Umbel's warriors and realize they'd lost a huge chunk. Geth put their army at barely three thousand swords, probably a quarter of what the tribes could field.

"Without Ceter though?" he mused aloud.

No one knew what had become of the warlock's army, the Thiring tribe. Melted away, back home, to the north where their wives and children and livestock awaited? Geth prayed like his life depended on it, like all their lives did. If even just a thousand of them had deserted, five hundred...

Ruddy must have been thinking along the same lines. He found Geth as he slid out of the saddle.

"How many swords would you say the king's got up in the Tooth?"

Geth figured in his head. "Several thousands, for sure."

"Battle-tested men, sworn to their king, committed to this war."

"True. And when you add that to our force..."

Ruddy forced a grin.

It wasn't a wholehearted gesture. The man was no fool, he knew the odds. But Geth loved him for making the effort.

"You know," he said, grimacing, "I never did get your name, Captain. If I need someone to save my skin, I want to know what to yell out."

"It's Worran. But don't mind if I still call you Wolf."

He waved Geth to follow all the way to Brant's own fire. Tents went up, meals went around. The lord retreated inside but Worran lingered cross legged across from Geth.

"The scouts are back," he said. "Our outriders haven't come across anything, but I've doubled the pickets just in case."

Geth nodded. "Good idea."

"Will he march south to meet us?" Worran eyed him from across the flames. "Or wait for us to come to him?"

Geth looked up. Brant had appeared, listening from the flap of hsi tent. Geth thought the question through before he answered.

"He'll wait. He could gamble, leave a smaller force to keep Hadean in check, then march south with the majority of his tribesmen to crush us. But he won't."

"Why not?"

"Because it's Hadean he fears. He won't risk him escaping the Tooth. He'll wait for us near Greenfell. That way he can set up one force against us, another against the king. If the two battles are waged within sight of each other, he can throw reserves from one to the other."

"Like we did at Copper Ridge." It was Worran's turn to nod.

Brant stepped out toward the fire. "Who can know Iyngaer's mind?"

Perhaps it was the day of hard travel. His earlier confidence seemed drained away. Geth opened his mouth to reply but the lord wasn't done.

"If the chieftain sends the greater part of his army south against us now, we'll be heavily outnumbered. That's what I would do."

Geth shook his head. "My gut tells me he won't."

"How can you be sure?"

"Because Hadean will launch a sally if he does. It will all have been for nothing if Iyngaer lets him out now. Worse, if Hadean breaks out, the men of Towerrock would break their fast on the Ilars' own supplies, everything they've stored up. There's no way the tribes could pack it up and take it along. They'd have no choice but to leave it behind."

"What if our pigeons never reach the king? Would he still risk a sally if he didn't know he had aid? He may not even know we're coming."

"I've sent Amalia with the message," Geth said. "Just in case. And Hadean's eyes on the wall wouldn't miss it if half the tribesmen suddenly disappeared. That could only mean one thing."

"Don't the Ilars have witches of their own to stop the Lady of Witchwood?"

"They have a powerful warlock, but Iyngaer cast him out." Geth flashed a grim smile. "His name is Agrem. He's on our side now."

That seemed to help Brant's confidence. The lord nodded, kneeled beside the fire. He waved both Geth and Worran closer, picked up a stick and began scraping lines in the mud.

"Assuming you're right," he said, "Iyngaer will likely line up here, just south of the town, beside the road. There will be no marching past him and he'll be close enough to watch the battle behind him at Towerrock as well."

A wavy line represented the river, an 'x' the fortress on its island. More lines denoted the besieging forces around the Tooth and the hills just to the east. Geth remembered the place Brant indicated.

"You're right. It must be there. We'll have no choice but to spread the lines thin to match Iyngaer's numbers, but he hasn't got many horses. Our own riders will help protect the right flank. We've just got to hold on long enough for Hadean to gain a foothold on the riverbank to the north of us. If he can get his men out and fighting, hitting the tribes from the other side, we've won."

Whatever he told Brant and Worran, the more Geth thought about it, the clearer it became just how slim their chances were. He'd sent Amalia with the cleat and word of their approach. Neary, Crookbow, and that lot would bolster their force as well. But Iyngaer had proved himself a fearsome warrior and wicked clever besides.

What else did the tree-top bastard have in store for them?

Geth sought out Worran the next morning as the army broke camp and prepared to march. "You saw Iyngaer at Copper Ridge, is it true what they say?"

"That he's a bloody devil?" the captain frowned, face as pink as ever. "It's true."

Geth didn't like what he heard.

"But he's careful too," Worran went on. "He didn't just charge into battle himself. He waited until Hadean did that. He probably didn't expect the lad to break his lines, true, but when it happened, he was ready to throw his own weight in and push him back."

Geth nodded. "I heard about that. From what they say, our young king split his tribesmen right down the middle, nearly won it all right then and there."

"Nearly. Until Iyngaer joined in with his best men. Next thing you know, the king was surrounded. We barely got to him in time."

"But you *did* get to him," Geth said. "And matched Iyngaer steel for steel. If he's a devil, I reckon we've got a few devils of our own."

Worran waved that off. "We've got a rabid wolf, I'll tell you that. I've seen his bite."

They shared a smile.

Geth's mind was already back on Iyngaer though. Worran's account matched everything Geth had seen for himself, that the chieftain was smart, knew how to turn a bad situation on its head or invent a solution no one else might dream of. He'd done as much in keeping Hadean alive those weeks when everyone thought he was dead, cementing his control over the tribes and unleashing the boy-king to incite civil war in Umbel.

But Geth had ended that before it started by killing the traitor, Eldric. By all the gods, he swore that leather-stinking treetop bastard would rue the day he'd let a fledgling king and his gutter-born swordsman escape Dues alive.

"We nearly finished it that day," Worran went on, shaking Geth from his thoughts. "The center held, and our riders eventually won out on the flanks."

"They say it was only by some Ilar magick that Iyngaer's army escaped."

"I was in the center," Worran said, "not far from the king, but that's what I was told. Something frightened the horses just when we broke through. Otherwise, it would have been a route."

Ceter. Geth knew his fearspell better than anyone. But the warlock was out of the picture now, one more reason to be hopeful. Geth looked the captain in the eyes, expression somber.

"It may come down to our horses against theirs again," he said. "And this time there won't be any magicks. Unless they're cast by us."

Worran nodded gravely. Geth looked past him, eastward, where his friends would be gathering already.

"I have to leave. Agrem is out there, gathering my file as we speak. And a few others I managed to scrape together."

"You're leaving?"

"We're still two days from the Tooth. There's a hilltop just south of Greenfell that overlooks our battleground. I'll meet you there."

Worran didn't look happy about it, but he saluted with fist to heart.

Geth didn't wait around to tell Brant. He took the horse he'd been loaned and rode due east, toward the cottage where he'd left the Seer. He didn't tell anyone about Crookbow either. *Let them get a pleasant surprise for once.*

Geth smiled, thinking of that. A warm wind had blown in from the south, however, warm enough for a man accustomed to the cold to loosen his cloak at the neck. He spurred his mount as hard as he dared until he'd reached the cottage sometime after nightfall.

There was no greeting from Eko, not this time. But Bird-man spotted him even through the dark and hollered a welcome. When Geth looked up, Agrem was already standing in the little house's doorway, outlined by firelight. The rest of the file came outside or crawled out of tents to greet him. Drayic, Red, Loura and the rest.

"Where the hell is Neary?" Geth said. He frowned at the tents, far too few to shelter fifty or more additional fighters. The moon lit horse tracks in the ground as well, but not an animal whinnied to either side. "And where the hell is Crookbow?"

The boys looked from one to another, lips tight. Kerrel finally stepped forward. "He came, but he's...gone, Captain."

"What the..."

Realization hit Geth like slap across the face, but Hack pushed to the fore with a curse of his own, leaving no doubt. "Thieving bastards! The sonsabitches stole our horses. And they stole Neary too!"

CHAPTER THIRTY-ONE

B link arrived with a bowl of venison stew and Geth was ushered inside to a place beside the fire. His head hurt but he slurped it down. Agrem passed him a flask of Ilar liquor. At least the Seer seemed back to his normal self.

"Don't worry, Captain," Hack said. "All the old gang is here. Drayic and his band as well. We don't need those bastards."

Geth looked down at the empty bowl in his hand, resisted the urge to throw it across the room. "Am I a fool for putting my trust in a bunch of thieves? If they've touched a hair on Neary's head, I swear to every god I'll have about a hundred balls gathered up in a pot for Blink's next stew."

"A hundred balls?"

"Give or take. This once, I'll kill the women too."

"You think they've got Ratcher?" Kerrel asked. "Nobody's seen him in days."

"Maybe he ran off, had enough of this war," Red-eye said. "Or maybe the Ilars got him."

Remembering the assassin's warning, Geth kept quiet. Red-eye patted his arm.

"Don't worry, sir. He'll be alright. You've got to think like that, always keep your hopes up."

"Is that so?"

Red-eye nodded, then looked around the room. Geth frowned, watching as the Umbelman seemed to gather himself.

"What is it, Red-eye?"

"I've got a message from Phelan, something he told me to tell you in private. But I don't suppose it's anything that can't be spoke here among the file."

Geth blew out a sigh. "Go ahead."

"He said—well, keep your hopes up still, Captain—but what he said was this: no matter what happens, you've been a good friend. The best friend in fact. No matter how this all ends, remember that. That's the message."

Geth blinked. A wave of emotion hit him, but he swallowed it down with a grimace. "Phelan said that, did he?"

"But keep your hopes up, that's what I say! There's only one way this ends. With us winning!"

Geth met those puffy pink eyes. He couldn't help but smile. Standing up, he pulled the green-cloak in for a brusque hug. He turned to face the others, one arm still around Red-eye's thin shoulders.

"Alright boys, from all the messages he managed to pass through, it doesn't seem like Phelan's been jailed at all."

His men looked from one to another as realization set in. Each had thought himself the sole messenger no doubt. Grins cracked faces and Bird-man snickered. Hack just looked confused.

"Does anyone else have any more words from him?" Geth asked.

They shared another chuckle but that was it.

"No? Good. Now let's go rescue the little bastard."

Talk of Phelan put a smile on Geth's face. But not for long. The little rogue would be half-dead of starvation by now, surrounded on all sides by bloodthirsty tribesmen. And even if Geth somehow managed to break him out of the siege, Melagus would have a cell in the dungeons with Phelan's name on it after the war was won.

Geth took Blink aside the next morning with that in mind. "I need you to head north. Ride for Point-fort."

"But I'll miss the battle?"

"Do it. And bring a shovel."

Blink's eyes fluttered a few times, exactly the thing that had earned him his name. He nodded finally and saluted with fist to heart. To be fair, he *did* look disappointed to be sent off.

But the man was useless in a fight, even if he could chop an onion like no other. It would be one less worry for Geth, knowing at least one member of the dead-man dozen was safe.

"Phelan buried something there, remember?" Geth waited for the next round of blinking. "Bring it all back to the Tooth. If we survive, I'll need it."

"If we survive?"

Geth didn't wait for the blinking to stop this time. "If we don't, take what you've found and ride for Pellon. Or Turia. And don't come back until someone besides Towdric wears the crown."

No blinking this time. The Umbelman's eyes went sober. *If there's anything to come back to,* they seemed to say. Geth left him with a slap on the back and turned his mind to making sure that day never came.

Without horses, the band had no choice but to make the distance to their meet-up on foot. Midway through the second day, Bird-man came back from up ahead with a green-cloak outrider from Umbel's army beside him. Geth sent his men to find food and a campfire among the ranks and headed toward Brant's tent, up on a rise looking over Towerrock's surrounds.

"Thram's balls." He hadn't reached the flap when he stopped, eyes fixed on the army below. The whitish stone spires of the Tooth thrust up into an iron-grey sky. Dark waters flowed past it on either side.

Brant came out of his tent to stand beside him, following his gaze. "We're too late. The ice is gone."

This once, the curses stuck in his throat. "Let's get a closer look," Geth croaked.

He led Brant several furlongs down the hill to the last pickets of their force. *Stay hopeful*, he told himself. *The months of siege must have worn down these bastards as well. Maybe Ceter's people have fled. Maybe they've had deserters as well...*

But Brant's expression presaged what Geth saw for himself. There, among the banners of bear, and hart, and all the rest flew the fox of the Thirings, Ceter's tribe. It was hard to make an accurate count of the divided army, but the nearer of the two forces—the one arrayed directly ahead—numbered at least eight thousand.

A smaller army clustered near the half-ruined town of Greenfell. Up close, Geth could see that the North River was actually still frozen mostly, except for a narrow band down the center. And yet dark water rippled freely on all sides of Towerrock. Shielding his eyes for a better look, Geth made out straight, clean edges near the fortress. The ice had been cut.

"Ice saws."

Geth cursed the earth-mother's mother. Not only had Iyngaer managed to hold onto Ceter's warriors, he'd used Geth's own ploy against him.

The only good thing Geth could see was that the chieftain had elected to leave a sizable force on the far side of the river. On the side where he stood, the east side, Iyngaer had set his fighters mostly around the town of Greenfell and further north along the banks. But his main army had already formed lines directly opposite Brant's position, further south. They stretched east to west across the road and into the fields to either side, using the river as an anchor for their right.

But there was nothing to anchor Iyngaer's left, leaving that side open for an attack with Brant's horse.

"He might have set himself further south," the lord said, thinking along the same lines, "and anchored against river to one side, hills to the other, but he'd be too far to send troops quickly to and from the siege."

Geth nodded. "We'll have to meet him with a very thin line, but our horses will outmatch theirs. In numbers and in strength."

"That's our only chance. A slim one at that."

It was true. Without a sheet of ice to charge across, Hadean's army would struggle to mount a sally, to exit the fortress at all really, much less gain a foothill on the riverbanks. Best Geth could tell, Brant's army would be on their own.

Eight thousand against three. Those were grim odds. They couldn't retreat now though, not with Towerrock on the brink of surrender.

"Well, I'd rather die under these dull skies," Geth muttered, looking up, "than live as a coward while my friends starve." He flicked a glance at Brant. It didn't seem like he'd heard, eyes still fixed on the enemy formation. By the look on his face though, he'd arrived at the same conclusion.

"So, it all comes down to our horses against theirs," Geth said.

Brant turned back to the big warrior. He opened his mouth, closed it again. Probably had nothing good to say.

But Geth forced a laugh. "Have you heard of the endless hordes of the Mog, out east?"

"I have." The lord couldn't resist a glance at the tattoos peeking out from under Geth's cuffs.

"It's all lies." Geth nodded, as much to himself as anyone else. "The Paellian armies are far bigger than the warbands of the Mog. But those stories seem true for one reason; the Mog are so much better fighting off the horse, they're like two or three lilies each."

Brant returned a weak smile. "Are you saying that, in actuality, because of our great skill, we outnumber the Ilar horsemen by three to one?"

"I was going to say four."

That smile broadened. Geth saluted with first to heart. Like so many times before, love for this brother in arms lit a fire in his belly. They could win. They *would* win.

"Truth be told, we're fighting Copper Ridge all over again," Geth said. "We've just got to hold in the center long enough to smash through the tribesmen on the flank with our horsemen. And there won't be any magicks against our mounts this time either."

"Our lines will be thinner," Brant pointed out. "And yet..."

Geth watched as the lord eyed the towers of the Tooth, lips curled in a frown. He followed his eyes, squinted out over the distance. "What the...?"

"Something tells me my cousin has something in store for the tribes."

Geth pulled at his mustache. "Iyngaer sure does have a lot of men positioned around the fortress."

"Maybe he knows something we don't."

"I think you may be right. According to Amalia, the Ilars have a spy inside the Tooth. That may be why Iyngaer's left so many swords to guard the siege. Even with the ice freed up, he's afraid. Of what, exactly, I couldn't say."

Brant muttered to himself, counting by the looks of it. "Almost four thousand swords between the far bank and this one. That's four thousand swords we won't have to fight."

There was some good news, Geth supposed. But scanning the lines of fur-clad tribesmen, his eye eventually found Iyngaer himself. He was impossible to miss, the giant bastard, even in armor rather than that white bearskin he wore in his hall. The chieftain stood among a force of several hundred reserves stationed directly between the lines arrayed to the south, and those nearer Towerrock, farther north.

Two fronts, Geth mused, *and a healthy troop of reserves ready to be thrown at either.* It was no accident Iyngaer positioned himself in the center of things. Those reserves were the men that would decide the battle.

"Then Iyngaer's the one to watch."

Brant looked to him, but Geth was just thinking aloud. The battle was about to start. And he had others to watch out for as well.

CHAPTER THIRTY-TWO

The horns had begun blowing, forming up Umbel's lines as blocks of warriors moved into position, tightening ranks and spreading into files just five men deep. Behind them, several hundred archers strung their bows, Stoney's lot among them. Geth's own file took a place of honor, right in the center of the ranks. They hailed him as he arrived. The fighting would rage hot there. Was it too much to hope every man in his dozen survived?

"I'll slaughter a lamb in your name, Red Awer," he murmured. "Just watch over my file. I'll slaughter an ox if that's what it takes—an elephant next time I'm in the Great South."

In the meantime, he clapped shoulders, offered nods and salutes of fist to heart. Faces brightened and backs went straight all around him. They knew his reputation. More than a few of these men had fought beside him before and lived to tell the tale. They believed he could lead them through it again.

"Kerrel," Geth said. I want you on my left. Stay close to my shield and kill anything that moves. Hack, You're right behind me."

"Yessir!"

"Dodger, Sweaty, Red-eye and Bird-man, you boys fill in behind Kerrel. In that order. Me and Hack will take on a couple lads from the next dozen over."

It was the best arrangement Geth could think of, except to send everyone but Kerrel and Hack to sit out the entire engagement. But that wasn't an option. Geth was just wondering what had become of Agrem when the Seer pushed through to take him by the shoulders.

"All will be well, mmmm?"

"You've had a vision, we're gonna win? We're gonna survive?"

"No."

"Thram's balls, what are you saying, man?"

Agrem leaned in close, face sober. "All will not live. And all will not win. But you hold the future." He moved his grip to squeeze Geth's hands. "Here, in these. This I have seen."

"The outcome of this battle is in my hands?"

"The outcome of the future. You will not crush it, mmmm?"

Geth looked down at his thick, callused palm. The Seer leaned in for a wordless embrace and left the way he'd come.

"Thram's hairy balls."

Horns ordered the army forward, there was no time to worry about any of that now. For the first time that day, Geth really eyed the enemy. Across a white expanse of snow-covered tussocks, Iyngaer's lines waited. Some banged their shields. Others hurled the usual insults and offal. The chieftain himself would be back behind them, among the reserves, his finest fighters, the same men that had cursed Geth before his Truslas, cheered him after. He planned on shocking them yet again.

But they didn't seethe back and forth or jostle for position as they had at Copper Ridge. They waited. It was Umbel's army that had to come to them.

Just outside of bowshot, another blast of the horns pulled Umbel's ranks to a halt. Geth stepped out in front of his section of line. It was time. To the left and right, other captains did the same.

"Brothers." He drew Cald's huge sword and held it aloft. "You know where we stand. You've been here before.

But today we don't wait for these shit-stinking, bastards, we go to them. When the horns sound, we cross that field."

The blood quickened in his veins just saying it. No one had worked harder than him to bring this battle after all. He hadn't prepared a speech, he spoke the words of his heart, of the deepest part of his guts.

"Those sonsofbitches are eating our bread, sleeping in our beds, while we go hungry and sleep on the dirt. While our friends and our king starve! Today, we take it all back! We cross that fields and we kill every man in sight. Because those are *our* fields, this is *our* country, and this is *our* war!"

Hack was the first to yell. A deafening roar followed from every throat, spreading down the line in both directions, cutting short other captains' words maybe. But the savagery in that noise couldn't be resisted. It swept a man up. You *let* it. It was the only way to survive.

Geth banged the white dog head on his shield. Others copied the gesture. The bashing of weapons only added to the din. Geth roared as loud as anyone.

Horns brayed one last time and the army advanced. "On me!" he shouted. "When I say so, shields go up! On *meeee!*"

They crossed the first yards at a walk, conserving strength until the bows twanged from across the field. Captains and sergeants called for raised shields and sped them up to a jog. Geth felt the blood pumping in his ears as snow crunched under his boots. He mouthed curses under his breath. The arrows fell behind them and the tribesmen knocked shafts for a second volley.

Geth hollered with all his might. "With me! For Umbel! For Hadean! For all that's ours!"

He sped up to a run, pulling the stretch of line in the center a little ahead of the rest. In doing so, they dodged the next fall of arrows. But the spears and swords and axes of the tribes bristled ahead. And the next volley would be loosed almost straight at them.

Geth lowered his shield and waved with his sword. "Shields down!" he bellowed.

"For Umbel!" came the cries.

"Arrrrgggghhh!"

The wordless roar of three thousand men rang in Geth's ears, left his own throat. An arrow thumped into his shield and stuck there as he ran, eyes just over the rim, crossing the final yards. His sword went back, his shoulder down. He aimed that dog head at the nearest spear, crashing into and through it with a tooth-rattling impact.

The world shook. For a moment, Geth was squashed breathless between his own shield and Hack's shield behind him. The Ilar line buckled but held. Geth found his footing at the same time as the tribesman in front of him, but that long blade of Cald's flicked out before his enemy could drop his broken spear shaft and draw. The first Ilar fell dead.

"One for the Wolves!" Hack shouted like a mad man. His blade rose to protect Geth's head, the sound of parried blows clanging above him.

A red-bearded Ilar with a spiked helmet dragged his dying countryman back and filled the gap in front of Geth. Chopping at the big warrior with an axe, the fool sliced clear through the iron rim of Geth's shield, tearing out a wedge of the plank as he wrestled the blade free. But in the time that it took to free the weapon, a lunge from Geth's long blade caught him above his armor, under the chin, sent him choking to his death on a mouthful of his own blood.

Red-beard collapsed backward into his fellows, allowing Geth a chance to flick a glance to either side. To his left, Kerrel held his own. But to his right, another green-cloak was hard pressed. A blow across the helm sent the man stumbling into Geth's side, opening up a gap wide enough for his opposite to dart a sword thrust in. The Umbelman cried out and dropped to one knee, only saved from decapitation by a parry from Geth.

Hack swung his sword over the big warrior's head to cover him as the Umbelman to the right was dragged back.

He hopped into the breach himself with a mad laugh. Geth's stomach tightened, fearing the worst. But the fool-hardy scratch fought like a devil, cursing with every swing.

We've just got to hold, Geth reminded himself. He couldn't spare a look over his shoulder to see how they fared. Ahead of him, the mass of leather and steel and bared teeth seemed to stretch back without end. He killed anyone that cam ewithin reach. He thrust with Cald's sword, suckered tribesmen closer then ducked so Red-eye, or whoever, could chop down from overhead as an Ilar unwittingly moved out from under the protection of his own second rank.

Screams and the clank of weapons punctuated the din of grinding shields, the rumble of thousands of feet on trampled snow. Red Awer's sacred mass stretched on. Time moved faster as arms slowed, weighed down with exhaustion or injury.

We've just got to hold! Geth kept on repeating.

In Geth's section of line, the enemies came, fought and died. But they kept coming. Geth drew heavy breaths, resting only when the tribesmen ahead pulled yet another wounded fighter back from the front ranks. He lifted his head when he could to steal a look up and down the line.

Best he could tell, they *were* holding. "This country is ours!" he screamed. A shout from somewhere to Geth's left reached his ears, heartening him even more. Something had happened near the river.

Hadean's sally?

Geth dared to hope. The Ilars ahead of him attacked with renewed vigor, but hacking with Cald's huge sword, Geth smashed clear through the helm of one and battered another off his feet for Kerrel to finish off. The bastards backpedaled as fast as they'd charged and Geth craned his neck leftward again until the source of the commotion became clear. Tribesmen anchoring their army beside the frozen water's edge scrambled to form up lines along the banks. A howl left Geth's lips as his eyes landed on the first boat to come splashing around the southern end of Towerrock's island.

Oars thrashed the water by the score, powered by helmeted green-cloaks crammed into shallow-drafted boats. His eyes strained northward, where Iyngaer had placed his forces in error. A barrage of arrows from Towerrock, thick as one of Blink's stews, fell among them as they tried to reposition, heading further south.

Geth turned his attention from the river on his left to the wide fields far to the right. It was there that Umbel's hope of victory rested, with Brant and his horse. Hadean's sally would take pressure off Umbel's thin ranks, providing the anvil to Brant's hammer. If he could take the beach.

Even as Geth watched, Iyngaer threw a portion of his reserves at the riverbank. A troop of bowmen turned their sights on Hadean's flotilla as well, still rowing for shore and badly exposed. Shields went up at the expense of hands on oars. The advance stalled. Green-cloaks fell dead over the sides of their boats or slumped over into their fellows.

Geth yanked Hack toward him, leaving it to the men behind him to fill his spot. "Hold the line!"

The green-cloak thumped his chest and laughed, crazy as anything. Geth left him with a prayer and pushed through to the rear of the line, hustling in search of Drayic.

"To the left!" he shouted, waving both arms as he sprinted back toward the position of Umbel's bows, halfway up the hill. "To the left! Hit the back of those lines!"

Drayic must have seen him coming. He appeared out in front of the ranks of archers, motioning the bows all to their left. Together, the pair got them moved close enough to loose their bolts dead into the backs of the tribesmen Iyngaer had arrayed to meet Hadean's sally on the banks.

Ilars fell dead in twos and threes. If not for that, the king and all his men would have been cut to pieces. The tribesmen didn't know which way to face, some hefting shields overhead or facing behind them, others swinging at the first boatmen to make land. Green-cloaks slid on ice and snow as they scrambled out of their boats to parry blows, but with Drayic's help, they had a chance. A man went down with a spear in the face as Geth watched. Another hopped over the gunwale with feet spread wide, hacking sideways through the guard of a waiting enemy.

"For Hadean!" they cried.

More green-cloaks piled out, scrambled up muddy banks, over the shingles of a rocky beach. Other boats ground up onto the icy edge of the water, spitting out warriors by the dozen, swords ready. Geth didn't see him, but he knew the king was among them. He craned his neck back to the right where Brant's horse had made some headway into Iyngaer's riders. Fighters from the back ranks of the tribes' main infantry line were already being hustled off to reinforce their cavalry.

The Ilar companies further upriver had begun the race down toward Hadean's landing as well.

"Thram and bloody Awer."

Whatever had sent them to the wrong position, he reckoned it didn't matter now. A hundred or more of Umbel's men held a patch of riverbank, allowing boat after boat to drop off fighters. But when those Ilars hit them from the north, the lot of them would be driven to a watery grave.

"A horse!" Geth cried. "Give me a horse!"

There was no getting through the Ilar ranks in front of him, but he could go *around* them. He wrangled a beast from a wide-eyed sergeant, spurred the beast to the right. Could he really hope to make it there in time? All the way around the line of battle and across the back of the Ilar position? Iyngaer and hundreds of reserves stood in the way. Geth climbed onto the animal and kicked it anyway. Hadean had no option of retreat. And those boats still on the water would have no way to make land and come to his aid once the tribesmen from the northern position arrived.

Horse hooves kicked up snow as Geth raced his mount around the last of Umbel's ranks. He pulled hard to his left, reaching the rear of Brant's horses in moments, but skirted farther north to avoid the bog of their assault. Yanking left again, the fight on the riverbanks finally came into view, furlongs ahead of him.

But there was no getting through. Directly between the big warrior and Hadean sat Iyngaer and his hundreds of reserves, the lot of them mounted as well. The treetop bastard hadn't even bothered to enter the fray.

"Tree-top bastard."

Geth craned his neck past them, at the river. A good number of green-cloaks had won land, but the first tribes-men from further north had begun arriving in twos and threes to bolster the defense on the banks. Geth's eye found Hadean at last, hacking desperately over his shield at the oncoming tribesmen, dead center of the tiny shield wall his green-cloaks had managed to lock together. There was nothing Geth could do. He faced his mount toward the hundreds of reserves around Iyngaer that stood between them and prepared to charge.

Another horn sounded, a strange one, like a woodsman's hunting horn. Geth pulled up, stood in the stirrups to see. Over his right shoulder, out of the north and east, a band of horsemen appeared, not a banner or emblem among them. Even so, there was no mistaking the fur cap of the rider at the fore, nor the proud grey mount he sat on.

"Crookbow, you sonofabitch!"

CHAPTER THIRTY-THREE

They weren't an army, Crookbow and his companions, but they stung the rear of the Ilars on the banks like a swarm of hornets on a naked man's ass. After the arrows of Drayic's bows, this second unexpected assault was enough to send many a tribesman fleeing the field altogether—or fleeing this world.

A rousing cry went up, from the walls of Towerrock if Geth wasn't mistaken. Troops of Ilars turning to escape northward came even closer within the range of their bows, drawing yet more volleys of death from above.

Now was the moment, Geth reckoned. The fate of the battle rested in one man's hands.

Iyengar.

Geth's eyes found him, taller than ever as he stood in his stirrups, waving his reserves toward the river. He had no choice but to enter the fray. Brant may have been stalled on his left, his main line might yet be holding as well, but Hadean's sally had won the riverbank despite ice and sword. Umbel's boats had already rowed back to the fortress and now returned with even more fighters. Iyngaer couldn't let them land.

Geth could see it in his head before anything happened. The chieftain and his company of horse would pile in behind the footmen already engaged with Hadean's men, lending shields to defend against Drayic's arrows and swords to press the king's assault. Superior numbers would force Hadean's shield wall back, forestalling the boats behind from unloading, and eventually picking those on the water to pieces with arrows of their own. The day—indeed, the war—would be over in the space of minutes.

"Iyngaer!" Geth kicked his mount straight for the chieftain, screaming as he rode. If he could slow the bastard down, win enough time for the boats to make land...

You're a mad man, he told himself. But there was no turning back anyway. When the first Ilar reserve turned his head to face Geth, it was already too late. Cald's sword swept through his parry, knocking him clean from the saddle.

That big sword wasn't made for fighting off a horse, but none of the riders he faced had spent years at war among the Mog like he had. He cut down another enemy and howled like the wolf they named him. A half dozen tribesmen wheeled to meet him. Like a true Easterner, he veered away before they could strike.

"Iyngaer!" Curling back again, Geth shouted over the din. "Iyngaer, it's me! Fight me, Iyngaer!"

The tall chieftain turned, and his eyes found Geth. He laughed and kept on his way. A dozen Ilars rode toward Geth already anyway. He weaved through them best he could, steering with his knees, trading blows first left then right, wending toward their leader.

But he was never going to cut his way through all those reserves. And with enemies thick behind him now, there was no path of retreat either. Cut, parry, wheel around as he might, the Ilar net closed on him, curses and clods of dirt and snow flying from horses and riders.

A swing from behind clipped the side of Geth's helm, blurred his vision. Still, he drove toward the chieftain. His breath came in panting gasps, blows raining down on his shield, deflecting off his sword, clanging off pauldrons.

Iyngaer hadn't taken the bait. Geth swore. He'd failed. In moments, he'd be dead. *And Hadean and Phelan and all the rest.*

But a familiar shout turned the head of the tribesmen in front of Geth just when his aching shield-arm felt too tired to rise. "Eat that!"

From predators, the Ilars hunting Geth became prey. The scream of a horse and crash of iron on steel announced the arrival of Neary and the band of thieves. Geth sucked in air as that woman with the hat like Crookbow's chopped a man's arm clear off, Vriana-like, shriek and all.

Iyngaer had to notice now.

How long had it been, how many boats had made land? Geth couldn't say. But the chieftain's reserves were in tatters—the rear at least. Up ahead, Iyngaer turned the rest of his riders en masse, swords pointed toward Geth, Neary, and Crookbow's thieves.

And away from Hadean.

Still, a few dozen horsemen could never slow three hundred enemies for long.

"Neary!" Geth cried. "We have to get to Iyngaer! Draw them out as much as you can so I can slip in!"

The grey-headed Umbelman grunted, slashing at Ilars, goading them to follow. He hollered at Crookbow and soon the entire band were retreating, drawing Ilar horsemen behind them and away from the main block. Geth spurred his mount against the flow of tribesmen, dodging as many enemies as he could, using his shield to fend off strikes, slipping ever deeper among their ranks.

"Iyngaer!"

The big chieftain's curses were audible even at a distance. Despite all his plans, superior numbers and the rest, the battle hung in the balance. He kicked his mount toward Geth, finding a home for his rage. Between the pair of them, Ilars scattered.

Cald's great sword met Iyngaer's blade with a thunderous clang as their two horses collided, shoulder to shoulder. The smaller Ilar steed skittered, bounced off the big southern beast and they parted again, horse-hooves hopping as each animal turned to circle back to the fight.

"There's no trial to hide behind now!" Geth shouted.

"Arrrggghhh!"

There were no words in any language for Iyngaer's fury. The giant tribesman snarled and tilted his weapon, charging back for more.

But this was the battle Geth wanted. The greater height of his mount helped him match the reach of his limby foe, as did the size of Cald's great sword. And few men west of the Lows had trained on horseback among the Mog. Geth knew he could win. He had to. Iyngaer's fighters surrounded the pair of them, watching and shouting for blood.

The chieftain didn't charge recklessly this time though, swerving to his right to avoid the collision with Geth's heavier mount. As he passed, he leaned half out of the saddle to swing up over his own shield arm, taking another chunk out of Geth's notched shield. The big warrior flailed with Cald's sword, whistling short of the mark even with the extra length of his blade. He looked down as he wheeled around for a third pass. His dog had lost an ear, the circle of his wooden shield like a pie with a slice cut out of it.

Years of fighting in the pits sparked an idea. Geth kicked his mount back toward Iyngaer, past rows of shouting Ilars he remembered from the Truslas. He marked the damage on his shield and angled the wedge just so. He closed with the chieftain in seconds, but veered at the last moment, leaning back and away.

Iyngaer stretched and chopped as he had before. Geth met that strike with the split in his shield. The blade bit even deeper, almost to Geth's forearm, but it stuck there just as he'd hoped.

Before Iyngaer could yank the weapon free, Geth was already kicking his mount away. At full stretch already, the chieftain cursed and went over the side of his mount, one foot still tangled in his stirrup. Ligaments tore with an audible snap and he screamed. He was already clutching at his knee when Geth turned for a final pass.

CHAPTER THIRTY-FOUR

Perhaps he should have ridden over the tree-top bastard and been done, but Geth slid out of the saddle instead, sword leveled. Even on the ground, with one leg twisted, the chieftain parried his first blow, fighting like the bear of his sigil. Sword and shield deflected more cuts until Geth finally skipped right and right again, toward that maimed leg, to sneak a thrust past the chieftain's guard.

But a backhanded slash from Iyngaer forced Geth on his heels before he could push the tip home. Blood colored a few inches of Cald's blade as it came free, not more.

"It ends now," Geth said. He hefted the weapon for one last blow, but the feel of cold metal against the side of his neck halted him midway.

"Go, Truslata."

Geth turned slowly. Ilars crowded thick behind him. A man with a forked beard Geth recalled from Dues pointed to one side. "Go. Leave Govendi or die with him."

Geth looked to the chieftain. Blood welled through the fingers of the hand at his side, but his eyes burned with unabated hatred. Only sturdy mail had kept Cald's blade from killing him instantly. Still, Geth didn't reckon he was much longer for this world.

Snatching the reins of his mount, the big warrior climbed back into the saddle. This once, he didn't dare curse his defeated enemy. The tribesmen parted to let him pass.

Outside the ring, Geth kicked his horse toward the riverbank, where last he'd seen the king. Without the aid of the reserves, Hadean's men had fought even deeper inland. A shouting Ilar with an antlered helm tried to stem the flow with men from the main, south-facing lines. But with less and less support, those lines began to wobble.

Umbel's forces pressed.

"Gods bless you!"

Geth didn't know who led Umbel's ranks, but whoever it was the man knew his business. With a shout, his green-cloaks pushed forward. The Ilar lines gave, and Umbel's fighters burst through like water through split seams.

"We've done it!"

The antler-helmed Ilar gathered a group of riders to him and turned them all back northward. Behind him, tribesmen in threes and fours threw down their shields and ran for it.

The rout ensued, fleeing men hacked down from behind, cornered and speared, trampled by Umbel's horsemen. Geth scanned the fray until his eyes found Hadean. The king met his eye. The lad pulled off his helmet, a broad grin across his haggard face. Geth laughed out loud and hooted for joy.

This was a true victory, nothing like the Ilar retreat at Copper Ridge. A few blocks of tribesmen kept their cool, locked shields and made good their escape. The Ilars on the west bank had never even entered the battle. But others, like Iyngaer and his reserve, had nowhere to go.

Hadean came riding toward Geth on a borrowed mount, his face gone somber. No time for congratulations just yet, there was still work to be done. The king eyed a stout ring of Ilar shields and swords back where Geth had left the downed chieftain. "It's a grim business ahead," Hadean said.

Geth frowned but nodded.

"Bring up the archers!"

Geth blinked. "Wait."

It was Hadean who frowned, hearing that. He raised a hand to forestall the arrows. Geth surveyed the wall around Iyngaer, two hundred men or more, brave fighters who wouldn't go to Vorda's hall without taking men with them. Iyngaer had regained his feet, leaning heavily on Fork-beard.

"Maybe there's another way," Geth said.

Hadean just watched him. Here was the same man that had executed his uncle without ceremony after all. But eying Iyngaer and Fork-beard over the rim of the shield wall, Geth knew what had to be done, just as he had known that night in the Tooth with the traitor Eldric. Agrem's words rang in his ear.

"Iyngaer!" The ire was gone from Geth's voice this time. He sheathed Cald's sword, approached with hands raised. "Iyngaer, let us speak!"

"Speak?" The chieftain called back.

"The Wolf to the Bear!"

CHAPTER THIRTY-FIVE

Hands up and far from his hilt, Geth crunched across mud, offal, and snow until the Ilar lines parted ahead of him. Tribesmen watched his advance, some with fear, others with malice. All it took was one fool to stab him in the back and it would all be for naught. But just as Geth stepped between the first row of shields, Agrem appeared out of nowhere to join him, those well-recognized spikes of hair the only defense he needed.

Geth stopped a few yards short of Iyngaer. Up close it was clear the chieftain struggled just to stand, even with a second fighter now joining Fork-beard to prop him up.

"Come to watch me die?" Iyngaer said through gritted teeth, eyes fixed on the big warrior. He ignored Agrem.

"None of your men have to die here. You have my word."

"None of my men." The tall chieftain cracked a hateful smile. "Only me."

"You're almost dead already. And this war is over. Hasn't the ground drank enough blood?"

"I die with a sword in my hand. And so do my men."

Geth opened his mouth, but the Seer assailed his chieftain with a string of Ilar curses. Geth knew those words, if little else, in their tongue.

The exchange went back and forth until it was Agrem who ignored Iyngaer, turning to address Fork-beard instead. Geth didn't know if the warlock had used his grapes-to-raisins threat, but Fork-beard and the other tribesmen forced Iyngaer down to a seat on the ground. Agrem knelt to inspect his wound.

"Is that it?" Geth asked.

"Mmmm."

Geth leaned in closer. "What did you tell them?"

"That he will accept. I have *seen* it."

"I will not accept!" Iyngaer called from over Agrem's shoulder. "I would rather die!"

The Seer turned, but Geth answered for him. "We'd rather you lived, your fighters too. And we'll so all we can to save you."

If the chieftain wanted to argue more, he didn't have the strength. Agrem knelt again, touched his neck, and called for a stretcher.

"Can you save him?" Geth asked

"Mmmm."

Geth recognized uncertainty in that expression this time. He surveyed the tribesmen to either side. The weight of defeat hung on their shoulders.

And yet there was hope in their eyes too. For his part, Geth felt a weight lifted off him. Many of these men had clapped him on the back after his duel with Othwid after all, or cheered his climb up that icy cliff, his swim across Balfega Meed. He sighed. Even the dog of war had had enough fighting for one day.

Fork-beard stood in for his wounded chieftain and met Hadean at the edge of the shield wall. An agreement was reached whereby the Ilars gave up their weapons but were permitted to leave. Under an escort of green-cloaks, the tribesmen began the march north right then and there. All save Iyngaer. He'd agreed to trade himself for his men. The stretcher arrived to bear the chieftain toward the walls of Towerrock, Agrem at his side, still treating his wound.

Geth turned to survey the aftermath of battle. Iyngaer's reserves were the lucky ones. The field was littered with the dead and dying. A good portion of the Ilar force had escaped, including the entire contingent on the western riverbank. But their army was broken. There would be no Misa of chieftains, no return of the tribes. Geth started back in the direction of the king.

A little man with greasy blond hair and a patchy beard barred his path.

"Phelan!"

Before Geth could do anything, Phelan reached back to smack him hard across the face. "What took you so long?"

Behind the little man, Kerrel grinned. A hearty laugh escaped Geth as well. He lunged after Phelan, pulled him into a bear hug. The unthankful bastard struggled at first but finally gave up. He buried his face into Geth's shoulder. By the way he hid his eyes, the big warrior knew he was crying.

"It's over," Geth said. "And don't you worry either. You're done with jail. For now, at least."

He released his friend, but Phelan shook his head. "Melagus isn't going to let it lie."

"I've got it handled, Phelan. I'm going to confess."

"Say it was you? Ha!"

"I've sent Blink to dig up what's left of the shine. I'm going to give it all back. As for the portion we've spent, who's gonna come at *me*, the Wolf of the Hills, for that?"

"Well, they won't come at you today. Not with all that blood all over you. And smelling like a sow's asshole besides."

Geth smiled. "I think I've earned a pardon out of the king, whatever I smell like."

Phelan looked as if he might have something to say about that, but Crookbow's approach cut him short.

"Have a good look, Phelan," Geth uttered out of the side of his mouth. "This one's a bigger thief than you."

Crookbow doffed that stupid cap as he arrived and bowed like he'd just stepped off stage. "Well?" He spread his hands, waiting.

Geth clapped three times with deliberate slowness. "For a minute there, I thought you'd double crossed me."

"I thought about it. I did. But I reckon you're not a man to be crossed. Single or double."

Geth snorted a laugh.

"But I'm holding you to your word," Crookbow said.

"Of course."

"And I'm keeping your horse too."

"Bloody thief," Phelan muttered.

Geth just shook his head. "You've earned it. The horse's name is Palladine."

They shared a smile.

Geth looked past the old brigand for Neary, but the Umbelman was nowhere to be found. The living tended to the dead and fires had been lit where tired soldiers hunkered down to share Ilar wine and whatever else could be found. But he didn't see the old green-cloak at any of them.

"Where's Neary?"

Crookbow frowned. "I thought I'd find him here, with you."

Geth bit down a curse. The sun had dipped and he shaded his eyes. He walked the field, calm at first, but with growing concern. Back where they had fought Iyngaer's horsemen, he finally spied a shock of white hair half covered in blood.

"Neary!"

Geth sprinted toward the downed Umbelman, sliding to a halt on his knees. He turned his friend to his side. Neary groaned but didn't speak.

"Kerrel!" Geth cried. "Find the witch!"

CHAPTER THIRTY-SIX

It seemed an age before Amalia arrived, looking haggard herself. The dozen had gathered by then, all of them alive by some miracle. Poor Neary had gotten the worst of it.

"Save him, Amalia." Geth had to stop himself from shaking her by the shoulders. "Do whatever you have to."

"Be quiet and let me work."

She knelt beside Neary, eyes closed, holding his head in her hands for a good long while. Time passed, Geth couldn't say how long. She needed his help to rise when she was done.

"Get a stretcher and get him inside the Tooth. Into a bed, beside a fire."

"You should find a bed and a fire yourself after that," Geth said.

"No time for that now."

A makeshift bridge—constructed for the sally but un-used, Geth reckoned—had been laid to replace the burned one. Geth and Kerrel took Neary across themselves. In-side, they were hailed by an impossible number of soldiers. Geth took one look at the women and lads and greybeards and realized what had become of the townsfolk Hadean had let inside the fortress. Each held a bow or quiver. And each had done his or her part.

The keep had undergone a transformation. Hadean ar-rived on their heels, ushering them toward his own cham-bers. But even as Geth hurried Neary across the ward, he took in the new opening that had been cut through the west-facing curtainwall, the tents everywhere, the archery targets. The door to the king's quarters was gone when they arrived, the bed as well.

They set their wounded friend down on the floor. Ker-rel lit a fire while Geth and Hadean piled blankets below Neary's stretcher and on top of it. Amalia stepped through the open doorway as they finished, shooing them all out-side.

Hadean led them down to the ward again. "Drink something. You've earned it."

A skin of tart Ilar berry wine came forth. After that, salted meats, presumably scrounged from the tribesmen's supplies.

"Amalia will keep him alive," Geth said. He didn't know if it was true, but he had to believe it.

"Let's hope so," Hadean replied. "I owe him a great debt. He must live to collect it."

The king forced a smile, but Geth couldn't match the gesture. He owed Neary as much and more. The rescue from the tower, the timely arrival with Crookbow, and again against Iyngaer's reserves—Geth knew he would have long since been dead if not for Neary.

The sight of even more archery targets in the inner ward turned Geth's thoughts back to Hadean. "Looks like you put your time to good use during the siege, my lord."

The king nodded. "They said I was a fool to let all these people inside the keep. And maybe I was. But they brought talents with them. And willing arms. We put them to work building the boats, fletching arrows. We taught them how to work a bow and put them on the walls. That left more experienced warriors for the sally."

"Boats." Now *that* made Geth smile. "Gods, but I've never seen so many. Guess it explains all the timber in the ward before the siege. And the rest."

Hadean's face reddened. Blankets hung in every entrance, not a door to be seen throughout the ward. No doubt the king wasn't the only one sleeping on the floor.

"Just wait 'til you see the greathall," Hadean said, reading Geth's thoughts. "We had to use all the tables as well."

Geth chuckled. "You even opened a new gate."

"To sally with the boats. Of course, we could have thrown planks out across the span of the burnt bridge. But they would have seen us coming, known exactly where we'd attack."

Geth thought it through out loud. "So, you trained up the townsfolk to aid the assault with their bows, then built boats and a gate to launch them from."

"We did what we had to."

"And you had to keep it all secret from the Ilars. You couldn't pierce the outer stones for the new gate until the last minute, I reckon."

The king ran a hand over his short, dark hair. "Truth be told, there was no keeping secrets from the Ilars. They had a spy inside. Even so, Melagus found a way to use that to our advantage."

Geth wasn't surprised.

"First he figured out who it was—"

"And had him hanged?"

Hadean smiled. "No."

"First time for everything," Geth muttered.

"He used him to feed false information back to Iyngaer."

If Hadean had been about to say anything, the appearance of the counselor himself cut him short. A sword hung at the worm's waist and a child-sized mail shirt swung from bony shoulders as he crossed the ward. But he looked as haggard as anyone, face gaunt, hair even thinner, an older version of himself.

"I've been looking for you," Geth said before Melagus could get in a word.

The counselor halted mid-stride, eyes narrowed.

"I'd like to turn myself in," Geth said. "For the thievery you've charged Phelan with. It was me. I've sent one of my men to dig it all up and bring it back. To be returned to the rightful owners."

Melagus sniffed. "You're saying it was you that squeezed through windows and cracked doors all throughout Towerrock?"

Geth turned to the king. "I throw myself upon your mercy."

"I didn't miss you," the counselor said with a sigh. "Not one bit."

Hadean cleared his throat. "But you're thankful for all Master Geth has done for the realm. Isn't that what you were going to say, Master Melagus?"

The worm wrinkled his lips. He managed a nod.

"On behalf of the entire realm," the king went on, "I...*we*...commend you, Captain."

Geth knuckled his brow. "Anything for my king. And my friends. But I'm a sergeant lord, not a captain. I have a file to look after."

"I think you've managed to look after far more than that. Your talents are undeniable on the field. And you've shown unmatched resolve, loyalty, and resourcefulness these past months. Far more than your share."

"Captain," Geth rolled it on his tongue. It had a ring to it. Men had been calling him that for a long time anyway.

"As such," the king went on, "I'll be needing more of your time. At my side."

Geth saluted with fist to heart.

But Melagus gave a snort. "Is it wise, my lord, to take such a mighty warrior away from the field? Where his talents clearly lie?"

Geth's fingers itched to find the bony bastard's neck, just for a few seconds, but the squelch of boots announced another approach. Brant saluted, his face unmistakably pale.

"Cousin Brant." Hadean frowned. "Have you been injured?"

"I'm alright, my cousin king. But all is not well."

Geth, Hadean and Melagus exchanged looks.

"News from the south," said Brant. "Just arrived from Umbel City."

He held up a hand to display a tiny note, the kind that arrived by pigeon. Melagus's eyes narrowed, but Brant didn't make them wait.

"It's our uncle, Lord King. He's moved his army south."

"South?" Hadean repeated.

Brant nodded, expression grim.

"While we've been fighting the Ilars, his armies have moved on Umbel City. My lord, Towdric has taken the throne."

A MESSAGE FROM THE AUTHOR

Thank you for reading HAIR OF THE DOG. To continue the adventure, download DOG DAYS at www.deankastle.com/books.html. To stay up to date with new releases, you can also join my newsletter at www.deankastle.com/newsletter.html. As a bonus, you'll receive THE HAND OF JUSTICE, a short story from Palladine's perspective about Phelan's infamous dice game and subsequent capture AND also THE WAY OUT, a short story featuring Ratcher.

Cheers!

DK

ABOUT THE AUTHOR

Dean Kastle is the author of the DOG OF WAR Epic, SWORD SONGS, the forthcoming LEGACY Series, and many short works. In addition to a love of 'story' in every medium, he's a rabid foodie and soccer fanatic. As far as he's concerned, Pluto is still a planet and the oxford comma is a matter of taste. He doesn't wear a beret or write with a fountain pen, but he does own a life-size replica of the Iron Throne. From that perch, he plots his next tale. Readers can connect with Dean on X, on Facebook, or by joining his newsletter. He lives in fly-over country with his wife, three kids and (yes) a dog.

Printed in Dunstable, United Kingdom

65234294R00234